THE TEN WORST PEOPLE IN NEW YORK

THE TEN WORST PEOPLE IN NEW YORK

A NOVEL

MATT PLASS

NEW YORK

This is a work of fiction. All of the names, characters, organizations, places and events portrayed in this novel are either products of the author's imagination or are used fictitiously. Any resemblance to real or actual events, locales, or persons, living or dead, is entirely coincidental.

Copyright © 2025 by Matt Plass

All rights reserved.

Published in the United States by Crooked Lane Books, an imprint of The Quick Brown Fox & Company LLC.

Crooked Lane Books and its logo are trademarks of The Quick Brown Fox & Company LLC.

Library of Congress Catalog-in-Publication data available upon request.

ISBN (hardcover): 979-8-89242-099-0
ISBN (ebook): 979-8-89242-100-3

Cover design by Nebojsa Zoric

Printed in the United States.

www.crookedlanebooks.com

Crooked Lane Books
34 West 27th St., 10th Floor
New York, NY 10001

First Edition: March 2025

10 9 8 7 6 5 4 3 2 1

For Elana and Paris

In times of stormy weather
She felt queer pain
That said,
"You'll find rain better
Than shelter from the rain."

"Strange Hurt" by Langston Hughes

CHAPTER

1

You wake in darkness in what must be the back of a truck. Metal claws trying to prize your skull apart, that's how it feels. Corrugated steel at your back, hard bench under your ass, and every lurch of the truck threatens to tear your shoulders from their sockets—a twisted mystery until you realize your hands are fastened at the base of your spine. And still you're buried by the darkness, swallowed by it, thinking, *please not blind*, until the pressure across the bridge of your nose tells you your glasses have been replaced with a blindfold, and that moment of understanding feels as good as anything that ever happened to you. Relief has you trying to stand, sliding up the flat wall of the truck. Your head hits the roof—this must be a cargo van—and strong hands force you back down. A flick of air against the cheek as an open palm slams into the side of your face. Blood in the nostrils, the taste of iron in your throat. You don't cry out, and part of you feels proud of that small stoicism. Behind the blindfold, your reptile mind hurls colored ink against your eyelids, as you wonder, *what the hell?*

Earlier, you were . . . home in your penthouse overlooking Brooklyn Bridge. You'd finished a workout, your shoulders and quads deliciously on fire. You remember watching the laundry boy hang shirts in the closet. You stayed in the doorway to see he didn't reach into your cufflink chest. When he'd gone, you made two calls: Thai takeout and a woman. Cheap eats and an expensive fuck—you fancied it that way around for a change. You remember the woman arrived before the food. She stood in the doorway, shorter and uglier than a woman should be, and you're thinking, *they screwed up my order*. After that, everything turned black.

The truck rolls on. You're a quick study and learn to reduce the agony in your shoulders by leaning into the corners. You once saw a movie where a blindfolded man memorized the twists and turns of his journey from the trunk of a car. Bullshit—this truck could be burrowing into the earth's core and you'd be no wiser. Your mind begins to clear. Still tasting blood, you run the options.

The Feds wouldn't hog-tie you in a truck. They'd gather like sleek crows in your lobby or swarm your office waving warrants. No law, then. A private matter.

Your heart rattles with the vehicle's suspension as you make a mental list of people who despise you. It's a long list, but you bite down on the fear and tell yourself this is not about revenge, not some deadbeat alone in his dark car with a jerrican of gas on the passenger seat. There must be at least two of them—one driving, one in the back with you—and a group effort means the goal is money. Good. Money you know. Money never failed you yet.

The truck shudders to a halt. Hydraulics sigh. Doors crank, letting in sheets of salty air. Fingers grip your biceps and you're on the move, flat-footed in your attempt to maintain balance. You're helped down, an awkward drop, but you don't fall, and in the stillness you open your senses to the night: traffic like brush strokes on a distant drum, a breeze laced with brine and diesel. A sound high above might be a gull. You're near water and a highway.

Is this place familiar?

No talking among your captors, only the occasional scrape of a shoe on gravel. You wish one of them would speak. You haven't said a word—they haven't gagged you yet, and you don't want them to. A dull *whump* as heavy boots jump up into the back of the truck. Rummaging sounds from within. The crunch of gravel as the boots hit the ground. A whispered conference—hissed, guttural—then a shove sends you staggering forward. A hand grips your shoulder, leading you on.

You hear the rattle of keys, locks turning. Another push forward and the atmosphere contracts. You're inside a building. Powerful hands guide you into what feels like a smaller space. You smell body odor, perfume. This new world feels compact and incubated, like . . . an elevator; you're in an elevator.

The car begins its ascent with a jolt, as if the first yard off the ground needs an extra pull. It's a particular mechanical tic, specific to this elevator car, and it's something that irritates you every time you give potential investors the grand tour.

You know this building. It's one of yours.

* * *

When the blindfold comes off, your eyes are reluctant to relinquish the dark. A human form stands before you, loose black clothes, black gloves, a pale face squashed like mashed fruit behind a stocking mask. The sight almost opens your bladder, and you reach for something to hold, remembering too late that your hands are bound. Toppling and unable to break your fall, your shoulder smacks against the ground with a sound like a whipcrack.

"Luca Benedetti, welcome to your reckoning."

A man, by his voice. Tall and athletic. You haul yourself off the concrete, your shoulder bright with pain. In the distance rises the blinking spire of the Freedom Tower—Manhattan trying to outdo the stars. You sense the presence of others behind you, but you won't look round in case you see one of them without their mask. Don't give them a reason.

"Why do you think you're here?" Tension in the man's voice.

"Money." Disgusted at the near-whimper in your voice, you say it again. "*Money.*"

The man tilts his stockinged head to one side. "Not exactly."

But you don't believe him, and already you're mentally scouring your own apartment. A few thou in the wall safe. Two watches in the leather roll—the Omega De Ville, the Patek Philippe Nautilus you brought in Paris. Your mind's eye falls on the Basquiat painting in the bedroom: a postcard-sized chicken-scratch that cost you thirty K in '79. You always had an eye for an investment, and that childish scribble would go for what—three, four mil?

"I can get you three grand in cash. Eighty in wristwatches. Other jewelry, maybe fifty, sixty thousand all in. That's it, until the banks open."

Your shoulder howls like it wants a divorce from your body, but your brain's obviously working because you didn't offer him the Basquiat—this scumbag wouldn't recognize fine art if it choked him.

The man says, "You think you can buy us off? Typical. Just one more reason why you deserve your place on the list of the Ten Worst People in New York."

His words seep slowly into your brain. "Ricky Talon's list? I'm a businessman. I shouldn't even be on that stupid fucking list. I'm suing Ricky Talon and I'm suing the *Talon Tonight* show, and I'm suing NBC, and I'm suing—" It hits you. "You want me to drop the lawsuit? Is *that* what this is about?"

The man smiles behind the stocking mask, his lips two squirming fish in a net. "This is about Mrs. Emily Garner of 333 Greene Avenue."

"Huh?"

"Emily Garner. A woman of color, a sitting tenant in a neighborhood where rents had doubled each year for three years. You offered her five hundred dollars to move out, and when she refused, you released cockroaches into her apartment. Ninety days later, Emily Garner was gone, and you'd installed a white couple at ten times the rent."

"I don't remember," you say. *It's true. There were so many.*

The man leans close enough to kiss or bite. "You remember Danny Araya."

Danny Araya. You know what's coming.

"Nine years old," the tall man says. "Stricken with polio, riding the elevator in his wheelchair. You wanted to sell the building, but the Arayas refused to leave because Danny's school had ramps and was only a block away. You waited a whole week before you disabled the elevator. Even then, the Arayas surprised you, carrying their boy up eleven flights all winter. One Sunday, the parents at work, Danny and his kid brother at home, an electrical fire starts in the wall. Toxic smoke fills the building. Danny's brother tries to carry him out, but

Danny's a deadweight. The younger boy panics and runs. Firefighters find Danny on the seventh floor. He'd crawled down four flights before the smoke reeled him in. What do you say to that?"

What *can* you say? You didn't start the fire. You felt bad about Danny. Didn't you donate to some kids' fund when the insurance money came in? Fires happen in old buildings, you know that better than anyone. You want to ask, what the hell? Instead, you do the one thing you shouldn't—you try to make a joke.

"I'll tell you, pal, this is the toughest tenants' association meeting I ever attended."

Overhead, a gull cries out.

The man says, "In twenty-four hours, this place will be sold and you'll add millions more to your pile. Just what Brooklyn needs, another office block. Of course, you can only sell the building now that it's empty. How did you persuade your tenants to leave? Rats in the basement? Blocked sewage pipes? Violence?"

"What do you want from me?"

A shove from behind. Strong arms hoist you onto the ledge that skirts the roof. Panic sucks air from your lungs. "Listen. There's a Basquiat painting worth millions." The city is a phosphorous pool, and trying to see the street below feels like trying to see the ocean bed in a storm. "I have powerful friends," you say.

"You know powerful people—not the same thing," the man says. "Luca Benedetti won't be missed."

He's right. No one scours the streets for you. No frantic fingers punch 911. Not your raptor ex-wives in their Florida condos, your wretched siblings, nor any of those deep-water predators you call friends.

Not even Clarissa.

Clarissa blossoms in your mind, your sweet daughter, whose little heart you've broken with your flying visits, your cancellations, and your occasional dismal trips to the Bronx Zoo. Clarissa, who calls you Daddy though you don't deserve it, who once drew a crayon picture of you and her flying an airplane into a golden heart-shaped sun.

"Please," you say. "I have a little girl."

"Then think about her, before it's too late."

Before it's too late? There's hope in those four words—a beacon in darkness. Something else . . . behind your back, you feel the cloth around your wrists. A scarf of some kind. You're thinking . . . a mask that looks like bodega pantyhose; a hog-tie made from a scarf . . . *these guys are fucking amateurs.* And if you make it out of here you'll take great pleasure in introducing them to the professionals, men who bind hands with cable ties, not scarves.

The man holds a phone up to your face—your phone. "Access code, please."

"Why?"

"You're going to send an apology to your social media followers."

You don't understand, but you give him the code—*what else can you do?*—and he taps away, then holds up the screen for you to read.

"I need my glasses," you say. "Inside pocket."

The man reaches into your jacket with nervous fingers, like maybe you keep a snake in there. More gently than you're expecting, he slides the glasses onto your face. Now you can read the text on the screen.

> *I can't live with the guilt another day. I'm sorry. I have lived the wrong life. I have taken when I should have given. I hereby instruct my lawyers to cancel the sale of Clearwater House. I instruct my finance team to make a one-time $10M donation to the homeless of New York. I beg you all for forgiveness.*

"A suicide note," you say.

"A promise. Confession is a powerful rite. It can bring about the most remarkable change of heart, make a man do the most unlikely things." The man smiles his mashed smile behind the net. "We just want you to do what's right, Luca."

* * *

And now you're alone again. But in the worst possible way.

You're falling.

Falling, falling through space as gravity bites and the wind plucks at your clothes. You are one of the ten worst people in New York, and you're about to die. Brick and glass blur as the ground rises to meet you, then the world inverts and you're no longer falling, you're flying, soaring upward, leaving the city far behind, breaking through the earth's atmosphere, upward, upward, until you sail into the flaming center of a golden heart-shaped sun.

CHAPTER

2

FBI SPECIAL AGENT Alex Bedford had seen her share of bodies, but when the sheet was pulled back, her stomach vaulted. Not at the waft of putrefied air that overpowered the scent of formalin, or at the crude Y-shaped autopsy scar—an oversized rosary stretching from shoulders to navel—but at the sheer, uncompromising lifelessness of the two-hundred-and-thirty-pound body. Forty-eight hours submerged in the East River had macerated the tips of Tyrell T. Dixon's fingers from mahogany to gelatinous gray. Crabs and other riverbed opportunists had eaten his eyelids and part of his upper lip, and the New York City councilor gazed up from the mortuary tray with a look of permanent surprise combined with the trace of an Elvis sneer.

In three decades on the job, Alex had seen worse. A young mother recovered in pieces from a wrecked Honda, the brisket-textured victim of a Bushwick tenement fire, a gang member's skull opened with a claw hammer. Dixon felt different. Alex had known the councilor in life—from a distance, anyway. This naked walrus, his fleshy upper arms spilling over the mortuary tray . . . Could he be the same man she'd been tracking for six months? The same fist-pounding political carnivore she'd studied in all those news reports, magazine profiles, long-lens surveillance images?

Dixon's body had been recovered half a kilometer from his stalled twenty-foot deck boat. Traces of alcohol and cocaine showed in the councilor's blood, but no indication of heart attack or stroke. Ignoring the creak from her fifty-five-year-old knees, Alex crouched at the rolling tray. She followed his arm down from the shoulder. No needle marks below the elbow, and none of the bruising you'd associate with handcuffs or cable ties. Soft hands, the remains of manicured nails, his skin tone the same as her own except for a lighter band circling his wrist—years of a watch strap blocking the sun. He'd come out of the water wearing a diamond-bezel Rolex Daytona and a hand-cut Zegna suit. *A life lived beyond the income stated on his tax returns.*

As Alex moved around the body, a blonde twentysomething pathologist's assistant waited with arms folded over her mauve scrubs.

"Suicide, right?" the assistant said.

Alex glanced up from the tray. "Is that your professional opinion?"

The blonde head bowed. "I just thought, you know, Ricky Talon's list."

Ricky Talon's list. The Ten Worst People in New York, a stupid late-night chat show meme with an online voting system for viewers at home. Alex had never seen *Talon Tonight*, but she knew Councilor Tyrell Dixon had been on the list. And so had that real estate guy who took a plunge from his own building. Dixon made it two deaths in two weeks from the same list—his demise would pour gasoline onto what was already a raging media fire, and Alex's investigation had just gotten ten times harder.

"What's a froth cone?" She tried to peer into Dixon's throat, but her head blocked the light. "It's mentioned in the autopsy report."

"Uh, froth in the victim's airway indicates air and mucus mixed with water."

"Meaning?"

"Meaning the deceased was breathing at the time of submersion."

Alive when he went in.

"Point-zero-four-percent alcohol to blood." Alex recited from memory. "Point-zero-three for cocaine. How would that affect a man of his size?"

"It might make him a better dancer."

Alex stared at the girl for a beat. "Tell me. Does the chief medical examiner share your sense of humor?"

The girl looked at her rubber shoes, the same mauve shade as her scrubs and her nail polish, and for reasons Alex wouldn't waste a second trying to understand, the matching colors made her feel old. Her mind skipped to a recent FBI conference: a Quantico instructor bitching over breakfast about entitled kids who dream of becoming celebrity FBI agents and take offence when they aren't immediately on first-name terms with senior officers. Alex Bedford had earned the *special* in special agent by majoring in respect, professionalism, and hard work. These new-breed behaviors grated like sand in the eye.

She said, "You can put him away now."

Alone in the chilled white corridor, Alex tried to huff the formalin from her nostrils. As she stepped into the elevator, she wondered if she'd been too hard on the girl. Maybe the dumb joke about Dixon dancing was a cover for her inability to answer Alex's question about toxicology levels. Maybe embarrassment had gotten in the way of a simple "I don't know."

The girl didn't matter. What mattered was that Alex, who prided herself on her ability to read people, was still trying to figure it out. As for Tyrell Dixon, instead of bringing him to justice, Alex would now have to bring justice to him. Fine. Some agents resented working on behalf of victims with ugly pasts, but Alex wasn't one of them. As her husband, William—a New York City firefighter—used to say, "You don't pause on the threshold of a burning house to ask if the occupants pay their taxes."

William's face filled her mind, her William, sweet William, smiling across the kitchen years before the end. A second face slotted into the mental carousel beside William: a beaming publicity shot of Councilor Tyrell T. Dixon. In life, her husband and the councilor had been very different men, but they'd shared one magic power: a look they gave you—dark, sparkling—that said they knew of a secret party and you were invited.

As the elevator returned Alex to the land of the living, she pictured Dixon on the mortuary tray and felt glad that the crabs hadn't gotten around to eating his eyes.

CHAPTER 3

Fifteen seconds passed between Jacob Felle hitting the buzzer and Floyd Shaw appearing at the door of the nineteenth-floor Manhattan apartment. Time enough for Jacob to regret coming straight from the airport, still groggy from red wine on the London-LaGuardia flight, from the grind of the immigration hall—a uniformed goon glaring at his British passport as if it had "Death to America" inked on every page—from the cab ride through the belching heat of New York City, the cabbie yammering about some list and how they'd have to shut it down if people kept jumping off buildings and boats, and "Man, that shit has to be rigged, because I voted every day for a month and my asshole of choice still didn't make the ten."

A heavier version of Floyd filled the doorway. "Jacob, brother-in-law, you still exist. Must be five years. I'll be damned."

The brown eyes had dimmed in the broad sandy face—hitting thirty-five did that—but unruly blond curls still tumbled to the collarbone, the same chilled-out-surfer look Floyd had rocked since university. Jacob braced for the trademark Floyd Shaw bear hug, but it never came. They stood smiling at each other, Floyd's teeth as white as his tee, Jacob wishing he'd taken time to brush before jumping in a cab. Eventually, Floyd stepped into the hallway and pulled Jacob into a stiff embrace, thumping a fist between his shoulders.

"So good to see you, man."

"You too, Floyd. Thanks for the invite. Is my darling elder sibling inside?" Jacob lowered his voice. "Anything I need to know?"

Floyd scratched at his nose. "Elizabeth popped out." He plucked at the leather lanyard that held Jacob's Lumix camera at his hip. "Suicide bomb?"

"Yep, suicide bomb masquerading as a professional-grade, 4K movie camera packed into a box the size of a Rubik's Cube."

"The man behind the camera." Floyd looked past Jacob to the elevators. "Your last doc picked up an award, right?"

"Three." Jacob scooped up his daypack. "Three awards and no money. About which, more later. I've a tiny favor to ask."

* * *

Jacob had seen Instagrams of Floyd and his sister's apartment, but nothing that prepared him for this. Through the square lens of the Lumix, floor-to-ceiling glass soaked exposed brick walls with sunlight, Afghan rugs floated over polished parquet, and in the distance an open-plan kitchen gleamed. You could ride a bicycle around this apartment, and Jacob couldn't help comparing it to his pleasant but Lilliputian flat behind Dalston Junction tube station in East London. His roaming lens arrived at Floyd standing under a framed *Time* magazine cover shot of his own sunburned face cocooned in a parka hood. The caption read, "A Shaw Thing: Explorer's Photographs Confirm Greenland Glacier Demise."

"You filming?"

Jacob lowered the camera. "Not especially. I see better this way."

"The artist, etcetera. Cool, but maybe don't film me?"

"Bad hair day?"

Floyd pulled at the end of his nose and sniffed. "Just be a bud. Hey, before I forget." He flicked something at Jacob that glinted as it arced through the air. Jacob caught a silver-colored key. Floyd pointed past Jacob to the front door. "You'll need to register."

"Register what?"

Floyd ushered Jacob back along the hallway. A black unit the size of a matchbox had been fitted to the outside doorframe. "Retina scan. Security measure."

"Worried someone will steal those massive posters of your face?"

"We had a break-in. Elizabeth got scared."

"Nope."

"Okay, I got scared. Look into the glass square."

Jacob brought his eyeball level with a tiny red dot behind the glass. Floyd punched a code into his phone. The dot turned green. "Jacob, seriously, thanks for coming."

"Glad to be here. When did you say Queen Elizabeth's due back?"

But Floyd had disappeared inside the apartment. His voice carried into the hallway. "You're in the first room past the bathroom. Grab a shower and a cold one, then join me on the balcony."

* * *

Jacob hefted his daypack onto the bed as a judder of jet lag disrupted his vision. A pair of skis stood in one corner of the bedroom, a didgeridoo in another, and against the far wall a tower of small boxes: shaving kits, with Floyd's face on the packaging. *For men who love a Close Shave.*

Two framed magazine pages hung by the window. The first, a fifteen-year-old *Yachting World* cover featuring a young Elizabeth on the deck of a sailing boat, her skin burned red by sun and wind, the gray eyes staring down the camera from under a messy crop of jet-black hair. "British Woman Navigates Globe in 100 Days to Highlight Rising Sea Temperatures."

Floyd on the glacier, Elizabeth on the ocean, and Jacob . . . what had Floyd called Jacob? *The man behind the camera.* It hadn't been a compliment.

The other framed article was from five years ago: "New Frontiers: New York Couple Honor Veteran Sailor at Opening of Club for Modern Adventurers." Floyd, Elizabeth, and an elderly man with kind amber eyes in a chestnut-brown face, standing outside a rust-colored brick building. Elizabeth's muscled shoulders—she always said nature built her for the water, not the mirror—appeared loose and relaxed, the photograph catching a rare moment of his sister at peace with the world.

New frontiers. Jacob hoped so.

Under the sharp needles of the shower, he began to reanimate, but the face that stared back from the bathroom mirror still looked pale and washed-out from the flight. In the spare bedroom, he paused with the towel pressed against his wet scalp, trying to prize from the corners of his tired mind what was wrong with the bathroom, with the whole apartment.

Pulling on a fresh tee, he pulled open Floyd's fridge and, jet-lag clumsy, knocked a square of card from under a Greenpeace magnet.

To Elizabeth & Floyd Shaw

Jonathan and Victoria Sands
Request the Pleasure of Your Company
at the Marriage of Their Daughter,
Samantha Sands
to David Lee.
Ceremony, followed by dinner and dancing.
September 7. One o'clock at the New York Public Library.

Jacob reset the card under the magnet. *Hard to imagine Elizabeth dancing at a wedding.* To reach the horizontal IPA bottles he had to move a takeout box containing a duck leg in dark sauce.

That settled it.

He found Floyd on the balcony, staring out at the distant metallic strip of the Hudson. Jacob reached for the Lumix, but he'd left it on the bed to appease Floyd.

"Elizabeth moved out, didn't she?" he said.

Floyd wiped at his nose with the back of his hand. "Not exactly."

"Floyd, the bathroom only has overpriced man products, the apartment doesn't look like a grenade exploded, and you're keeping meat in the fridge. Elizabeth's dead or she left."

Floyd leaned his chest out over the balcony.

Jacob did the same, and the heat and hum of the West Village rose up to meet him. "Jesus, Floyd. At least tell me she knows I'm here."

"I'm sorry."

"Mate. I haven't spoken to her in four years."

"I know."

"I assumed she'd given her blessing."

"I know."

"Where is she?"

"I'm not completely sure."

A bank of office windows glowed in the afternoon sun. Jacob watched his hopes dissolve in their orange fire. "Want to tell me what's going on?"

"I'm working up to it." Floyd stared across the river at Jersey City, arranged like a squat, ugly army on the far bank of the Hudson. "How's England?"

"You'd know if you bothered to visit. No change since we were at uni. Still beautiful. Still cold. Still vulnerable to promises to restore its former glory."

"Aren't we all, dear boy?" Floyd said, in a terrible British accent. He flicked his beer bottle to make it chime. "Let's hit the Village. I need another beer and we need to talk."

CHAPTER

4

ALEX BEDFORD FOUND her partner Pat Coombs in the parking lot of the NYU Langone Medical Center. Coombs perched on the hood of their Chevy Impala, brogues up on the fender, a phone at his ear, the other hand holding a half-eaten bagel. The scent of salt and burnt oil wafted in from the East River and a low evening sun cast a halo around Coombs's pink hairless skull.

"Thirty minutes works," he said into his cell when he saw Alex. He killed the call and offered her the rest of his bagel. "Well?"

Alex waved the food away. "No evidence that he jumped, fell, or was pushed. And unless you tell me we just found a suicide note, our dear Councilor Dixon's death will be recorded as misadventure. Misadventure, my ass." She walked all the way around the car. Better than putting her fist through the windscreen. "Who were you just talking to? What's happening in thirty minutes?"

"We have an audience with Mr. Ricky Talon at NBC studios." Coombs spun the remains of his bagel at a trashcan, missed, cursed, and slid down from the hood to finish the job. "I'll drive, you can read up on the background."

In the corner of Alex's vision, orange tracer-fire heralded an incoming migraine. And she had no Excedrin in her bag. "A corrupt councilor swallows half the Hudson River the day we secure his arrest warrant, and our first play is to interview a talk show host?"

"Come on, Alex, two men from Talon's list turn up dead? The media was hot enough for 'Ricky Talon Drives Luca Benedetti to Suicide.' Imagine what they'll do with Tyrell Dixon. It's going to be a very public shitshow and Murphy doesn't want us on the back foot."

Supervisory Special Agent Brett Murphy. Alex's boss. Trust Murphy to put optics before police work.

Coombs had the driver's door open. "We can talk on the way. I know you always have an alternative theory, and you know I always love to hear it."

* * *

Crawling north in rush hour traffic did nothing to halt the gathering storm of Alex's migraine. Hexagons of sun glare paraded across the East River, and the shifting points of light stung her eyes. She flipped down the visor, her skin more gray than russet brown in the rectangular mirror—no amount of moisturizer could compete with night after night of broken sleep.

"Dixon didn't trip over his shoelace," she said, lowering the window to let fresh air into the car. "Option one, we have a pair of random suicides, Benedetti and Dixon."

"Why random? Maybe Talon's public shaming proved too much for them."

"Benedetti I don't have a handle on, but no amount of public shaming could make Tyrell Dixon change his choice of necktie, never mind drown himself in the Hudson."

"How about this," Coombs said. "Dixon got a tip-off from the DA's office that we had the warrant and decided to follow Benedetti's lead."

"I can't buy that, Pat."

"You have a better opinion of the DA's office than I do."

"Dixon wouldn't fold at the first flashing blue light. He'd fight the charge, and he has friends in high and low places to help him do it." Alex massaged her temples. "Which brings us to option two—homicide. Plenty of people had reason to keep Dixon out of a courtroom. We know there's a link between Dixon and the Maranzano family. What if Philip Maranzano got wind of our arrest and did a little urgent housekeeping?"

"How do you drown a guy like Dixon and leave no sign?"

"He had coke and booze in his blood."

"City councilor. Goes with the job. And how does Benedetti fit in?"

"Dixon took kickbacks from construction, Benedetti's empire was real estate, and Philip Maranzano has his claws in half the construction projects in the city. How about Maranzano takes out Benedetti *and* Dixon?"

"The building Benedetti jumped off was empty, awaiting sale. He locked it from the *inside*, and only the security firm had spare keys. Those keys never left the safe. I'm telling you, Luca Benedetti was a stone-cold suicide." Coombs inhaled as he adjusted the seat belt over the bulge of his stomach. "You know what I think, Alex? You can't let go of all those nights wasted on the Dixon stakeout, eating radioactive Chinese and pissing into a GoGirl flask. You want this to be something it's not."

"I nearly had him, Pat."

"I nearly played wide receiver for Ohio State, except I was never any good at football and I didn't go to Ohio State." Coombs turned the Impala away from the water, taking them west toward Rockefeller Plaza. "So, are we going to talk about option three?"

"Which is?"

"Crazy *Talon Tonight* fan starts knocking off the list one by one."

"You just said Benedetti was a stone-cold suicide."

"Unless it was made to look that way."

"Now who's reaching?" Alex remembered something her partner had said before they got in the car. "You wanted me to read up on something. We get an analyst's report already?"

"Better than that." Coombs pulled a copy of the *Enquirer* newspaper off the dash. "Option four. Voodoo, baby."

Alex flattened the paper against her knees. Her skull pounded so hard she had to bear down to stop the print swimming before her eyes.

Curse of the Worst Claims Second Victim

Crooked councilor Tyrell T. Dixon is the latest victim of a VOODOO CURSE threatening Ricky Talon's "Ten Worst

People in New York." That's the bombshell claim of TV medium and spiritualist to the stars, Jade Powers.

"First Luca Benedetti, now Tyrell Dixon." Powers spoke exclusively to the *Enquirer* from her chic Jersey City condo. "My sources in this world AND THE NEXT tell me that we're dealing with a curse of diabolical proportions."

"Pat, why am I reading about a bullshit curse?"

"Sidebar," Coombs said. "Down the page. See who else Talon fingered for the chop."

She found the list under the heading "The ~~Ten~~ Eight Worst People in New York."

1. Emil Hertzberg, AKA Miss Piggy—Hedge fund billionaire and suspected PERV
2. Carl Bigney—Anti-immigrant ex-hipster and RACIST TV commentator
3. Laurie Cullen—CLIMATE-CHANGE-DENYING prof bankrolled by Big Oil
4. Cardinal Joseph Clement—Catholic priest embroiled in CHILD-ABUSE claims
5. ~~Luca Benedetti—SLUM LANDLORD with history of displacing poor tenants~~
6. Bekah Baxter—Social media FASCIST agitator
7. Dallas Johncock—Conspiracy NUTJOB known for trolling the parents of dead kids
8. Clara Wilter—Insta-famous daughter of family firm behind US OPIOID CRISIS
9. ~~Tyrell T. Dixon—CORRUPT city hall councilor with underworld ties~~
10. Delase Carter—Rap artist known for his RACE-BAITING comments

"Can they do this?" Alex dropped the newspaper into the footwell. "I mean, these people have money. How is Talon not getting sued to hell and back?"

Coombs yawned as he pulled up at the curb. "Ask him. We're here."

* * *

"The public decides who makes the top ten, not me." Ricky Talon spun his chair to face windows overlooking the green slab of Central Park. "And if anyone wants to try and litigate half a million online voters . . ." His hand swept across the boardroom table with a flourish—*be my guest.*

Talon had high coiffed hair and the scrubbed rosy face of a child, his default expression a class-clown grin. Faint yellow traces lined the gaps between the square teeth, and when they shook hands Alex had picked up a sour trace under the cologne. A secret smoker.

"You and your team have no access to the voting system?" she said.

"Even if you want to manipulate the narrative?" added Coombs. "Bump a newsworthy someone up the list?"

"You'd make a good showrunner," Talon said with no hint of a smile. "Absolutely no meddling in the voting. *Verboten* by Vikram here, and his stormtroopers down in legal."

Vikram, a thin young man with a permanently downturned mouth, said, "We *are* dealing with a small number of legal issues, but with the names generated, shall we say, democratically, we feel that the risk profile is within tolerance."

Talon pushed back his hair with the heel of his hand. "What Vikram is trying to say is that since we launched the Ten Worst list, my ratings can be seen from space. And all that extra ad revenue will pay for a lot of Vikrams."

"Legal issues?" Alex addressed her question to the lawyer.

Talon answered for him. "Nothing to worry about. We've heard from the lawyers of—keep me honest, Vikram—two of Benedetti's ex-wives?"

Vikram held up three fingers.

"Three. Well, let them try. I'm nothing if not *careful.* No accusations on the show, no new claims of wrongdoing—anything I say is already in the public domain. We don't even define what we mean by *worst*. Ten worst at what? Playing Scrabble? Eating noodles with chopsticks? You see where I'm going, Detective?"

"Special agent," Alex corrected him. "Mr. Talon, we're going to need your whereabouts on the nights Luca Benedetti and Tyrell Dixon died."

Talon picked an invisible spec from his lower lip. "I don't know where I was five minutes ago. My assistant Emelda keeps my diary, you can speak with her." He glanced at the lawyer, then back to Alex. "Am I a *suspect*? Do you think I might be murdering people to improve my ratings?"

"We just want to rule you out."

"Oh, I'm not offended." Broad smile. "And it's not the worst idea to boost viewing figures that I've heard pitched at NBC."

"Two men are dead, Mr. Talon," she said, putting enough steel into her tone to send his smile into retreat.

"Of course." A beat as Talon reset his expression to solemn mode. "Terrible business, despite them being . . . well, a nasty business. How can I *help*, Special Agent Bedford? I expect you'll want to speak with my production team."

"We'd appreciate it."

A new light shone in Talon's eyes. "*Talon Tonight*, official partner to the FBI."

"I'm sorry?"

"Nightly updates, ride-alongs, interviews with your team—we'll show you in a super-awesome light, of course. Whether you solve the case of the copycat suicides or catch the crazed Ten Worst killer, we'll make sure you look *amazing* doing it. What do you think?"

Alex closed her notebook. "Thanks for the time, Mr. Talon."

CHAPTER

5

Jacob soon realized that when Floyd said "hit the Village," he meant take the elevator down to the Village Tavern, located on the ground floor of his building. Jacob stepped into a basement with lights so low they had to be a safety hazard. Neon ceiling lamps lent each table an eerie glow and the thudding bass made him feel old, but Floyd had said that "lower Manhattan died years ago," and this way they wouldn't have far to stagger home.

Their server recognized Floyd. Jacob could tell from the way she sneaked a better look as she set down Floyd's Shock Top and Jacob's double Laphroaig.

"Are you—?"

"No." Floyd lifted his drink without meeting her eye.

She departed with a stiff back, and Jacob tried to follow her into the dark with his Lumix camera. "What was that about?"

"Can we not film?" Floyd said.

Jacob let the Lumix drop to his hip.

"I'm not exactly a stranger here," Floyd said. "Or maybe it's hidden worlds."

"Huh?"

Tiny pink spots appeared on Floyd's cheeks. *Hidden Worlds* on the Discovery Channel. 'Floyd Shaw takes you places you've never been.'"

"That one passed me by. Maybe if you'd returned my calls the past four years . . ."

Floyd swallowed beer, setting his glass down half empty before Jacob took his first sip. "Canceled after one season. Climbers are the new rock stars—a pun the media won't tire of. Explorers, it transpires, are colonialists and cultural appropriators."

"Damn. At least you're still the face of Close Shave razor blades."

Floyd drained his glass and excused himself to the restroom. He returned with a bounce in his step and punched Jacob's shoulder before he sat down. "Good to see you, man. You look lean."

Jacob held up his whiskey. "The low-cal malt diet. Floyd, I've a question for you."

"You want to know why Elizabeth cut you off four years ago."

"Hell yes, but that can wait. First, I want to know when you started doing cocaine?"

Floyd frowned like he might deny it, then something tapped Jacob's knee. Floyd's fingers tried to pass him something below the table.

"I'm good, thanks," Jacob said. "I hung up my coke boots a few years back."

Floyd made a *suit yourself* face and slumped back in his chair. "So, what's this tiny favor you need?" he said. "You go first. I'm still working up to Elizabeth."

"Seems a little pointless now, but okay." Jacob took a pull of whiskey. "I'm your classic art-house wanker, right? My last film on women's boxing picked up a Sundance special mention, but it barely covered costs."

"Ever considered making something people would pay to see?"

"Yes, actually. But it's all about finding a subject that will connect with the audience. I've been looking for something human, relatable, but also with scale . . . big and crunchy."

"Give me a *for example*."

"For example, you."

Floyd's brown eyes sharpened.

"Not just you," Jacob said, leaning forward. "The whole New Frontiers eco-adventurers concept. I could embed with the club like a kind of war correspondent, join modern pioneers as they risk their lives to raise awareness of a dying planet. Working title, *The Rebirth of Adventure*. A chance for me to step out from behind the camera."

Floyd watched Jacob over the lip of his glass. "You just had this idea?"

"I had this idea five years ago when you opened the club. But out of nowhere Elizabeth cut the cord and you both stopped taking my calls. Then two days ago my phone rings and you tell me to get my ass out here on the next flight without telling me why."

Floyd pushed back his chair. "I need another bump. Then I need to tell you why you're here."

* * *

"You know me," Floyd said, three minutes later. "I want to save the world as much as the next guy."

"Unless the next guy's Elizabeth."

Floyd rapped the table, as if congratulating Jacob on a difficult pool shot. "In Elizabeth World, if you don't leap out of bed each morning to man the barricades, you might as well tattoo 'lazy fascist' on your forehead." Floyd sucked on his top lip. "We had a canoe trip planned down the Amazon to raise awareness over illegal logging. Then I get a call from these guys." Floyd shook the chunky black chronograph circling his wrist. "My timepiece sponsors still think explorers are cool. Problem is, they also sponsor the Brazilian Grand Prix. They heard about the blog and didn't want me embarrassing the Brazilian government."

"And you told Elizabeth you wanted to cancel the trip."

"Do I look like I'm tired of life? I said *maybe* we postpone until after the Grand Prix. Oh, Jesus . . . I'd betrayed her. The man she'd married would never help a crooked government greenwash its dirty laundry. After that, we exist in miserable silence for weeks, until one day I get back from Trader Joe's and her stuff's vanished. I found my sponsorship contract in the kitchen sink under a box of matches."

"Subtle."

"Yeah, well, little bitch that I am, I burned it. The thing is, it wasn't just me." Floyd pursed his lips, as if the words tasted sour.

"About a year ago, Elizabeth changed the business model at New Frontiers. Membership became free if you promised to burn your commercial contracts—and I mean literally burn them. Obviously, ninety-nine percent of the membership said, 'Screw you.' She closed the club down—a unilateral decision, I didn't get a say. New Frontiers has been closed ever since."

Jacob rubbed at his eyes.

"Sorry, man." Floyd huffed back a nasal blockage. "You'd set your heart on those interviews. I could give you a personal exclusive on my Greenland trip, or a disastrous K2 ascent I made a few years ago, but that's all."

"Forget the interviews. She's sick again. It's back. That's what you're telling me."

"That's what I'm telling you."

Sick again.

Jacob aged seven, crouched at the top of the stairs, eavesdropping on his parents. "The teacher could have lost an eye." There would be more psychological tests. Jacob, already a dedicated secret listener, knew about the tests. He also knew that Elizabeth had wrecked a psychologist's office. The psychologist had described her as the scariest child he'd ever seen.

Jacob aged nine, summoned with his sister to the kitchen where their mother stands at the window, her face a porcelain mask. A policewoman tells Jacob and Elizabeth to be brave. A secret weakness in their dad's heart . . . he won't be coming home . . . Later, Jacob is reading Batman comics by torchlight under his duvet. From Elizabeth's room comes a sound like a fox with its leg caught in a trap. The wall between their bedrooms shakes with the force of a hurled chair, followed by the crack of a smashed mirror, the wrench of a shelving unit pulled to the ground, a scream that seems to rise forever. And the one person who can reliably calm Elizabeth down won't be coming home.

Jacob aged twenty-five, hosting Christmas in London for his mother and the newly married couple. Elizabeth in better spirits than Jacob can remember, full of her upcoming solo round-the-world sailing expedition. Floyd his usual cheery self, but refusing to remove the scarf around his neck. Elizabeth oddly attentive to her husband, touching his hand, filling his wine glass. Jacob recognizing his sister in a rare state of contrition.

Enough.

"Why didn't you call me, Floyd?"

"Forbidden."

"Why bring me here now? What's going on?"

Floyd's eyes flickered yellow in the neon. "You can still find her at New Frontiers, haunting the place with a few hangers-on. I want you to tell her that she needs help."

"Why would she listen? She hasn't spoken to me in four years."

"Elizabeth loves you, man. You know that."

Floyd's eyes drifted to the TV screen above the bar, and Jacob followed his gaze. A man grinned from a photograph: black, late-forties, green necktie under a tan suit. Cut to footage of a body bag being loaded into an ambulance, police divers in wetsuits. A headline rolled across the screen. "Breaking News: Councilor Tyrell Dixon's Email Confession Confirms Second 'Redemption Suicide' from Ricky Talon's Ten Worst People in New York."

CHAPTER

6

Six twenty AM, downtown Manhattan, and the windows of the Federal Plaza building blazed in the morning sun. Alex's boss had summoned her for a six AM meeting, then texted ten minutes before the hour to say he was running late. Alone on the twenty-third floor of the FBI Criminal Investigations Division, Alex rummaged in her desk drawer. Her frantic hands found a desk diary, two nutrition bars, a fabric armpit holster for a .40 caliber Glock, and finally a small plastic bottle. The rattle of Excedrin sounded like church bells. Two migraines in two days. That felt new.

She dry-swallowed the pills rather than waste sixty seconds walking to the water fountain. While her laptop booted, she prowled the open-plan office, pulling down window blinds, each ray of sun a needle in her eye.

The overhead light flickered, and her name rang out across the office.

"Alex, what's with the blackout blinds? We expecting an air raid?"

Supervisory Special Agent Brett Murphy leaned into the doorway. Under the strip light the skin below his eyes appeared almost translucent. Five years and one rank Alex's senior, Murphy wore his checkered sportscoat like a uniform, both buttons closed.

"I was experiencing a little personal carpet-bombing. I took a pill."

"Need a day in bed?"

"All good." She'd already used her annual allowance of sick days. A decade ago, a colleague exceeded his allowance by two days. His nickname was still Sick Note.

"You saw the news?" Murphy said, as he filled a paper cone from the water cooler.

"CNN said Tyrell Dixon emailed the Department of Justice with a suicide note that named names. Is that true?"

"Suicide note barely covers it." He perched on a desk a few cubes away—the days of male agents perching on the desks of female subordinates were over, even females who'd reached the relative safety of their sixth decade. "Total mea culpa. Names, dates, bribe amounts, emails, contracts. All the kickbacks, the cronyism, the look-the-other-ways. Dixon cleared two decades of shit off his chest before his leap into the big blue. This will cause the biggest shake-up in local government since forever. Just a shame it won't have your name on it."

Alex massaged above her ears where the pain pooled. "So now we think Dixon took his own life?"

"Yes, thank God."

"What are we thanking God for?"

"For not sending us a serial killer."

"You're sure we're looking at two suicides?"

"From the same list? I know, it stretches the imagination. But Benedetti locked himself in his building before he took a dive—his keys were found *inside* the lobby. And we've nothing to say Dixon didn't follow suit. Think about it. Dixon's email would have earned him twenty years in a two-by-ten, or a bullet in the back of the head while he's walking his pooch. A dip in the Hudson seems preferable to both."

"I guess," Alex said.

"Maybe it's not that weird, Alex. One showboating scumbag repents and another showboating scumbag sees how many headlines it gets and wants in on the act. The main thing is that it's no longer FBI business. Don't look so glum. Your investigation applied some of the pressure. It's not like you don't deserve credit."

"I'm supposed to feel good about driving a man to suicide?"

"Depends on who you talk to." Murphy huffed through his nose. "You should be happy, Alex. Dixon's confession eats everything, including your miss with that NYC council whistleblower last year."

You should be happy, Alex.

Because there's nothing a good agent enjoys more than seeing her FUBARs filed on a high shelf to collect dust. However high that shelf, she doubted Murphy would forget the gleeful call from his equivalent at the NYPD. "Hey, Murph, we got a guy walked in the shop, says he works at city hall and we should be looking hard at Tyrell Dixon. Funny thing is, this guy says he lifted his skirt to you six months back. Spoke to a Special Agent Alex Bedford. She said she'd call him back, but she never did."

One of many things Alex should have done around that time. Your spouse, they say, is your other half. Lose him and you might find you're half a person living half a life.

"So, what happens now?" she said. "We're not done looking into Talon."

"I saw your notes. He claims to have been at his New Hampshire vacation place when Benedetti hit the sidewalk, and at an awards dinner in Chicago the night Dixon died. Sure, check it out, close the loop, but we've done our diligence here. You can leave Benedetti and Dixon to the NYPD—let them deal with the media bullshit."

"Can I at least see the email Dixon sent? I'll correlate it with our intel and send anything I find over to the PD."

"Just send them your case file." Murphy made a dismissive gesture with his fingers, flicking the work at the NYPD. "Let them do the work for once."

"For once, sir?"

Murphy closed his eyes—knowing he'd screwed up. "I'm sure your dad was a fine police officer before he retired, and the New York Police Department is a fine institution. But we're the FBI, Alex, and we have enough serious crime to keep us busy without needing to step out of lane. Besides, you're due at that DEI course in New Jersey from tomorrow."

The Diversity, Equity, and Inclusion two-day course. She'd forgotten. *Dammit.* "Can't you send someone else?"

"You volunteered, sport."

She did. And not only for that. On a bad William day a few months back, she'd signed up for DEI training, a community outreach program, school education visits, even an FBI yoga class. *Busy, busy, busy Alex Bedford.* No slipping.

"Take Pat Coombs, if you must." Murphy was already heading for the door. "And bring us back a transgender sign for the bathroom."

When Murphy had gone, Alex leaned back in her chair, thumbed in her earbuds, and set her phone to an old recording of Jacqueline du Pré playing Elgar's Cello Concerto in E Minor. Murphy was happy to believe they were looking at two suicides if it meant the case stayed with the NYPD, and Alex wasn't going to change his mind any time soon. She spun slowly in the chair, taking in the empty office panorama as the exquisite ache of du Pré's cello filled her ears. Eventually, the music did its job: the clouds in her mind parted to reveal clear skies—a space for thoughts to form.

What had Pat Coombs said? Luca Benedetti was a stone-cold suicide.

Unless it was made to look that way.

* * *

Alex's agency password accessed the NYPD mainframe and a few clicks later, Luca Benedetti's case file. In the dark office, the incident report glowed on screen.

Injury Extent: Fatal
Injury Reason: Fall from roof of Clearwater House, Greenpoint, Brooklyn (20-floor apartment building, closed for renovation)
Injury Cause: Suspected suicide

Luca Benedetti had died between two and four in the morning, but his broken body lay on the sidewalk until a private security patrol cruised by at six AM. The first responder from the NYPD had secured the scene, and a subsequent search confirmed that Clearwater House had been locked from the inside. No sign of forced entry. Benedetti's keys had been found on the floor inside the lobby.

On the floor? Not in his pocket?

She scrolled down the report. Weighing two hundred pounds, Luca Benedetti would have reached 120 mph before he hit the ground, and the ambulance team wouldn't need medical training to know he was beyond saving. One of her first cases for the bureau had been a spate of college suicides linked to an early web forum: nine young lives hurled themselves off buildings across five different college campuses. She didn't remember all the victims' names, but she remembered the pictures.

Benedetti's last goodbye: *I have lived the wrong life . . . I beg you all for forgiveness.*

Who was he begging for forgiveness? His family? Tenants? The crime scene tech who spent an hour scraping his brains off the asphalt? She clicked into the autopsy folder for the coroner's report.

> Cause of Death: Multiple blunt-force injuries, fracture of the thoracolumbar spine, rupture of the aorta, severe head trauma
> Verdict: Death by suicide

Alex, who hadn't lit a cigarette for thirty years, blew imaginary smoke at the ceiling. The report said suicide, the clock on her laptop said 7:25, the Excedrin was working its magic, and she'd wasted enough time. Maybe Pat Coombs would fancy a prework coffee at the diner across the street.

About to click out of the NYPD case file, she noticed a folder named "Images." Alex didn't need to see the photographs, but—ridiculous, perhaps—it seemed like cowardice not to look. The first image she opened was a close-up of a blood-soaked eye resting where an ear should have been, the arm of a pair of spectacles growing up from the socket as if the wire had sprouted organically from the cheekbone. The second image was the body from above, pancaked against the sidewalk like Wile E. Coyote after a canyon fall. Alex's temples throbbed as she clicked back into the first image and stared at the crooked arm of Benedetti's spectacles protruding from his eye socket.

She'd seen something like it before.

Or rather, she hadn't.

In that early college campus case, Alex still raw as an uncooked shrimp, five of the nine college kids who jumped to their death had worn glasses. All five folded their glasses away into a pocket before they jumped. Habit? Some kind of subconscious preparation for the afterlife?

She flipped back to the incident report. The first responder from the NYPD had been Probationary Police Officer Leo Diaz out of the Eighty-fourth. She wrote the name in her notebook, then sat back in her chair, tapping her teeth with the end of her pen.

She reached for her phone.

Graham Bedford picked up on the third ring, which meant he was in his recliner facing the TV, a mug of black coffee resting on one arm of the chair, his phone on the other.

"Dad, when you were in the police department, did you catch many suicides?"

A grunt from the depths of the recliner. "Too many, sweet pea. New York's a merciless town if you're not winning."

"Find any of them with their spectacles on?"

"Can't say I remember." A beat, then, "Come to think of it, no. No, I didn't."

"Thanks, Dad. Be good."

Alex dropped her phone into her jacket pocket. She wasn't a psychologist, but the college case had taught her something that her dad—an NYPD veteran with thirty years' service—had just confirmed: suicides remove their glasses before they jump.

CHAPTER

7

Cooked in his clothes from thirty minutes on a subway train with broken AC, Jacob stood in a parking lot, gazing through the Lumix lens at the square brick and boarded windows of the abandoned Jumping Jack Power Plant, an upturned packing crate of a building. Beyond the waterfront of Brooklyn's Sunset Park, a strip of ocean scattered the evening light, and the air tasted of gasoline from the nearby Belt Parkway. To the north, Liberty raised her torch as if trying to hail a cab.

He skirted the building until he reached a double door with a brass plate. New Frontiers. The brass had darkened over the years. Under Jacob's hand, the door gave an inch.

She might be inside.

Elizabeth, his sister, whom he'd called Lizbat before he could pronounce her name. Who taught him secret languages and read him pirate stories from the top bunk bed. Who got kicked out of school after beating a boy in the playground for stealing Jacob's new mittens. That's what the adults had never understood. They saw a young girl hitting out randomly at the world. But Elizabeth always had a reason, and that reason—Jacob instinctively understood—was fear. Fear of being ignored, fear of a world without a father, fear of shame being cast on an already-broken family, fear of her own powerlessness to protect the crumbling world around her.

If Elizabeth was back in the bad place, it meant she was scared.

The scent of rusted iron met Jacob as he stepped inside. Graffiti tags covered the walls, the concrete floor buried under twisted metal shelving, the only sound the wash of traffic from the nearby parkway.

His "Hello?" echoed in the overhead pipework.

On the far wall, a three-foot horizontal arrow in luminous green had been sprayed over the graffiti. The arrow pointed to a metal staircase. Jacob listened to the building breathe. Holding the Lumix at chest height like a police bodycam, he picked his way across the rubble.

A turn in the staircase brought him to a different world, a broad airy hallway leading to a steel door. Life-size monochrome photographs lined a pink wall. Five men—four white and one black—each with his own name plate. Jacob focused the Lumix on the first image, a vintage shot of a mustached colonel-type behind the wheel of an early motorcar.

Stephen Allen Reynolds, sailor, whaler, soldier.

Jacob Felle, sailor, whaler, soldier sounded better than Jacob Felle, semi-successful documentarian. He moved on down the hallway, his lens sweeping over a smiling man in a leather flying helmet, a slight tweedy figure in a garden, and a triumphant hunter lifting the horns of a lifeless antelope.

Tom Baldwin, pioneer balloonist.

Byron de Prorok, archaeologist, anthropologist, author of travelogues.

Fritz Duquesne, Boer War veteran, big-game hunter.

The final photograph was more recent: late sixties or early seventies, a narrow-shouldered man standing on the deck of a sailboat, one knee cocked on the rail, coils of rope over his shoulder, snow-capped peaks puncturing the sky behind his head.

Leonard Harris, sailor, inspiration, friend.

Jacob recognized the amber eyes in the chestnut-brown face. This was a younger version of the man in the magazine cover photo hanging in Floyd and Elizabeth's apartment. Elizabeth had told Jacob about Leonard, back when they still spoke on the phone. She'd been keen to introduce them when Jacob visited New Frontiers, a visit that had never happened.

Why hadn't his sister added an image of a pioneering female? He'd once heard Elizabeth say that feminism was the smartest trick men ever played on women, but like many things she said over the years, he hadn't fully understood what she meant.

At the end of the corridor, he turned to frame the gallery with the Lumix. This would make a fine panning shot, ending with Leonard Harris, sailor, inspiration, friend. If Leonard was still alive and liked telling stories, maybe there was a movie to be made after all.

* * *

What had he expected? A leather-bound gentleman's club where you might find Phileas Fogg taking bets to circle the world? A high-tech lab where professional explorers could pore over 3D renderings of mountainsides or undersea trenches? Jacob ran the Lumix over a vaulted industrial-sized loft space, a ghost ship of empty leather sofas, half-drunk coffees, magazines left open on tables. Two unmanned concessions stood under a wall of leaded glass—one a coffee kiosk shaped like a silver Airstream, the other a pop-up apparel shop for the outdoor activity brand Arc'teryx, with a set of empty coat hangers on a rail.

He weaved between the sofas toward the only other exit, a sliding wooden door at the rear of the loft. The door slid open to reveal the paper-white dangling body of a man, chin on chest, naked except for a pair of undershorts and skinny as a blade of grass. Jacob stumbled backward. He would have fallen if his thighs hadn't hit the back of a sofa. The man's head lifted. Green eyes lit up a face dense with orange freckles. The man wasn't suspended by his neck—*thank Christ*—but by one hand gripping a metal bar over the doorframe.

"You're handsome," the man said, unsmiling. "Six or seven. I'm a four. Henry's a ten."

"Lucky Henry," Jacob said, annoyed with himself for stumbling. "I appreciate the feedback. Is there a New Frontiers meeting tonight?"

The man dropped softly to the ground. He had the lean physique of a teen, but the lines around his eyes put him over thirty. The ragged ginger scalp suggested he cut his own hair.

"We're not taking members."

Jacob detected a French lilt in the accent—*members* was *mem-bears*.

"I'm looking for Elizabeth Felle. I'm her brother."

"Elizabeth never said she had a brother."

Which shouldn't have come as a surprise. Or driven a tiny splinter into Jacob's heart.

"I'm Jacob Felle. Good to meet you."

Iron rods closed over Jacob's hand. "Claude Lemieux. Is that thing on?"

He meant the Lumix. "No," Jacob lied. "Is she here?"

"Nah, sorry, bud."

"Is she coming later?"

Lemieux shrugged. "Wouldn't know—haven't seen your sister since this place hollowed out. I just came by to pick up some shit and got distracted by my old hang bar."

"Can I wait in case she shows up?"

Lemieux frowned as he scratched his rib cage. Without a word, he pulled the door closed, leaving Jacob staring at the wooden slats, wondering if Elizabeth was quietly slipping out of a rear entrance. Thirty seconds later, the door slid open again. The orange man now wore a pair of cargo pants, but his torso was still bare. His smile illuminated the freckled face.

"Can't talk man-to-man without pants. Come the fuck in, Jacob Felle."

CHAPTER

8

*Y*OU'RE CRAZY AS *a box of crickets, a tin-hat loony-tune.* That's what the world says about Dallas Johncock. You dare to educate the common man and they shut down your TV station, kick you off social media, put you on a list of the ten worst people in New York alongside kiddie-fiddlers and Nazis. Suicide cult or serial killer, the media says. Either way, Ricky Talon started the coolest new craze in town.

Forget about it. You know a CIA kill list when you see one.

A hot summer evening, eighty-five degrees, and still you're shivering as you pass St. Paul's Chapel to reach Fulton Street. Maybe it's this location that chills your skin. You just crossed the 9/11 Memorial Plaza: site of the greatest hoax ever visited on the American people.

Who are you kidding?

It's the *anticipation* making you shiver. Tonight could change everything. That's why you're here despite the list, despite everything... What the senator is offering you is just too good to turn down, and every nerve in your body feels like someone turned the pegs on a guitar until the strings are ready to snap.

Your throat tightens as you launch the video app on your cell. Your long face stares back at you. "Calling all truth-seekers. Tonight, I meet with Senator Patrick Charles Duval. The senator promised us the truth. He knows we are legion; we are tired of being lied to, and we will spread the word like fire in a cornfield."

You stumbled on *cornfield*, but there's no time to rerecord, because here comes the car, a long stretch job with tinted windows. You can't see the driver, but the plate matches the WhatsApp message you received an hour ago.

"Know then, truth-seekers, that if you're seeing this, I've been disappeared, and you must tell the world."

The car halts beside you. The engine purrs, a panther pretending to sleep.

You set the clip to auto-upload three hours from now.

Be bold, Dallas.

As you reach for the door handle, the panther growls and leaps forward. You can only watch from the curb as red taillights swish around a corner, leaving you alone in the dusk.

CHAPTER

9

ALEX LEANED OVER the bathtub to prop her phone on the toilet seat, the movement releasing a waft of coconut oil from her shower cap. She set a radio app to NPR—an arts discussion, earnest voices—then slid down until the water warmed her chin, and immediately knew that she didn't want to be in her tub, any more than she wanted the tumbler of Rioja perched beside the faucet or the fennel salad she'd prepared for her postbath meal. This was what single people did. Took baths, listened to the radio, drank wine . . . Did they all endure their leisure time like a factory worker waiting for a shift to end?

She closed her eyes and saw Luca Benedetti, who died with his glasses on.

Tyrell Dixon on a metal tray; the email he sent the DoJ.

The bath was cooling. She tried to turn the hot water faucet with her big toe. NPR had shifted from arts to news, and Alex was surprised to find Ricky Talon's dead men relegated to the fourth item. "Today the NYPD confirmed no evidence of foul play in the deaths of Luca Benedetti or Tyrell Dixon."

She reached for her phone and googled *Dixon suicide*. The first result was a YouTube clip of the latest *Talon Tonight*. Barely twelve hours old, the clip had nine million views.

"Ricky, if your list encouraged a little personal reflection in those two crooks, then I can only congratulate you for shining a light in the darkness." Alex recognized Talon's guest, Paddy something, a jut-jawed candidate for the upcoming mayoral elections.

"Nothing to do with me," Talon said with fleeting grin at the camera.

"Well, I can only hope that number one on your list is also in a reflective mood. I'm talking about Mr. Emil Hertzberg, Miss Piggy himself, a man who has never seen the inside of a jail cell, despite what happens to those poor young girls who board his yacht. Why no jail? Because Mr. Emil Hertzberg has powerful friends. And that, Ricky, is exactly the kind of corruption that I will target if I am lucky enough to be elected mayor of New York City."

Just before Alex killed the clip, she heard Talon say, "I think I just heard your campaign manager orgasm."

She called Pat Coombs.

"Alex, everything okay?"

"Just tearing greens for a salad." She smiled at the realization that she felt it kinder to lie than to place the image of her wet naked body into her partner's mind. "Can you meet me at the diner by the office?"

"Tomorrow before work? Sure, I'll see you there at seven."

"I mean now."

"Something new came in?"

"No, I just want to kick some ideas around."

A beat. "It's kinda late, Alex."

"Shit, you're right. I forgot criminals clock off at five."

Another beat. Coombs said, "Are you okay?"

"Why wouldn't I be?

"You sound a little . . . I don't know."

Alex heard the shrill in her own voice. "It sounds like you *do* know."

Her partner sighed into the phone. "Down time can be difficult. I get it."

"The lonely widow wants to meet up so she doesn't put her head in the gas oven?"

Coombs surprised her with the sharpness of his tone. "Your head wouldn't fit an oven, Alex. It's too full of dead goons."

"Huh?"

"You're gonna tell me that we can connect Talon, Benedetti, and Dixon, aren't you? Well, let me spell it out. Both Talon's alibis check out—a maid saw him at his New Hampshire vacation place on the night Benedetti croaked, and we have him on camera at a Chicago awards dinner while Dixon was drinking the Hudson dry. The NYPD found no signs of foul play in either death, and did you see our future mayor interviewed by Ricky Talon? The list is already being weaponized. Oh, and you received a direct order from Murphy to stand down. Is that enough or should I go on?"

Alex lay in the bath, her fury seeming to heat the water around her.

Coombs broke the silence. "Look, I'm taking my boys out. Bowling and pizza if you want to join us? We can talk through any damn thing you like over a beer."

An olive branch and the offer of a distraction. Not subtle. But kind.

"Aren't the Mets playing?" Alex said. "You guys always go to the Mets."

"See ticket prices this year? We'll watch the game at the lanes. Bowling and pizza is part of what Harriet and I call Operation Scale-back."

"Nothing wrong with skittles and beer." *Now they were making small talk.* "Thanks for the offer, Pat, but it can wait. And I have plans for later."

"A date?" he said. She heard him inhale sharply, scared he'd said the wrong thing.

"A Google date," she said, letting him off the hook. "I want to spend some time with the erstwhile Luca Benedetti. Tomorrow morning I'm meeting the uniform who was first on scene after Benedetti's body hit the sidewalk." Before Coombs had time to object, she said, "Enjoy bowling and say hi to the boys."

Alex climbed out of the bath and reached for a towel. She'd lost weight, and not in a good way. "No sign of foul play, my ass," she said to the mirror.

CHAPTER

10

Claude Lemieux had natural springs in his heels. He bounded down the hallway ahead of Jacob, chattering over his shoulder. Did Jacob know that Claude had been the first man to free solo the Princess Tower in Dubai? What a blast, man. Next up was the Burj Khalifa, also in Dubai, and currently the tallest building in the world, an eight or nine for real. Claude wouldn't be first up the Burj, but he'd be first to do it without a rope, and yeah, he'd be arrested, but a week in a Dubai jail was a small price for eternity. Cause that's what *first* means, man. When you're first, you're first forever.

At the end of the corridor, someone had carved the words "Anarchists Only" into a wooden door. In front of the word *Anarchists*, the word *Armchair* had been added in black Sharpie. Claude waved Jacob in with a shy smile.

"We used to call this the den."

The room had the cluttered air of a school staff room: magazines, a trestle table strewn with papers, books scattered like broken birds. No Elizabeth and no other exit, but in one corner a man in a pink shirt and beige chinos fiddled with the controls of an espresso machine.

"Henry Duval." The man in the pink shirt wiped his hand against his leg and offered it to Jacob. "Good to meet you, Jacob. Espresso?"

"I'm good, thanks."

Henry was half a head taller than Jacob, square in the shoulders, with nutmeg eyes and ash-brown hair swept back from a high ivory forehead. As Jacob took the proffered hand he noticed taut skin over the stump of the fifth knuckle. Henry's pinkie finger was missing. The sight was jarring, and Jacob hoped Henry hadn't sensed him flinch.

Claude placed both hands on the trestle table and launched himself up and over, twisting acrobatically to drop onto the couch with a *whump*. "You can ask him if you like. Henry doesn't mind."

"Ask him what?" Jacob said.

"Nicely done," Henry said with a twitch of a smile, holding up the hand with the missing finger. "Claude's referring to my absent digit. This, Jacob, is what happens when you fail to settle a Yakuza debt on time."

Claude made a snorting sound from the couch. "Believe that if you want to. So, Jacob. Were you, Floyd, and Elizabeth all at the same college in England?"

"Floyd and I went to Exeter. Elizabeth was at Southampton. She could have gone to Oxford, but Southampton meant she could sail at the weekends."

Why tell them that? Like they wouldn't already know Elizabeth was smart. What else will you tell these men? That you and your sister attended boarding schools the Felles could never have afforded before your father's life insurance paid out? Schools you despised and begged your mother to release you from—to no avail.

Claude flexed his fingers, staring at the ridged muscles down his own forearms. "You came all the way out to the Rotten Apple to see your sister, but you didn't call ahead?"

"I was hoping to surprise her."

"Brave man," Henry said. "Please, have a seat."

Jacob pulled out a chair. He had to move a stack of magazines—climbing, sailing, hiking—and as he placed them on the floor, he found himself staring at Henry's bare toes on wooden floorboards—no socks, no shoes. Jacob straightened and said, "Assuming Elizabeth doesn't show tonight, any idea where I'll find her?"

"If it's a surprise you're after, try Montauk," Claude said, flashing a grin at Henry.

"What's at Montauk?" Jacob said.

"Nothing much." Henry took a seat at the end of the sofa and rested a hand on Claude's shoulder. "I believe your sister used to sail down that way, but not for a while now."

"Right." Claude looked at his lap. "I was thinking of someone else." He dug a hand down the side of the sofa cushion, produced a phone and started to scroll. "First time in NYC, Jacob?"

Fine, let's change the subject.

"I was here when Floyd and Elizabeth had a tiny place up in the Bronx," Jacob said. "I can work the subway and I know to ask for *warder*—like in *prison warder*—if I want water."

"Then you're practically a New Yorker," Henry said. "Which hotel are you at?"

"I'm at Elizabeth and Floyd's place."

"Ah." A beat. "And how is the mighty Floyd?"

"A little less mighty than the last time I saw him. He mentioned the club had closed."

"Too many people wanted to ride the fame train." Claude pulled on an imaginary steam whistle. "Which isn't a crime. It's just a bit, you know . . . Floydy."

Jacob surprised himself with the heat in his voice. "Floyd's a good guy."

Henry raised his palms in apology. "Claude didn't mean any offence. We all loved the Floyd. You know, I've got Elizabeth's number in my phone. Want me to let her know you're here?"

Like you didn't already.

Jacob stood to leave. "If she shows up, I never came by. Surprise, remember."

Claude pointed a long finger at Jacob. "Your secret's safe with us."

*　　＊　＊　＊*

Jacob leveled his eye to the retina scan and listened for the click of the lock. As he entered the apartment, Floyd's bedroom door opened wide enough for Floyd to squeeze through the gap. Thrashy guitar music spilled from the room.

"You're back early." Floyd breathed stale beer into Jacob's face.

"She wasn't there. Am I interrupting something?"

"A few friends round for poker night. New Frontiers was empty?"

"I met a skinny climber called Claude and someone called Henry. I got the feeling they warned Elizabeth, but I may be imagining it."

"Henry Duval." Floyd's lips curled. "Interesting."

"Is it? Are you okay, Floyd?"

"Never better."

"Then why are you acting like a policeman guarding a crime scene? Worried I'll clean you out if I join the game?"

Behind Floyd, the bedroom door opened to reveal a long-bodied man with wiry hair under a trucker cap, and a deep sunburn that broke to pearl-white at his neckline. He had what looked like a pink mop tucked under one arm, until the mop twisted out from the armpit and became a young Asian woman—Chinese or Chinese heritage, Jacob thought—with large liquid eyes, black jeans ripped at the knees, and a singlet covering a body so thin it seemed to bow in the middle. The way she closed the bedroom door made Jacob want to know what was inside.

The man offered Jacob his hand.

"Roland van Buren." Flat tone, no smile. "You must be Jacob."

Jacob took the hand—slender fingers, iron in the grip.

"Roland's a mountaineer," Floyd said. "We climbed together. He's a fellow victim of the Elizabethan purge of New Frontiers."

"Another climber," Jacob said, and when van Buren raised an eyebrow at him, "I just met Claude Lemieux."

Van Buren tilted his long head to one side. "Lemieux, ginger hair, no filter—talks too much. Met him a couple of times before the club fell apart. Different circles."

The girl with pink hair shook Jacob's hand. "Chloe Zhang. You're the filmmaker right?" The liquid eyes appraised him. "I saw your documentary on female boxing and identity."

"Oh, that was you?" Jacob said.

"Not exactly a blockbuster, huh?" She gave a *what-can-you-do?* shrug. "I remember Elizabeth recommended the film to everyone at the club, back when we were all on better terms. It had a cool title. What was it, *Hit Like a Girl?*"

"That's the one." Jacob tried to sound nonchalant, but his heart leapt. *Elizabeth liked his film?* She never said. He banked the warm feeling before it evaporated.

"Is that why you're here?" van Buren said in his toneless voice. "Making a movie?"

"Honestly, I'm not quite sure why I'm here," Jacob said, glancing at Floyd.

Floyd scratched his scalp with both sets of fingernails. "Jacob, man, we need to talk."

* * *

The Village Tavern was busy and they stood at the end of the bar. Floyd wedged himself into the corner so he could face the room, his eyes sweeping the neon basement.

"Go on," Jacob said when they both had a drink in their hands.

Floyd wiped his nose. "This is a shitty thing to do, but I think you'd better leave."

"Leave?"

"Well, you know the old joke. You don't have to go home . . ."

But you can't stay here.

"You're kicking me out? I only landed yesterday—and I'm only here *because you called me and told me to come.*" Jacob's chest tightened. "I haven't seen Elizabeth yet. I haven't given her your message."

"Yeah, I kinda changed my mind about that."

"Claude or Henry called Elizabeth. Elizabeth called you."

Floyd shook his head.

"Yes, she did. She called and gave you shit for inviting me. And you folded."

Floyd shook his head more violently.

"Then what's changed?"

"Nothing . . . Look, there's a Virgin flight at noon tomorrow. Or you could take the Amtrak down to Philly for a week and fly home from there. Philly's cool."

"Yeah, or I could spend a month in the Bahamas eating caviar. I'm a documentary maker who survives by making dumb TV ads for local firms. I don't have endless funds."

"Give me your hand."

"Huh?"

"Hold out your hand."

Floyd pressed something into Jacob's palm.

"I'm sorry. Truly. But you need to leave. Meanwhile, have a little fun on me."

Jacob opened his hand to find a small plastic coke baggie in his palm. He closed his fist quickly. Floyd was already pushing his way through the drinkers toward the door.

CHAPTER

11

Nine in the evening. Tomorrow, Alex would meet the cop who found Luca Benedetti's body, but first she wanted to learn about the man who terrorized tenants for three decades before he landed on the sidewalk outside Clearwater House with his spectacles poking up through an eye socket. A glass of Pinot Noir within reach of the sofa, she put in her earbuds, balanced her laptop on her thighs, and allowed Yo-Yo Ma to gently soak her in Bach's Cello Suite no.1 in G Major while she waited for her mind to clear.

William's photo on the mantle watched over her.

"I'll eat later," she told her husband. "I'm fine."

A Google search for *Luca Benedetti, Clearwater House* unearthed a string of news items connected to his suicide, several mentions of Ricky Talon's list, but nothing she didn't already know. By page four, the results had widened to include Benedetti's personal life—between divorce hearings and business litigation the man had spent half his life in court—and items related to his umbrella company, Clearwater Holdings.

Alex read until her eyes swam. "Time for one more page?" she asked William.

The warm breeze of his voice filled her head. *Don't be too long or I'll be asleep.*

At the top of page five, a name caught her eye. *Clearwater Community.* The link took her to a four-year-old news article in the *Bronx*

Gazette. A fire at the Clearwater Community Nursing Home in Morrisania had claimed three lives. Staff had done their best to evacuate the building, but three elderly residents proved too slow or too confused to make it out in time. The CEO at the time, one Kelly-Anne Pinstock, described the fire as a freak accident. An image sat beside the text: Kelly-Anne Pinstock was late fifties or thereabouts at the time the photo was taken, with a blancmange complexion and a hairdo like the Liberty Bell.

The elderly victims were Walter Thomas, Jeanette Spalding, and Leonard Harris. The names meant nothing to Alex and she didn't recognize them from the grainy photographs.

But imagine. A whole life lived and to die that way at the very end.

She called her father, and for no good reason panic gripped her until he picked up.

"Hey, Dad, guess what!"

"What?"

"I love you."

That deep chuckle. "I know you do, sweet pea. Hold on . . ." a pause, muffled shouting from another room. "Your mother says don't eat chia seeds. She read an article."

"Tell her I love her too."

"She knows."

"Tell her anyway."

Alex wished him good night and promised to visit soon.

Luca Benedetti owned Clearwater House and Clearwater Holdings. Maybe he owned Clearwater Community Nursing Home too.

She opened another browser.

CHAPTER

12

Jacob downed his sixth Nikka and placed the empty glass beside the uneaten burger on the bar. Past midnight, and he was alone in the Village Tavern except for two women drinking at a small table. He allowed himself a flight of fancy in which he joined the women and hit it off with the better-looking one. His imagination skipped the sex and went straight to the morning after, waking with their legs tangled like garlic stems. Then followed an imagined week of heady romance that culminated in his new love begging him not to fly back to England.

He knew he was searching for a reason to stay.

His phone history reminded him that he'd tried to call Elizabeth eight times that evening. After call three, he'd stopped leaving voicemails.

As for Floyd . . . Floyd was a changed man. The coke, the tension in his face and voice, his new friends.

Jacob remembered the cold strength of Roland van Buren's grip. Jacob had credited Claude Lemieux with a strong handshake, but van Buren had fingers that could crush rocks. The girl with the pink hair—Chloe Zhang—the way she'd shut the bedroom door so Jacob couldn't see inside—what was she hiding? Crumpled sheets? That didn't feel very Floyd, but right now *Floyd* didn't feel very Floyd.

Chloe remembered his film and that had felt good.

Elizabeth liked it—that felt even better.

But alone in the neon wasteland of the Village Tavern, Jacob remembered the one review for *Hit Like a Girl* that had lodged forever in his chest. "Felle is technically gifted but fails to genuinely connect with his subjects."

The reviewer could have been describing any one of Jacob's romantic relationships. Jacob said the right things, did the right things—what was the line from that Strangler's song? "We moved into a basement with talk of our engagement"—but he'd never allowed anyone to fill the hollow space behind his rib cage.

And now even his own sister wouldn't speak with him. Floyd could deny it all he liked, but Jacob sensed Elizabeth behind Floyd's insistence that he leave town. She didn't want to meet with him—fine. But the fact that she wouldn't let Jacob stay with his brother-in-law . . . ? Elizabeth had never been vindictive; that was new.

The same question he'd asked himself outside New Frontiers: if Elizabeth was lashing out, it meant she was afraid. So what was she afraid of?

He raised his hand for a final Nikka, then headed for the bathroom. Fuck it, one line from Floyd's coke baggie, for old times' sake. Something wasn't right and a bump in the nostril might stop him feeling sorry for himself. It might jolt his fatigued brain into forming some kind of plan.

CHAPTER 13

IT WAS ONE in the morning before Alex confirmed that neither Luca Benedetti nor his company, Clearwater Holdings, appeared in any of the articles about the fire at the Bronx-based Clearwater Community Nursing Home. The Clearwater connection was likely be a coincidence.

She splashed the last inch of wine into her glass. There was one more thing she could try. The City Register Information System website asked for her credit card, and Alex hesitated. The FBI provided free access, but that would mean logging in with her work creds—she wouldn't put it past Murphy to have had her actions in the system flagged. In the end, she entered her personal card details and, twelve dollars later, *Clearwater Community Nursing Home* generated a single record: a change-of-use document filed two years after the fire by Elmhurst Realty. The building converted to a storage facility and the name reverted to its postal address: 1930 Foch Boulevard.

Business ownership records were available state-by-state. Alex launched the entity database on the New York Department of State's Division of Corporations site.

ENTITY NAME: ELMHURST REALTY, INC.
ENTITY STATUS: INACTIVE

REASON FOR STATUS: DISSOLVED BY PROCLAMATION
SERVICE OF PROCESS: CLEARWATER HOLDINGS, INC.

There it was. Luca Benedetti and Clearwater Holdings owned Elmhurst Realty, and Elmhurst owned Clearwater Community Nursing Home. Three deaths and not one mention of Benedetti's name. How many cops and journalists did he have to pay off to make that happen? Alex couldn't see a connection with Tyrell Dixon, Ricky Talon, Talon's dumb list, or any other damn thing, but if nothing else, she now felt she knew Luca Benedetti a little better.

She drained her wine glass. Yo-Yo Ma had last drawn his bow an hour ago, but she'd hardly noticed. William had hated all classical music—he was a Springsteen man, heaven help him—and they'd spent many an evening with their respective earbuds in, legs entwined on the couch, lost in their own private musical worlds, deliciously together and apart at the same time. Alex didn't need the headphones now. Could have blared Bach at max volume from the Bose speakers either side of the fireplace. Could have fetched her cello down from the attic crawl space and played until her fingers bled.

Ignoring the click in her knee, she walked to the mantle to kiss her husband's photograph good night. In the morning she would be meeting the cop who found Benedetti's body. Meanwhile, she'd run out of reasons to avoid that big, empty bed.

CHAPTER

14

Jacob stood over his sleeping brother-in-law. Waves of morning sun drenched the master bedroom where Floyd lay twisted up in a sheet, blond strands across one cheek, an arm trailed on the floor like a stray tentacle.

"Wake up, Floyd."

Floyd groaned into his pillow. "What are you doing in here?"

"You didn't answer my knock."

"Close the curtain."

"Get up. I'm out of here by noon, like you wanted. Meanwhile, you promised me a Greenland interview. I'll give you fifteen to shower and fix your hair."

* * *

Floyd had always loved a camera, and he knew what worked. As Jacob screwed the Lumix onto its travel tripod, his brother-in-law pulled on a plain gray sweatshirt and emptied the pockets of his cargo pants to remove any odd-looking bulges. Jacob positioned Floyd on a dining chair below the framed *Time* magazine cover, the image of Floyd's face out of focus, but the iconic masthead still recognizable.

"My mouth tastes like a rabbit hutch." Floyd tousled his hair and smoothed the front of his sweatshirt: windswept yet fundamentally neat, the Floyd Shaw brand. "Does this top work for your shot palette?"

"It's doing its best." Jacob closed a window blind to take the glare off Floyd's forehead. "Black would be more slimming. Give me an audio level?"

Floyd extended two middle fingers at the lens. "Why are we doing this? Without the rest of New Frontiers, you don't have a movie."

"In my game, you bag footage when you can. I might not see you for another four years. Move the chair three inches to the left. The sunlight's picking out the old-man wrinkles around your eyes."

That earned Jacob another finger. "What time's your flight?"

"We have about an hour before I head out." Jacob dropped his eye to the viewfinder. "Okay, let's do it. I want to hear about the Greenland Expedition." He rolled his hand to show they were recording.

Floyd straightened his spine. "Picture the five of us in full ice kit, holed up in a cabin in Ilulissat. Guides and dogsleds at the ready to gather evidence that the Kujalleq glacier was melting faster than the 'experts' had predicted."

Staring down the Lumix lens always woke the creative urge, and in the edit suite of his mind Jacob projected scientific data over Floyd's face.

"The Greenland government was dragging its feet on our permit, trying to placate an oil giant that didn't want its offshore rig associated with climate change. Our weather window was closing, so we broke camp before dawn, did what we needed to do, and got back just as the mother of all ice storms hit the coast. We got slapped with a savage fine, but we got our pictures."

Jacob zoomed tight on Floyd's face. "Devil's advocate. Imagine the environmental impact if everyone ignored the permit law."

"It's like chemotherapy and cancer." Floyd stared down the barrel of the lens. "The worse the sickness, the stronger the medicine required. Our photographs hit the cover of *Time* and our message reached millions." He stopped and shook his head. "Can we erase that bit about chemo? Makes me sound like a ghoul."

"Sure, let's jump to your K2 climb. You said it was a disaster. How so?"

Floyd stopped Jacob with a raised hand. "Gimme a minute." He disappeared into the bathroom and returned a few minutes later, dropping onto the chair with a thump. Tiny beads of sweat formed along his hairline. "What were we talking about?" he said.

Jacob lowered his eye to the lens. Now was the time, while Floyd was getting up on his coke high. "Before I forget, Floyd. When I visited New Frontiers, Claude said something about Montauk and Henry kinda shut him down. Mean anything to you?"

"Not really." Floyd massaged the bridge of his nose.

"Any reason Elizabeth might be there?"

"How would I know where she is? I don't even know where she's staying." Floyd slapped his hands together. "Oh—I get it. That's great. Nice work, Jacob."

"What?"

Floyd ripped the radio mic off his lapel. "You don't want an interview, you just want to find out how to reach Elizabeth. Do you even have a flight booked?"

"I'm worried about her. You've made me worry about her, Floyd. I've a right to know where she is."

Floyd stood, eyes bulging, then made his way to a kitchen drawer where he retrieved a square wall calendar. He spun the calendar across the room and it skidded to a halt against Jacob's feet. "This is what you're looking for, much good it'll do you. Elizabeth canceled everything. See for yourself."

As Jacob reached down for the calendar, a voice turned their heads to the doorway.

"I'm interrupting."

Floyd's buddy Roland van Buren leaned his long torso against the hallway. Behind him, Chloe Zhang lowered a canvas shoulder bag to the floor.

"We're done." Floyd sounded more sad than angry. "Jacob's heading out."

"Floyd," Jacob said. "We need to talk."

But Floyd had disappeared along the hall. The front door banged shut. Van Buren peeled himself away from the wall and scooped up the canvas bag. "He's under a lot of strain." Said with a jerk of the head in Floyd's direction and no warmth in the voice. "It's been good to meet you, Jacob. I think it's best if we hang out when you're next in town." Emphasis on *next*.

"Are you telling me I can't talk to my brother-in-law?"

Van Buren gave that some thought. "I don't think we're there yet, and I hope we never will be. But Floyd's—what would you Brits say?—he's a good mate. You stand by your mates, right?"

Without waiting for a reply, van Buren followed Floyd out of the apartment. With a flick of her pink bangs, Zhang trailed after them. She paused to give Jacob a smile that he might have read as an invitation to follow, if she hadn't closed the apartment door firmly behind her.

Left alone, Jacob retrieved the calendar Floyd had hurled across the room. It was already flipped to September and though today was only the third of the month, all thirty boxes had been crossed out in thick black Sharpie. Elizabeth—assuming she'd been the one wielding the Sharpie—had been making a point.

He tilted the calendar to the light. Beneath the black lines, faint blue ballpoint entries remained visible, and under today's date he could just make out the words *Montauk YCRM*.

Jacob put *Montauk YCRM* into Google.

A yacht club.

He started to pack away his film equipment.

So van Buren and Zhang had a key to Floyd's apartment, and one or both of them were on the retina scan. *Weird*. Floyd really had changed if these were his new playmates.

Maybe Elizabeth leaving wasn't as one-sided as Floyd made out.

Camera and tripod packed, daypack over his shoulder, Jacob rode down in the elevator. In the building lobby, he searched on his phone for directions to Montauk YCRM, hoping it wasn't too far away.

CHAPTER

15

THE MORNING AIR tasted burnt, a prelude to rain. Probationary Officer Leo Diaz's cruiser was already parked under the dappled shade of a maple tree when Alex Bedford climbed out of the Impala. She flipped her FBI credentials at Diaz through the cruiser windshield. He joined her on the sidewalk outside Clearwater House, a century-old apartment building and the last of Luca Benedetti's properties to receive a site visit from its owner.

"Appreciate you coming out," she said. "You were first on the scene?"

Diaz was young with an olive complexion and deep brown eyes that held Alex's gaze as if he were a mouse watching a cobra. "The security patrol called it in. I secured the area while we waited for the security firm's spare set of keys, then my partner and me took a look inside. Do we have a problem?"

Scared they'd screwed up. Maybe they had. "Benedetti was dead when you arrived?"

"No doubt."

"Still wearing his spectacles?"

"They were kinda twisted up in . . . it."

"Where was the body, exactly?"

Diaz pointed without turning his head. Alex's instinct told her that he was trying not to look at the sidewalk where Benedetti's body had detonated.

"Must have been a shock to see him like that," she said.

"One of the EMTs lost his breakfast."

"My first jumper suicide made me puke on a new pair of boots."

"Hope they weren't suede."

"Leather and a half size too small, but I thought they made me look taller. There's a number you can call, you know? I hear your generation's better than mine at asking for help."

Diaz nodded. "My Cap told me to avail of the generous resources provided by the police department to safeguard my mental health."

"Good for him."

"He said that after I made the call, I should remember to scratch the word *pussy* into my badge." The brown eyes jumped as he remembered who he was taking to. "Sorry, ma'am."

Alex stared up at Clearwater House, the edge of the roofline stark against blue sky. She experienced a moment of wooziness. *Please let it be vertigo and not the stirrings of another migraine.* In her mind's eye the flailing figure of a man hurtled down toward her. "I'll grab my flashlight," she said. "You fetch a crowbar."

* * *

Officer Diaz prized out the wooden boards nailed over the main entrance to Clearwater House, and they passed through double entrance doors into a lobby bathed in cold blue service lights. The air was surprisingly warm. Perhaps because Alex associated the building with death, she'd expected the chill of a mausoleum.

Diaz scratched his cheek. "Locked from inside, same with the other entrances." He pointed at a dusty corner of the lobby. "We found his keys right about *there.*"

Alex tried to picture Luca Benedetti alone in the lobby, readying to end his own life. Everything she'd read about him in the last twenty-four hours—and there was plenty of tabloid history to read—suggested a heart calcified by years of playing the public villain. Hard to believe he'd drop his keys on the floor after fastidiously locking all the doors. But if someone else had been involved—if Maranzano's people had dragged Benedetti here and thrown him off the roof—then how did they get out and leave the doors locked and the keys on the inside?

"Who had access to the spare set of keys?"

Diaz shook his head. "See where you're going, but the security firm keeps its keys in a lockbox under a camera, 24/7. The Clearwater set had never been checked out." He gave her a sideways glance. "You believe what the TV is saying? Some kind of copycat suicide?"

"It's possible," Alex said. "What do you think?"

"Huh?" Uniforms weren't used to being asked their opinions by FBI agents.

"What's your theory?"

"I, uh . . . Doors locked on the inside, keys on the lobby floor. Why he jumped—no idea, but he jumped for sure."

"Fair enough," Alex said. "I want to see the roof. Is the elevator working?"

"Yeah." Diaz sounded relieved he'd passed the test. "We used it to get up there."

With a lurch that jogged her stomach, the elevator left the ground. Alex shared Diaz's relief—twenty flights of stairs would have shredded her knees.

* * *

A warm salt breeze tugged at her jacket as she walked the lip of the roof, trying to identify the spot where Benedetti's feet last stood. The Freedom Tower loomed in the east, four hundred feet taller than the twin towers it had replaced. Some days Alex looked at the glittering black syringe and saw a monument to rebirth and resilience. Other times, she wondered if the city had offered up a juicier target for next time.

"Right about there, ma'am," Diaz said.

She flattened her belly against the concrete lip. In the dark, Benedetti couldn't have known what lay below. Did it matter to a suicidal mind if its body splattered against the sidewalk, impaled itself on a railing spike, or crashed through the roof of a parked car?

"I have lived the wrong life. I will not live with this guilt another day."

A fake suicide note donating millions to charity was hardly something Maranzano's men would think of. And why would Maranzano risk a pattern when he didn't need to? A suicide and a boating accident would attract far less attention than two suicides with identical last-ditched attempts at rehabilitation and redemption.

Alex's phone buzzed. Pat Coombs.

"How was bowling, Pat?"

"Awesome. I kicked the boys' ten-year-old asses. Spoke to an NYPD buddy first thing, and I thought you'd want to know. The Ds on the case scraped Talon's phone records along with Benedetti's and Dixon's. No connection between any of them."

In other words, let it drop, Alex.

"Today's DEI training," Coombs said. "If we want to make Trenton by midday, we need to hit the tunnel by ten."

He said something else, but Alex had stopped listening. Officer Diaz walked stiffly toward her, a cartoon cop with his patrolman's hat and gun belt silhouetted against the sun.

"I stepped on this." Diaz held out an object the approximate size and shape of a butter knife. He'd put gloves on to pick it up—good man. "Guess we missed it first time around."

Alex pulled on her own gloves before taking the object. Iron, light for its size, with a hammered-flat blade and a loop at one end that her thumb could fit through. The edges were rough, the surfaces uneven, with only the faintest trace of rust.

"What is it?" she said.

Diaz chewed his lip. "Construction fixing? It's heavy, I thought maybe . . ."

"A weapon?" Alex tested the blunt edge. "You wouldn't bring this to a knife fight unless you planned to spread your opponent to death. Benedetti's corpse had no wounds that correspond to this shape."

But Benedetti's corpse had been soup in a skin sack.

Alex slipped the iron object into a clear evidence bag. "I'll have it checked out. Well done, by the way, for not just back-heeling it into a corner."

The young officer managed to look simultaneously pleased and embarrassed.

* * *

Alex watched Diaz ease his cruiser away from the curb. She stayed on the sidewalk to clear her head. No one believed Benedetti's death to be anything other than a suicide, and she'd found nothing solid to challenge that view, except . . .

Her fingers closed around the bagged iron object in her pocket as Clearwater House loomed above her, and a phrase surfaced from the dark waters of her mind.

The call of the void.

Standing at a cliff edge—or the ledge of a skyscraper rooftop—people can experience a strange and terrible desire to jump. Alex had never felt it. For a year after William succumbed to the evil tumor in his brain, she swam alone in an underwater world: looking without seeing, listening without hearing, her innards scooped out by the futility of waking and work and being alive. But even in her most saturated moments of despair and anger—volcanic, earth-splitting, sky-rending anger—it never occurred to Alex to take her own life. Maybe it was a sign of weakness. Maybe she should take a lead from Officer Diaz and carve *pussy* into her badge. Or maybe she just wasn't built to quit.

Maybe Luca Benedetti wasn't either.

CHAPTER

16

Spears of afternoon sunlight attacked the train that carried Jacob the length of Long Island. He had the carriage to himself, the vibrations rattling the Lumix as he filmed tree-lined avenues, parkland, stretches of sparkling ocean, residences that became grander and more isolated the further east he traveled. Four hours after leaving Grand Central Station, he found a taxi behind Montauk station that took him to Star Island—one road in and out—and the sprawling low-rise campus of the Montauk Yacht Club.

The sun was low by the time he found a seat at an outside café with line of sight to the club entrance. He'd called that morning and confirmed that Elizabeth was still booked to speak at seven. Whether she'd show was another matter.

Then, there she was.

An older, more muscular version of his sister climbed out of a battered maroon station wagon and marched across the parking lot with that familiar, lightly swaying motion, as if compensating for the rolling lilt of a boat deck. Gray strands in her cropped black hair matched the gun-metal sweatpants and track top. She carried a daypack on her shoulder. A bandage covered her left arm from wrist to elbow.

Jacob, baseball cap low over his eyes, shrunk down as she passed, but Elizabeth didn't glance in his direction. He was on his feet in time to see her flash an ID and exchange words with the reception staff. A young gym-built man in a tight-fitting polo shirt escorted her through an internal doorway.

Jacob approached the remaining receptionist. "Has she gone in already? Typical."

"Can I help you?" The young woman showed teeth in a friendly smile.

"My sister, Elizabeth Felle." Jacob offered her his driver's license. "I'm filming tonight's talk. Just point me in the right direction. I'll find my way."

* * *

The function room the receptionist directed Jacob to was empty. He continued along the wooden hallway, past mounted regatta photographs and a stuffed trophy cabinet until he reached a fire door with glass panels. He was about to go through when, on the other side of the glass, a door opened and Elizabeth's head appeared, checking the hallway in the opposite direction. Instinctively, Jacob pulled back before she turned his way.

Footsteps, too heavy to be his sister.

"Uh, Miss Felle, that's a private office. I'm afraid you can't be in there."

"I'm so sorry. I was looking for somewhere to get changed."

"Like I said, the ladies' locker room is at the far end of the hall. Let me escort you."

Jacob's sister had navigated the world's oceans solo. There was no way she'd misunderstand simple directions to a locker room. As two sets of footsteps receded, he peeked around the window frame to see the gym-built receptionist hold a passkey to a card reader and usher Elizabeth through another set of doors. Fifteen seconds later, when Jacob tried the same door, he found it locked.

He retraced his steps to the empty function room, with rows of folding chairs and a low stage. He'd lost his chance to catch his sister alone. Maybe that was for the best. In a crowd, she couldn't run.

CHAPTER 17

THE COMFORT SUITES Hotel was charisma-free but FBI expenses-friendly and only a short drive from the Trenton office. Alex Bedford found Pat Coombs in the first place she looked, the hotel bar. He glanced up from his paperback at the sound of Alex's carry-on, the scrape of its sticky left wheel against the polished floor.

"Alex, you made it. Thanks for popping in."

"You didn't get my message?"

"Yeah, at about one thirty when I was heading up to the conference room."

The way Coombs flattened his book on the bar—*Stalingrad*, with an old tank crunching rubble on the cover—told Alex he was pissed. As the sole representative of the New York FBI office, he'd have had to pay attention to a half day of DEI training instead of zoning out and letting Alex take notes. *Serve the lazy goat right.* Alex waved to the barman, pointing to Coombs's red wine to indicate she'd have the same.

"I assume your tardiness has to do with the visit to Benedetti's place?" Coombs said.

She described the object Officer Diaz found on the roof. "I sent it to the lab."

Coombs wrinkled his nose. "Murphy's going to love that."

"Heaven forbid we should be thorough." Alex's wine arrived and she took a welcome slug. "Now stop moaning and indulge me for a moment, will you? We have a list of famous—infamous—names. Two of them commit suicide within a month. Both make spectacular and highly unlikely appeals for redemption accompanied by a game-show giveaway."

Coombs shrugged. "But aside from that, zero connections between the deceased, and zero sign of external interference in their death. Did you see *The Alanson Show* the other night? He had some psych expert comparing Dixon and Benedetti to alcoholics at step nine of the twelve-step program—making amends for their past sins. Bad guys do bad things, Alex. Some repent and try to make good."

"Step nine, sure. But as far as I know, step ten isn't throwing yourself off a building or a boat. I don't buy it, Pat. Egos like theirs don't quit while they're still winning."

"You're back to thinking Ricky Talon's murdering celebrities to maintain his ratings?"

"I said indulge me, not mock me." Alex finished her wine and raised a hand for another. "Assume for a minute that some bad, mad, or sad person is working their way through Talon's list. Who's your money on for next victim?"

Coombs motioned for the barman to make it two fresh drinks. "Okay, I admit this is kinda fun. I'm a psychopath with a shopping list. I'm free to move because the FBI and the NYPD are dumb as rocks and nobody's listening to humble genius Alex Bedford."

"But you know that three's the magic number," Alex said. "Do number three, and however carefully you arrange the scene to look like a suicide, the list goes into protective lockdown and we go into overdrive."

Fresh drinks arrived. Coombs swallowed wine and said, "So for number three you pick the hardest target. Might be your last chance."

"None of them are soft targets."

"But who's the hardest?" Coombs inhaled a scoop of air. "Cardinal Clement? We know how good the Catholic Church is when it comes to protecting its own. Did you see *Talon Tonight*?"

"Of course not."

"Last night it was a journalist who wouldn't shut up about Cardinal Clement. Historical abuse cases, cover-ups, the Vatican hiding priests in far-away parishes. Clement will be spooked to hell and back—he won't raise his head for a while."

"So not Clement. Who else?"

"How about Miss Piggy?"

"Who?"

"Emil Hertzberg, hedge fund gazillionaire and—if rumors are to be believed—child-molesting son of a bitch."

"Why do they call him Miss Piggy?"

"I swear you must live on Mars, Alex. Here . . ."

Coombs tapped at his phone and showed Alex a photograph of a middle-aged man in an open-necked pink linen shirt. Square teeth protruded below small roundish eyes under long lashes, the cheeks red from alcohol or too much sun, the lips plump and pursed. The image had a caption: *Emil Herzberg, AKA Miss Piggy.*

"Hertzberg splits his time between a parkside townhouse-cum-fortress and a mega-yacht called the *Bella Figura*," Coombs said. "The yacht never stays in one marina for more than two nights, and Hertzberg is surrounded by ex-special forces security. You'd have more luck trying to kill Kim Jong-Un."

"Has none of the child abuse stuff stuck?"

"Hertzberg has high-level protection from likeminded acquaintances, or so the rumor goes. But let's not get into government as one big pedophile ring." Coombs checked his watch. "Tell me, why would anyone start murdering people on Ricky Talon's stupid list? In the grand scheme of things, they're a bunch of no-mark bottom feeders."

She had no answer that didn't involve the word *crazy*.

"More to the point, Alex, what has you convinced we're dealing with two murders?"

She had no answer that didn't speak to the feeling in her gut: men like Dixon and Benedetti didn't take their own lives—they had their lives taken from them by other men, or, if they got lucky, by the passage of time.

Coombs shook his head. "You're out of answers and I need to leave this bar before I order another bottle." He nudged Alex's carry-on with his toe. "Planning to shame the New York office tomorrow?"

She looked down at her battered Samsonite carry-on. The wheel had squeaked forever, so why hadn't she replaced it? She could afford good luggage with William's firefighter pension on top of her salary. And of course, they had no children. The young, pennywise Alex Bedford had promised the older, wealthier Alex a set of fabulous luggage. Young Alex couldn't have known that, for so many reasons, older Alex wouldn't give a shit.

"Let it go, won't you?" Coombs voice was like a finger snap under her nose.

"Huh?"

"Anyone could have dropped the Dixon tip." Coombs smoothed a palm over his hairless scalp and let the hand rise to order himself a final drink. "You see the *Times* today? Another five city officials indicted courtesy of Tyrell Dixon's email bonanza. No need to complete step nine, Alex. You already made amends. Time to let it go and move on."

"That's what Murphy said."

"You know he's leaving us for training school."

"Murphy says that every year."

"Shelly in admin told me he put the papers in. You know where that leaves you."

"Picking up a two-dollar goodbye card when I stop for gas?"

"You're in line for Supervisory, Alex. You should have kicked on years ago."

"We've had this conversation, Pat. I'm an investigator, not a people manager."

"A laudable—and frankly baffling—lack of ambition considering your record and how damn good you are. Is this about the Dixon screw up? You dropped the ball once in two decades. You'd just lost your husband. Come on."

"What's your point?"

"Do I have to spell it out? You screwed up, but Murphy rates you. He'll give you an easy, tune-up fight to get you back in the ring. Meanwhile, city hall will try to bury the whole Dixon thing, and if they can't they'll scapegoat some poor schmuck. Poking your nose into non-Bureau business makes you that poor schmuck."

Alex pressed her hand to her heart. "I swear to support and defend the Constitution of the United States against all enemies, foreign and domestic, unless it makes me look bad, in which case I'll hide behind busy work and let someone else carry the can."

"Joan-of-fucking-Arc," Coombs said mildly. "Tell me again why you joined the FBI?"

"Because I was a good enough cellist to get a music degree but not good enough to make it my living."

"No, that's why you're not playing for the New York Philharmonic. You joined the FBI—or so you told me over cocktails at that Halloween party years ago—because you need a bachelor's degree to become an agent. You said your dad would have wept if the first person in your family to graduate college ended up in a PD uniform handing out speeding tickets."

"You make it sound like I had no choice but to be a cop."

"Your father's daughter—that's what you told me." Coombs held up his hands in surrender. "I'm only saying, Supervisory could be good for you. Fresh start, new challenge."

A familiar ache pulsed in the bone above her ears. She chased down two Excedrin with a gulp of wine and dropped cash on the bar.

CHAPTER

18

JACOB HAD NO intention of setting up his camera—she'd spot it immediately. Instead, he took a seat at the back of the room, pulled his cap even lower and stared at his lap while the audience formed around him. By seven, the room was full. Jacob's left neighbor wore suede deck shoes, and his right neighbor crossed long, elegant legs under a linen dress.

"I'd like to welcome our guest speaker for the evening." Jacob didn't dare look up, but the voice was male and olive-oil smooth. "Cofounder of the New Frontiers club for modern adventurers and one of the few women to have sailed singlehanded around the world in under a hundred days. Let me introduce you to one of the *best* people in New York. Give it up, Montauk Yacht Club, for Elizabeth Felle."

Clapping, a few generous whoops from the crowd. Then it was Elizabeth's voice coming through the speakers.

"I want to tell you a story, Montauk. It's the story of the most amazing woman you never heard of. In 2006, the sailor Galia Moss made history, but she barely made the papers."

Her voice cracked on *amazing* and the crowd quietened. Jacob sensed his two neighbors lean in, as if every part of their anatomy had been conscripted into listening to his sister. He'd seen this before.

Elizabeth's stage-awkwardness combined with her absolute conviction made watching her speak in public like watching a bear walk a tightrope.

"Galia was the first Latin American woman to sail solo across the Atlantic Ocean. She worked with an NGO to donate a home to a Mexican family for every eight nautical miles she sailed." Elizabeth had found her rhythm, the words echoing in the high ceiling. "I know better than most that solo sailing is a selfish pursuit. It requires financial and emotional sacrifice from the people you love. Galia found a way to turn her selfish dream into something that enriched society. That's the message that I want to share tonight . . ."

Forty minutes later, Elizabeth closed her talk with a call for action. Everyone in that room had an opportunity, right now, to consider how they personally could enrich the society they lived in. She asked for questions, and when the heartfelt applause subsided, an audience member two rows ahead of Jacob took a roving microphone and asked if Elizabeth planned to make any more daring solo trips herself.

She held up her bandaged wrist. "I get older, but sailing doesn't get easier." Light laughter rippled through the room. "So probably no. Any other questions?"

Jacob had planned to wait until after the talk before he made his presence known. Later he wouldn't be able to recall what made him raise his hand for the roving mic.

"I have a question," he said, looking full into his sister's face.

She barely flinched, her reaction contained within her eyes, which seemed to darken almost to black before recovering their natural smoky gray. "Please," she said.

Jacob hesitated, mind blank.

Elizabeth smiled down from the stage. "You came *all this way*, and you've nothing to say?" More laughter.

"You have a gallery in the hallway of New Frontiers." Jacob grasped at the first thing that came into his head. "One of the photos is Leonard Harris. He was a pioneering sailor too, wasn't he? I always wanted to learn more about Leonard, but I never got the chance to ask."

Her smile hardened as she walked to the other side of the stage, addressing the crowd as she went. "Leonard Harris joined the original New Frontiers club in 1957, long before my time. He was the only African American member, in fact he was the only African American solo navigator that he *knew of*. That changed because Leonard changed it." Elizabeth cleared her throat. "Sadly, Leonard is no longer with us, but his legacy lives on."

She walked back across the stage and stared at Jacob. "I can tell you from personal experience that a life you love can end at any time. So I suggest we treat today as if there'll be no tomorrow. Now . . . I believe I'm standing between you all and your first cocktail of the evening. If there are no more questions . . ."

* * *

Jacob hovered by the door, pretending to adjust the Lumix while the audience drifted out. Finally alone, she turned on him. A student of his sister's moods since childhood, Jacob had labeled her various expressions. The look she gave him now was *How Dare You?*

"Is that thing off?" she asked. "I won't say a word in front of your third fucking eye."

Jacob showed her that the Lumix wasn't recording.

"Has Mum finally drowned in a bucket of Chardonnay?" she said.

"She's alive and wondering why she had to lose a daughter as well as a husband."

Like I'm wondering why I had to lose a sister as well as a father.

"Floyd sent you, then," Elizabeth said.

"Floyd doesn't know I'm here. Your friend Claude mentioned something about Montauk and I saw tonight marked in an old calendar—I thought maybe you'd show."

"Claude, huh?" Elizabeth leaned against the back of a chair. "Claude is lacking a certain . . . filter. Did he tell you how handsome you were?"

"A seven on a good day. I'll take it."

"Wise man. Why did you ask me about Leonard Harris?"

"It just came to me. I couldn't ask what I wanted to ask in front of everyone."

"Which was?"

"Why you cut me off four years ago."

She shook her head. "I can't do this right now."

"You owe me an explanation."

Red spots of color formed on her cheeks. "You think we'll talk and everything will be resolved? This isn't a fight over who gets to sit in the front seat of the car."

"I'm worried about you."

"Not your job."

"You've changed. Floyd's right about that. What are you doing in a yacht club? You used to despise the posh yachties."

Elizabeth glared at the ceiling, her fists clenched at her sides.

"Look at you," Jacob said. "The anger's back. Tell me it isn't."

"At least I'm honest about it."

"I don't even know what that means."

A lie. He knew exactly what she meant.

Jacob the fatherless teenager, his anger a straitjacket he could never remove. He remembered the first time he'd walked into a boxing gym, the blessed relief of learning that you could climb into the ring and hammer the hell out of a training partner—hit as hard as you liked, let it all go—then bump gloves and warm down together. But he'd never learned how to carry that feeling with him when he left the gym. Every time he unwrapped his hands at the end of a session, he felt the straps of the straitjacket tighten.

"Why did you cut me loose?" Jacob said now. "What did I do?"

"Nothing, that's the point."

"Then tell me what's frightened you enough to turn your life upside down."

She surprised him with a weary smile. "Okay. I guess you deserve an explanation. I need to grab my bag from the locker room. Ask in reception where we can get dinner around here. I'll meet you out front and we'll take a stroll and sneer at the boats."

Jacob waited by the reception window watching yacht lights twinkle on the dark water. In his hand he held a yellow stickie with three restaurant suggestions. It took him ten minutes to realize that Elizabeth wasn't coming.

* * *

He'd missed the last Montauk-to-Manhattan train. The receptionist at the Montauk Yacht Club offered him a deluxe suite—the only room available—at a four-figure price. He searched on his phone for room at a cheap hotel, found nothing. A plastic box on the reception desk held taxi business cards.

"How much for Montauk to Manhattan?"

He heard the smile in the voice at the other end of the line. "Brace yourself, buddy."

* * *

From the rear seat of a four-hundred-dollar taxi ride, he left a voicemail. "Floyd, I know you don't want to hear this, but I found Elizabeth and you were right. She's in the bad place again."

Hear that, Elizabeth? The bad place, where your fear overwhelms you and you react by pulling out clumps of your school friends' hair. You bloody Dad's shins as he tries to restrain you, and, when you're older, give your husband bruises he has to pass off as snowboarding accidents. But even in the bad place, however scared you might have been behind the anger, you never hurt your little brother.

Through the cab window, a harvest moon sprinkled silver dust over the ocean. How had she concluded her talk at the yacht club?

I can tell you from personal experience that a life you love can end at any time.

In the twenty-six years since their father died, had either of them really dealt with the loss? Was the thirty-five-year-old Jacob still in denial, reading comics under the duvet while his older sister smashed up the bedroom next door?

I'm not saying a word in front of your third fucking eye.

At Montauk Yacht Club she'd reacted to his camera the way a vampire reacts to light. No change there.

In the glistening waves flashing past the window, an idea slowly formed.

She wanted him gone. Okay, then. What was that worth to her?

CHAPTER

19

Alex shivered in her summer jacket. Eighty-four degrees outside and they'd cranked up the air conditioning in the lecture hall. Beside her, Pat Coombs checked football results on his phone. From behind a lectern, a small man with a voice like sand being poured into a metal box made the case that diversity, equity, and inclusion was the FBI's superpower.

Her phone vibrated in her pocket. Incoming call from area code 540, which meant Stafford, Virginia, the FBI headquarters at Quantico. Alex's spine stiffened. The lab techs typically emailed their reports and a phone call suggested they'd found something worth calling about. She nudged Coombs and nodded to the back of the room. He shook his head.

She went anyway and earned a snippy comment from the lectern: "Reminder, we will be breaking in ten, as per the agenda in your pack."

By the time Alex made it to the corridor, a lab tech named Norris Percy had left a voicemail asking her to call his direct line.

"Mr. Percy. Alex Bedford. What have you got?"

"Well, ma'am, your item's soft iron, between ten and twenty years old." Percy's Alabama tones put the taste of peach cake in Alex's mouth. "Soft iron has low carbon content, which explains the lack of rust. Exposure to elements would explain why there's no blood or DNA, if that's what you were hoping for."

Made of iron and clean of prints. She could have told him that. "Okay, what is it?"

"Well, it could be construction equipment, some kind of fixing, but the shape and the lack of carbon got me thinking it could be a pea ton."

"A what?"

"P-i-t-o-n. Climbers jam it in rock and loop rope through the hole. They prefer soft iron because it has zero carbon."

"So it stays rust-free if they leave it in place."

"Exactly." Percy sounded disappointed that she'd stolen his punchline.

"Why would it be on the roof of a twenty-floor building?"

"I figured you'd want to look into maintenance crews from a few years back. Maybe they used climbing equipment before health and safety came in."

Alex thanked Percy and asked him to mail the full report. His reply was lost in the vibration of another call coming in. Her boss, Murphy.

"Tell me you're in Trenton, Alex."

"I'm in Trenton."

"But you didn't make it for yesterday's session. Car broke down? Train crash?"

Behind Alex, agents filed out of the meeting, seeking coffee and restrooms. She moved down the corridor for quiet. "I had a few things to finish up on the Dixon case."

"You're not on the Dixon case." From behind Murphy, a voice called his name. "I gotta go. No more 'Where's my FBI agent' calls, okay?"

Three beeps told her Murphy had hung up.

A rangy, loose-limbed agent passed Alex in the hallway. "Hey, how about you send Ricky Talon our way," he said. "We could use help thinning out the ten worst people in New Jersey."

Alex opened Google Maps on her phone. She found what she was looking for just as Pat Coombs appeared in the hallway with a question on his face. The neon strip above his head seemed to fizz and bleed into the air. She dug her knuckles into her eye sockets as a wave of nausea shivered her skin. Not now, with two hours of DEI joy still to go.

"Princeton, this afternoon when we're done," she said. "You're welcome to come."

"Where are we going?"

"Mountaineering."

She left him in the corridor while she went to find a toilet to throw up in.

* * *

The young sales associate in the lime green bandana pinch-zoomed the image on Alex's phone. "Yup, it's definitely a piton. A few years old, but totally serviceable."

Eastern Mountain Sports offered serious gear for serious climbers. The two Excedrin Alex had swallowed over lunch had worn off, and the chatter of schoolkids by a bouldering wall scratched at her temples like a crown of barbed wire. While she was flashing her badge at Lime Green Bandana, Coombs had wandered off into Apparel. She saw him in the distance, lifting the arms of a purple mountain jacket, making it dance.

Lime Green Bandana handed back her phone.

"Could you use it to climb a twenty-story building?" Alex said.

"If you like that kind of thing."

"You don't?"

"Urban climbing's the hot craze. In my humble opinion, it's for look-at-me assholes who think real mountains are for boomers." Lime Green Bandana made a face. "You said you're from New York? You could check out New Frontiers."

Alex jotted the name in her notebook. "New Frontiers?"

"Club for adventurers. I was a member years ago, before I moved out this way. If it's still going, it might be worth a visit."

"Why?"

"They always had plenty of urban climbers and no shortage of look-at-me assholes. You want to find someone who'd leave a piton in a skyscraper, New Frontiers is a good place to start." A shriek from the school party drew his gaze. "Sorry, guys. Gotta go."

As they walked back to their rental, Coombs beckoned for the car keys.

"Is it that obvious?"

"You look like pale sweaty death, Alex."

She handed over the keys. "You drive. I'll google New Frontiers."

Coombs had the driver's door open, his chest against the frame. "Seriously, Alex?"

"Why not? The killer snatches Benedetti and forces him to unlock his building, locks the door from the inside, leaves the keys in the lobby, takes Benedetti upstairs and makes him post his suicide note, then throws him off the roof. Then he scales *down* the outside wall, pulling out the pitons behind him, except he leaves one on the roof by mistake."

Coombs shook his head at the sky. "This isn't a Batman movie. You think Maranzano has an army of climbing daredevils doing his dirty work?"

"It's not Maranzano. Too sophisticated. But it's still a lead, and last time I checked, the 'I' in FBI still stood for investigation."

"See today's *Times*?"

Coombs slapped a copy of the *New York Times* on the roof of the car. Alex liked that her partner still bought a physical newspaper—Pat Coombs was one of the few people she knew who never scrolled idly on his phone. William had been the same, happiest when seated by the window of their apartment, a pot of strong coffee on the side table, a book in his hands.

"Global warming." Coombs tapped the front page. "A military coup in Somalia, storm damage in Florida, a mass shooting in an Oklahoma Walmart."

"So?"

"The media's tiring of Benedetti and Dixon." Coombs adjusted the driver's seat. "The curse of the worst has worn off, Alex. Your iron shoehorn isn't connected to Benedetti, and Benedetti isn't connected to Dixon."

"You're probably right, Pat."

Coombs gunned the engine. "You only say that when you think I'm wrong."

CHAPTER

20

Sunset Park still tasted of gasoline and sea salt, but the Jumping Jack Power Plant seemed smaller in the sallow dusk. Jacob found the entrance door locked. His finger traced the letters of the brass plaque set into the wall. When he pressed his ear to the door, the only sound was the wash of his own blood.

He'd known that coming here was a long shot. He had no address for his sister, knew none of her friends, and had given up trying her number. Floyd had kicked him out—after Montauk Jacob had spent the night at a grim but affordable hotel in Jersey City, then wandered the streets of Brooklyn all day, periodically returning to New Frontiers to try a door that refused to open. Maybe he should give the world what it wanted and head back to London.

His feet took him out of the parking lot and down the slipway toward the waterline where waves lapped against stone. The sky darkened with cloud, the ocean black and empty. Lost in the rhythm of his thoughts he almost missed the battered maroon station wagon parked behind a dumpster—the same car he'd seen his sister climb out of at the Montauk Yacht Club.

* * *

Jacob squeezed between clawed thickets and brickwork to reach a ground floor window of the Jumping Jack Power Plant. Through foxed glass, he could just make out a handle in the center of the casement. He searched around his feet for a fist-sized lump of rock, then pulled his tee over his head and used it to wrap the rock. He'd never broken into a building before. *New frontiers.*

* * *

Before he was halfway up the stairs, an angry shout filtered down from the main room. Jacob walked the edge of the pink hallway to avoid creaking floorboards. Another yell, female, angry, unmistakably Elizabeth. Jacob ran the play in his mind. *He goes through the door. She's already at fever pitch, won't listen, screams at him to leave. He refuses. She storms out. His chance is gone.* He needed something to make her listen, something to short circuit her rage long enough that he could make his pitch.

He padded back down the stairs and unbolted the front entrance—instinct said he might want to leave in a hurry—then made his way back to the window he'd smashed to enter the building. He sucked up a lungful of musty air and rested his palm on the jagged glass in the frame.

Boxing had taught Jacob a new relationship with pain—over years of hard sparring, he'd learned to reframe hurt as merely a means to an end. Now he dragged his palm over the splintered glass and rode out the shiver that ran up his arm to his shoulder and back down to his fingers. When he turned over his hand, an inch-long cut had already begun to weep.

At the top of the stairs, Jacob paused in front of Leonard Harris's photograph. Leonard smiled encouragingly as Jacob set the Lumix to record and knocked hard on the door.

* * *

Elizabeth looked more disgusted than surprised as she peered at him through a crack in the door. "Did Floyd give you his key?"

Jacob showed her the blood etched into the lines of his palm. "If I'd known Floyd still had a key to this place, I wouldn't have nearly slashed my wrists getting in."

The bones of Elizabeth's face looked ready to burst through the skin. They both watched a drop of blood fall from Jacob's hand and ping against the wooden floor. She pulled the door open. "Two minutes to clean you up. Then you're out of here."

* * *

Whoever Elizabeth had been shouting at had disappeared. Alone with his sister, Jacob perched on the arm of a sofa, then stood up again. Damned if he'd take the low-status position. He watched Elizabeth pluck a vast red leather handbag from a chair and produce a plastic first-aid kit and a bottle of Evian. A ship's horn sounded somewhere out in the bay.

"Give me your arm," she said.

Jacob let her swab the cut and wrap it with a cloth bandage. She lifted her own bandaged wrist. "Matchy-matchy. What a little brother thing to do."

"A little brother so worried he'll climb through a broken window."

"Okay, let's hear it," she said. "What's Floyd been telling you?"

"He wants you to stop what you're doing with New Frontiers before it's too late."

"Floyd brought you three-and-a-half-thousand miles to tell me that?" She massaged her wrist through the bandage. "What's he doing with himself, now that I'm gone?"

"Eating real food. Keeping the place tidy. Smiling without permission."

"Putting that gunk up his nose?"

"After his wife left him an empty apartment and a box of matches."

His sister fixed him with a look: *Patience Wearing Thin.* She reached into her handbag for a ball of crimson wool speared by knitting needles. Jacob watched her fingers find the edge of her work, loop the wool, *click, click, click.*

"When Floyd called me in London," Jacob said, "I had this idea to make a film about New Frontiers, *The Rebirth of Adventure.* After I learned you gutted the club of members, I had a new idea. *The Death of Adventure, how internal rifts destroyed the dream.*"

"What are you talking about?" Elizabeth dropped her knitting onto a sofa.

"I'm going to make a movie from the outside. You'll see a lot of me from now on."

Livid spots bloomed on Elizabeth's cheeks. Her voice was dangerously soft. "We're not children, Jacob. I told you already, this isn't a fight over who sits in the front of the car."

"Yeah," Jacob said, sensing that his entire childhood might burst out through his rib cage. "We know how this goes. Your face gets red, your voice goes soft, then all hell breaks loose. Elizabeth loses her shit and we all run for cover. Fine, I'll go. But I'll be back tomorrow and the next day, sticking my nose in until you see sense. You can punch holes in the wall, but you won't hurt *me*, Elizabeth. Never did, never will." He held up his newly bandaged hand. "I'm your brother. You've always looked after me, and now it's time for me to look after you."

He had no name for the look she gave him now.

Hold your ground. Hold her eye. She's expecting you to fold.

Her hands dived into her handbag, brought out a notebook and a pencil. She scribbled and tore off a sheet. "Come here tomorrow morning. We'll talk. Then you'll leave."

Jacob took the page, a Brooklyn address he didn't recognize. "What's this? Chinese takeaway? Real estate office? Fool me twice, shame on me."

Elizabeth was already at the door that led to the den. "A friend's place. Don't believe me? Don't come." He watched her slide the door closed behind her.

With its scattering of leather sofas and abandoned coffee cups, New Frontiers seemed to echo in silence—vast, empty. But also awake with possibilities. As Jacob opened the door to the gallery, a woman walked toward him. Fiftyish, compact and useful-looking in a square-cut navy suit, dark circles ringed her eyes, a color-match for the tight curls of her hair.

"The door was open." She showed Jacob a badge. In her other hand she held a phone with an image on the screen. "I'm looking for someone who can tell me about this."

CHAPTER

21

ALEX KEPT WALKING forward, using the power of her FBI badge to usher the young man back through the doorway. Having picked her way over dirt and rubble on the first floor, then forced her bad knee up a set of stairs and into a bizarrely pristine pink portrait gallery, she wanted to know what was behind that door.

Very little, it turned out. Empty sofas and dusty windows. The abandoned Airstream coffee cart made her wish she'd stopped for a cold brew on the way. And standing in the center of the room, this young man—white, mid-to-late thirties, handsome in a quiet kind of way, with light brown hair cropped close to the skull and a camera slung around his neck.

"Are you a member here?" she asked. "This is New Frontiers, right?"

"It was." He gestured to the empty sofas. "Closed down a while back."

British accent, and not the kind from TV shows where the men wear frilly cuffs and the women are sewn into petticoats. There was a wariness about him that pricked her interest, but people react to the badge in different ways, and this guy probably never encountered an FBI agent outside of a movie. Something else: his stance, light on the balls of his feet and evenly balanced. She'd seen it in Bureau colleagues who went deep into martial arts—they seemed to float an inch off the ground. This young man didn't float, not quite. But she could tell he'd have quick feet and quick hands.

"Are you here alone?" she said.

A fraction of a beat. "I think so. I just arrived. Haven't checked everywhere."

"And you're here because . . . ?"

"Here at New Frontiers or here in New York?"

She smiled at him—*Answer how you want.*

"I'm looking for my sister," he said. "She was one of the club founders. Looks like I missed her, though." He cast around the room, as if to confirm it was empty. "Is there anything I can help you with before I leave?"

Alex showed him a photograph of the piton on the screen of her phone. "Do you know what this is?"

He peered at the screen. "Looks like a climbing spike."

"We found it on the roof of a building that had been burgled," Alex said, tapping two Excedrin pills from her bottle and swallowing them dry. "If someone can tell me how it might have got up there, I can rule out the roof as a means of entry."

The young man shook his head. "As far as I know, most climbers don't use this old kit, and when they do, they remove the spikes as they go. Green climbing."

"Green?" Alex swapped her phone for her notepad.

"Leaving a piton in a rock wall is like throwing an empty Coke can out of a car window. But look, I haven't been on a rock face for twenty years. I'll tell you one thing: you'd have to be pretty skilled to scale a building with this old kit." He massaged a fresh bandage on his left hand. "You'd be better off breaking a window to get in."

Pretty much what she'd expected him to say. Alex felt suddenly tired. "Could I get your name?" She turned to a fresh page in her notebook.

He gave it to her, spelling the surname before she had to ask. *F-e-l-l-e.*

"Thank you, Jacob, I think I have what I need."

She left him in the vast empty room, feeling his eyes on her back as she stepped out into the portrait gallery.

On edge, Mr. Felle? A little too eager to help?

Perhaps. But contact with the law makes even the most law-abiding citizen remember the red light they ran. In a club for adrenaline junkies, it would be a miracle if they didn't all have some infraction to hide. *Admit it, Alex. This guy confirmed what the shop assistant told you yesterday. Time to consign your piton to the storage room where it belongs.*

She was almost at the stairs when she stopped. Turned. Walked back along the hallway. Back past the explorer, the mustached colonel, the triumphant hunter, until she faced the only nonwhite occupant of the gallery, a narrow-shouldered man on the deck of a sailboat, kindness in the amber eyes.

Leonard Harris, sailor, inspiration, friend.

Something in the face... and where had she heard that name?

She pulled out her notebook and flipped pages. *Hell, yes.* One of the victims of the fire at the nursing home Benedetti owned had been named Leonard Harris.

* * *

"Pat, it's the same guy. There's an obituary on the *Sailing* magazine site from four years ago. *Pioneering African American Sailor Dies in Fire.*" Alex rested her chest against the open door of the Impala, inhaling sea breeze and diesel. "Benedetti was connected to Leonard Harris, and Leonard Harris is connected to New Frontiers."

"Loosely connected."

"Sure, so tell me with a straight face that you still think this is a copycat suicide or some crazy person working their way down a random list of names."

Her partner's response was a *humph* sound. Alex said, "Jacob Felle, UK citizen, says he's visiting New York to see his sister. Immigration should have an address in his ESTA application. I want to know if he was in the country for Benedetti or Dixon. And get me a membership list for New Frontiers."

"On it. Should I brief Murphy?"

"Leave Murphy to me." She looked back at the flat roof of the New Frontiers building, barely visible above the warehouses.

"We're on to something, Pat. I can feel it."

CHAPTER

22

W̲HILE FLOYD'S LOFT was big enough to ride around on a bicycle, Jacob could have driven a compact car through this spotless DUMBO apartment. Elizabeth met him at the door in gray coveralls, her cropped hair flattened under a headscarf.

"You're not wearing your camera," she said.

"My *third fucking eye*? I left it at the hotel for your benefit."

"I thought you were staying with Floyd."

"So did I. Floyd had other ideas."

She led him down a hallway as wide and sterile as a hospital corridor. "Before we talk, I need a favor." In the hallway stood seven feet of burnished teak, sitting on a hand truck. Elizabeth nodded toward an open door. "Can you manage?"

"Building bridges with my sister, one wardrobe at a time." Jacob tilted the hand truck to take the wardrobe against his chest—it felt like slow dancing with a bear. "Did you overhear my conversation from the den?"

"What conversation?"

"With the FBI lady who turned up at New Frontiers?"

Jacob couldn't see his sister's face, but he thought he heard a catch of breath. "Go left a bit," she said. "No, *my* left. What FBI lady?"

Jacob circled the hand truck into a bedroom dominated by a king-size bed with a rose-colored comforter. Fresh laundry spilled across the bed. Dumbbells under the window, two books on the bedside table, packing boxes against the wall. As he set the wardrobe upright the reflection of his own face slid down to meet him in the polished teak. "She came by about a burglary. They found a climbing piton on the roof and she wanted an expert opinion."

"Seriously, an FBI agent came to New Frontiers?" Elizabeth held two corners of a laundered sheet and flicked the other end toward Jacob. He caught the loose corners and a waft of lemon rose from the fabric. "Why didn't you come and fetch me from the den?"

They walked toward each other to join the corners of the sheet, then back out again, folding lengthways then square, the way they'd done it as children helping their mother.

"She got what she needed and she left." Jacob leaned against the wardrobe. "But her visit got me thinking." Outside, a police siren wailed, joined by the howl of a fire truck. A shiver of vertigo ran down Jacob's spine, the same as when he'd first leaned out over Floyd's balcony. "You're not going to like this."

Elizabeth raised an eyebrow at him.

He pressed back against the teak, relishing the solid wood against his shoulder blades. "The first time I turned up at New Frontiers, Claude was in his boxer shorts. And your pal Henry wasn't wearing any shoes or socks."

"They're not gay, if that's what you're thinking. Not as far as I know."

"No, it felt more like I interrupted them getting ready for something. Then I see you at the Montauk Yacht Club. What were you doing in that office before Mr. Muscle Receptionist escorted you to the locker room?"

Elizabeth pulled a white linen shirt from the pile of laundry and began to fold. A hint of tornado flickered in her eyes. "You saw that?"

"You've never been lost in your life," Jacob said. "You had a reason to be in that office. Then yesterday an FBI agent turns up at New Frontiers to talk about a burglary. I checked. The FBI doesn't deal with burglary."

Her cheekbones shone white as scars. "Now you're an expert in the FBI?"

"I'm an expert in you, Elizabeth. You're planning something. Maybe it will happen on the water and that's why you were skulking around Montauk Yacht Club. Maybe it's something else. I just know that it's important enough to have decimated New Frontiers and destroyed your marriage. It's big enough that you're worried about jail time."

Her breath shortened. "And you're here to tell me to stop before I get hurt."

"Hell no."

That raised both her eyebrows.

"I'm here to tell you to let me in," Jacob said. "Climate crisis protest, refugee sit-in, antiwar demo? Whatever it is, let me document the action. A proper production. Imagine your message picking up an award at Cannes. Your manifesto streamed into a million homes."

She stared at him, as if utterly lost. Then she gave a great barking laugh.

"What did I say?" Jacob asked.

"I need a cup of tea." She rose from the bed and disappeared through the door. Left alone on the bed, Jacob followed.

On his way to the kitchen, he passed another bedroom, and the filmmaker in him couldn't walk past an open door without glancing inside. A linen bathrobe splayed across the bed with arms outspread like a gunshot victim, the monogram *H.D.* in red stitching over the heart.

"Where are you," Elizabeth called out.

His sister was agile but never light on her toes. The slap of feet on wood gave Jacob the millisecond he needed to pull his head back into the hallway and pretend to be examining a photograph on the wall: a younger version of Henry Duval alongside an older man—Henry's father by the shape of the jaw and the set of the eyes. Father and son wore light blue uniforms and stood over an antiquated cannon and a pyramid of cannonballs. Both men carried muzzle-loading muskets and regarded the camera with the same joyless smile.

"This apartment belongs to Henry," Elizabeth said. "His father is a US senator and an American Civil War enthusiast. Senator Duval calls this dress-up *reenactment*. Henry thinks it's practice for the next one."

* * *

Chamomile softened the air as they took stools at a concrete worktop the length and shape of a surfboard. A card on the worktop caught Jacob's eye, similar to one he'd seen at Floyd's.

To Elizabeth + 1

Jonathan and Victoria Sands
Request the Pleasure of Your Company
at the Marriage of Their Daughter,
Samantha Sands
to David Lee.

"I asked them to remove Floyd." Elizabeth blew on her tea. "The plus one is Samantha's way of saying I should get back in the game."

"Not tempted to take Henry?"

Elizabeth quartered a lemon and squeezed a few drops into her tea. "Henry's not my type."

"The man looks like a film star."

"You date him, then." She sucked the remaining juice from the lemon segment and tossed the rind into the sink. "Henry Duval is a sweet rich kid with a Confederate flag for a father. He's a good guy, a good friend, but he's a little too"—she hunted down the word—"*biddable*."

"So how long are we doing this for?" Jacob said.

"Doing what?"

"Making small talk so that you don't have to respond to what I said in the bedroom."

She watched him through chamomile mist.

"Don't forget," he said. "I've seen you this way before."

"Balls."

"At college when you formed that animal liberation group. You were talking about kidnapping lab technicians and blowing up testing facilities. And you'd have done it too, if you hadn't realized your co-members *weren't* serious at the exact same time they realized you *were*. My point is, you must be up to something big if it's put you in this state."

"What state?"

"Gutting New Frontiers after all your work to build it. Leaving Floyd. Creeping around yacht clubs. Running away from me. All sounding fine to you?"

After a beat, she said, "I haven't been back to England in years. How is the hoary old bitch? Please, humor me."

"If I must . . . England's falling apart."

"About bloody time. Leafy churchyards, simpering vicars, fetes selling homemade cake, sleepy cricket matches on village greens."

"I love that stuff."

"Everyone loves that stuff, dickhead. It's the only export we have left. But the price of idyll at home is misery abroad. The West has deliberately bred hypocrisy, cruelty, and stupidity. That's our birthright, Jacob."

"Our birthright is that hideous pair of ceramic dogs Dad bought in Malaga."

Elizabeth smiled and became, for an instant, the exact image of their mother when their dad made a bad joke. She carried their mugs to the sink, and Jacob watched the muscles bunch in her back as she rinsed the crockery.

"You know, he tricked me," she said into the sink.

"Dad?"

"Floyd. Behind the jungle machete, he's a coward. It took me years to work it out, but he must have known all along."

"I know he loves you, and it wasn't always one-way traffic. Remember the first time I brought him home from college on Easter break? You pretty much kidnapped him."

She tilted her head at the memory. "The men at Southampton were so cynical and weary. Floyd had a spark, an American thing. Plus, I was still rescuing strays back then. You remember his dad died in final year—we had that in common." She turned with dripping hands. "Enough Floyd. Let's talk about you. Who are you when no one's watching?"

"Me?"

"You say you want to get involved? You want to help?"

"Yes."

"But in *my* thing. What's your thing? And don't say it's trying to keep our family together after Dad died. No one asked you to do that." She gave him a rare look, one that felt like the sun coming out from behind a cloud—*Talk to me*. "Seriously, I want to know."

"My thing could be a movie that makes a difference," he said. *And seeing that you're okay.*

She thought about that. "A movie's not good enough. I need doers, not watchers."

"I can do."

"Really? From what I've seen, you live your life behind a lens. Stand back, observe, tell other people's stories. What's *your* story, Jacob, and when are you going to start living it?"

Jacob's story. Who'd pay to watch that?

Mr. Almost—the nearly man. Good at everything, not great at anything. Creative, but never able to unlock the potential. Afraid, perhaps, of what might happen if he did. "You know your problem," *his last girlfriend had said, moments before she left his key on the hall table and closed the door behind her.* "You won't be happy until you've left a mark on the world—but you don't have the guts to admit it."

Three thumps rattled against the front door of the apartment. Elizabeth motioned for Jacob to stay seated. He heard the click of a latch, a male tone, the words indecipherable, but rising and falling like a runaway roller coaster.

Floyd. *Bloody Floyd.*

"Jacob, are you in there?" Floyd yelled from the hall. "You okay?"

Jacob slid down from his stool. He heard the door slam.

Elizabeth appeared in the kitchen. "You told him you were coming here."

"I didn't. I swear."

Her eyes were cold glass. "Jacob, it's been great to see you, and I appreciate the concern. I know this is hard for you to hear, but it's time you went home."

CHAPTER 23

Supervisory Special Agent Brett Murphy didn't offer Alex or Coombs a chair in his office, which left them cradling open laptops on the crooks of their arms. Morning sunlight slanted through the blinds, picking out a triangle of dust the cleaners had missed when they wiped Murphy's desk.

"Okay, so we have a connection," Murphy said. "Who do we like at New Frontiers?"

Alex consulted her notes. "We haven't been able to find formal membership records, but based on a few online forums, New Frontiers had over a hundred members."

"Many climbers?"

"Unfortunately, yes. We're still trawling. But it's going to be a long list."

"Wonderful. What about the Brit you met there?"

"Jacob Felle. TSA confirmed he didn't come through border control until after Dixon's body was found. Our assumption is that he wasn't here for Benedetti or Dixon."

"So he's a no."

"File under *Person of Interest*," Coombs said. "It looks like he's related to the club founders, plus he has a sheet for marijuana possession and minor assault back in the UK."

"Narcotics?" Murphy looked almost disappointed. "Is that what this is all about?"

"Unlikely," Alex said. "Possession of a personal amount when he was twenty-two, and the assault was a drunken pub fight a decade back. Scotland Yard said, 'He's no villain.' Good news is we now have a DNA sample if we need it. He's a filmmaker. Art-house stuff with decent reviews."

"Is that relevant?"

"There's some careful staging in the suicide plus redemption motif."

"Which might make sense if he'd been here for either of the deaths." Murphy pursed his lips. "Who else have we got?"

"The founders," Coombs said. "Elizabeth Felle, sister of Jacob Felle, and her husband, Floyd Shaw. Aside from that, we're sticking a pin in a very long list of names—running them through the system to see if anything pops."

Murphy frowned. "Why does the name Floyd Shaw ring a vague bell?"

"Celebrity explorer, because apparently that's a thing. Had a show on the Discovery Channel called *Hidden Worlds*. 'Floyd Shaw takes you to places you've never been.'"

Murphy raised an eyebrow at Alex. "Like the roof of Clearwater House when you were meant to be in Trenton?"

She chose to ignore that.

Murphy picked at a fingernail. "Floyd Shaw used to work in television, and we have two dead men from Ricky Talon's chat show list. A Shaw-Talon connection?"

"Not that we've found so far. Talon's alibis check out, and it's hard to see why he'd start knocking off people from the list he created—the definition of shitting in your own backyard." Alex closed her laptop and slid it into her bag. "My working theory is that Talon is not involved. We have the Leonard Harris, Luca Benedetti connection, but that's all. So for now, we start weeding the New Frontiers membership and we take a closer look at the nursing home fire that killed Leonard Harris."

Murphy raised an eyebrow at her. "Is that it?"

"We also go back to where we started. Councilor Tyrell Dixon's so-called suicide note and all those emails he sent to the DoJ."

"The NYPD and the analysts gave those emails a thorough scrape, Alex."

"They didn't know what to look for." Alex headed for the door. "If there's a Benedetti-Dixon connection, we'll find it in Dixon's emails."

She held the door for her partner, but Pat Coombs was rooted to the spot, staring at his phone.

"Cardinal Clement," he said. "Six on Talon's list."

Alex's heart dropped in her chest. "What about him?"

Coombs showed her the news headline on his phone. "Ten Worst Go to Ground, but Cover-Up Cardinal Clement Won't Be Cowed."

"The Cardinal plans to speak on the steps of St. Patrick's this afternoon," Coombs said. "Our killers won't get a better chance."

CHAPTER

24

PEOPLE NEED TO see their superheroes in costume, but it's too hot for your damn robe. Sweat prickles under your zucchetto and threatens to steam your glasses, but you must be still as you address the crowd from the steps of St. Patrick's Cathedral. Here, spread your scarlet chest and let lightning bolts take aim, open your throat to the airborne virus, allow your sin to draw down the crashing plane.

If that's His will.

Daniel is your lesson for this field of six thousand wilting flowers. God can still draw a crowd. You clear your throat into the microphone and the people fall silent. You hear traffic and the distant chant from the knot of protestors corralled on the far side of the street. They have a scarlet banner. *Vatican Sex-Abuse Denier. Shame on You Cover-Up Cardinal Clement.*

You tell the crowd that Daniel so trusted God that he walked into a lion's den. That draws an *ahhh*—they like this one. You wonder if the hidden agents of law enforcement will like it too. The FBI has the plaza covered from every angle, according to the agent hovering in your peripheral vision. She's dwarfed by Bishop O'Brien's personal security guard who stands beside her like a marble column.

Daniel, you tell the crowd, remains unafraid because he knows his fate resides not in the hands of his enemies nor in the lion's jaws.

God chooses who He rescues and, like a good exam invigilator, God cannot converse with you while you are taking the test. That draws a ripple of laughter from the crowd—how they clutch at any reason why God might choose not to answer their prayers.

Movement in the third row. Two protesters have infiltrated the congregation. O'Brien's personal security guard reaches them first, pulling down their banner with a massive fist. A ripple of anger passes through the crowd. Six thousand people await your reaction.

Shame on You Cover-Up Cardinal Clement.

It isn't a cover-up when you hear it from a colleague in Holy Confession, when you immediately seek guidance from your superiors, when you remove the wrongdoers from their positions and demand assurance that it will never happen again. It isn't a cover-up when you protect the faithful from the damage of a public disgrace.

Only God is sovereign, only He can judge. You're here, aren't you? You're making it easy with your chest bared for the sniper's bullet.

If that's His will.

You describe how an angel closed the lion's jaws, and how King Darius fed Daniel's enemies, along with their wives and children, to the hungry beasts. Let that sink in. Their wives. Their children. Don't expect mercy, you say. And don't expect to understand God's ways.

Six thousand faces wait for the twist, the warm bon mot to lift them and send them on their way, but today your lesson will be served cold. You step back from the lectern, another sermon delivered, another angel sent to close the mouths of the lions.

O'Brien's personal security guard lumbers forward to lead you safely from the stage. Your head barely reaches his chest as he shepherds you toward the cathedral. A glass of wine awaits under cool vaulted ceilings. The guard keeps a steady hand on your forearm. Up ahead, a wooden door opens within the vast double portal of the cathedral. The spherical Bishop O'Brien appears in the doorway. O'Brien drones on like an old nun, but the wine will be excellent.

You're close enough to see the sweat on O'Brien's bald head when you hear a shout. The FBI lady sprints at you across the plaza. She grips a gun in her hand, but it's pointed at the ground. O'Brien's personal security guard puts his body between you and her, a human shield. His huge hand clamps your chin, forcing you to look up into the granite plane of his face.

Tears run down the cheeks of O'Brien's personal security guard. "You don't even recognize me, do you?" he says.

CHAPTER 25

SEAN WANNAMAKER WAS thirty-six years old, six-foot-three, two-hundred-twenty-five pounds, and until five hours ago the head of private security for Bishop O'Brien of the Diocese of Manhattan. He had no sheet, no outstanding warrants, and no living next of kin. He did have a new nickname courtesy of an *Enquirer* headline. "Ten Worst Terminator Arrested in Cathedral Clash with Cardinal Sin."

Alex Bedford entered the Thirteenth Precinct by the underground entrance, avoiding the massed cameras on the front steps. In the observation suite that annexed the interview room, she found Murphy perched on a desk staring at the monitor.

The screen showed an overhead view of four chairs around a table. Wannamaker filled one of the chairs, his blond scalp centered in a knot of shoulder muscle. Murphy's gaze never left the screen, so he missed Alex's eyebrow raise at her boss's latest off-duty wardrobe: purple and yellow striped shirt over green checked golfing trousers. She would never have let William mix patterns that way, and despite the seriousness of the moment she allowed herself a tiny smile at the conceit that Murphy's wife secretly hated her husband.

"Congrats, Alex. I heard we found Talon's list all over Wannamaker's search history."

"Half the crazies in New York probably have their bedrooms papered with Talon's Ten Worst list. We'll need more than Google history."

"You bearing up?"

Alex tearing across the plaza, her Glock fused to her hand. The giant releases Clement. The massive shoulders flex. Alex screams for her colleagues to hold fire. The giant drops his pistol and she kicks it away. The giant disappears under a mound of cops. Time, having slowed, accelerates again.

"I'm fine. Wannamaker was on his knees when we took him to the floor."

"And how's Cardinal Clement?"

"Shaken."

Murphy muttered something to himself. When Alex asked him to repeat it, he said, "Never mind. You showed restraint, Alex. Armed assailant. Credible threat to life."

"If I shot him we'd have another corpse and no suspect. When does his brief arrive?"

"Wannamaker refused representation, an early Christmas gift, and one we should unwrap before he takes it back."

She was half out the door when she stopped. "Wannamaker's gun has never been fired."

"Your point being?"

"If we had to go to court tomorrow, the best we'd get is possession of an illegal firearm and threat to life."

Murphy stretched out his arms, as if warming down after lifting weights. "See what you get from Wannamaker. He's bought us time, if nothing else. Right now, the media's running with the *Ten Worst Terminator* as a lone-wolf crazy. There are worse places for us to be."

* * *

"My name is Alex Bedford. I'm with the FBI."

Wannamaker hadn't looked up when Alex entered the windowless interview room or when she'd pulled out a chair and started the tape running. As she took her seat, the extra-large male cop glued to the wall lowered his brows in silent greeting.

"Mr. Wannamaker. Sean. Do you need water? Coffee?"

She might have been talking to dried cement.

"I was at St. Patrick's. Do you remember me?"

Not a flicker.

"I saw you say something to Cardinal Clement. What did you say?"

Wannamaker flexed his fingers and the muscles in his forearms moved like iron rods. Alex was glad of the steel chain that tethered his wrist to the table.

"What did you say to Cardinal Clement?" *Keep using the name.*

Wannamaker rolled his spine upright until his square face came into the light. Alex had expected tears—in her experience, big men didn't break, they shattered—but the cornflower-blue eyes were clear. When he spoke, his tone was measured as if he was dictating a memo, his voice almost effeminate—a gym juicer?

"I told him that God sees him."

Alex opened her pad to a fresh page. She wanted Wannamaker to see the white space that was his to fill.

"What does God see when he looks at Cardinal Clement?" she said.

Wannamaker touched the pads of his fingers to the table, walking them up and down an invisible keyboard. "The first time, I ran straight to my mother. I lied. I told her I was homesick. She said Saint Sebastian was a good school, the priests were good men."

Alex's mind leaped ahead. A Catholic boarding school and Clement a staff member. Something nagged, a memory of another case she'd heard about. Across the table, Wannamaker's pupils dilated. She was losing him to his memories.

"You said that was the first time you ran away?" Alex clicked her pen and made a show of recording a note on her pad. "It happened again?"

Wannamaker's eyelids fluttered, and for a moment Alex thought he'd gone. The words came in a rush of air. "The second time, I went to Father Thomas's house. He had little fists of white hair over his ears and a kind smile. I told him what the priests made me do. Father Thomas told me I was brave. He left me to make tea, and he must have made a phone call, because fifteen minutes later Clement was in the room. I knew Clement—he'd visited the school to tell us about

Jonah and the whale. He sat on the sofa in a suit and promised me that everything would be okay. The doorbell rang and it was my mother. She was crying. She gave me the biggest hug, and for a moment I thought she'd come to rescue me."

Wannamaker's hands clenched on the interview room table. "We sat in Father Thomas's sitting room, and I listened to Clement telling my mother that I was a good boy. But then he started to say other things. They'd had problems with me at the school, I made up stories about teachers and other boys. It wasn't true. I wanted to scream, but my tongue was too thick. My own mother asked me why I was making up stories."

"They sent you back?"

"*She* sent me back."

A column of anger rose inside Alex, one she had to sidestep if she wanted to remain useful. "Sean, did you take a job with Bishop O'Brien so you could get close to Clement?" And when he didn't answer, "Why Clement? Why not the priests at your school?"

Wannamaker tried to cover his face with his hands, but the chain was too short and he had to lower his head to meet his palms. "The priests only hurt *me*. Clement turned me against my own mother. She lost her son that day."

With a jolt like the snap of an elastic band, Alex's memory served up the case that had been nagging at her mind: a Catholic academy in Massachusetts—Framingham School for Boys—an abuse ring involving the local chief of police, a magistrate, a senior local politician, all provided with access to young boys by the priests who ran the school.

Could this be a copy of that case? Wannamaker was just young enough; the dead men on the Ten Worst list just old enough.

"Sean, is that how you knew Luca Benedetti and Tyrell Dixon? Did they visit you at school?"

Wannamaker erupted. His wrist chain clanged and the fists landed on the tabletop with a crash that Alex felt in her feet. She scrambled out of her chair as her cop chaperone jolted into life. Three more cops charged into the interview room. It took all four to force

Wannamaker back into his seat. One of the cops had his elbow under Wannamaker's chin. Alex saw the blue eyes roll back to the whites.

* * *

Murphy was on his phone when Alex returned to the observation suite. He waved for her to wait outside. Through a glass panel in the door, she watched his thin mouth move without pause.

Her cell buzzed. A syrupy female voice, Texan, or thereabouts. "This is the office of the Catholic Diocese of St. Patrick's Church. I'm hoping to speak with Miss Alex Bedford of the FBI."

"This is Special Agent Alex Bedford."

"Oh, how wonderful. Miss Alex, I do apologize for the hour. I'm calling to let you know that Cardinal Clement would like to thank you in person for what you did today."

"That won't be necessary."

"It would be his pleasure."

"But not mine." Alex ignored the sharp breath at the other end of the line. "Tell Clement he's lucky to be alive. And tell him Sean Wannamaker was right. His God sees him."

CHAPTER

26

Jacob stretched out on his bed at the Skyview Hotel, filming the sun rays burning triangles onto his belly. Elizabeth had been about to let him in—he'd blown it. Floyd had blown it for him. After Elizabeth had shown him the door, Jacob had raced down in the elevator after Floyd, but his brother-in-law was nowhere in sight and not answering his phone. Jacob had marched back across the Brooklyn Bridge, stopping first at a basement bar to feed his self-pity. He'd arrived at his budget Jersey City hotel late afternoon, a sticky, inebriated mess, and now he had nothing better to do than stare at his own belt buckle through the Lumix lens.

He tried Floyd's cell again, a reflex habit at this stage. Voicemail.

Standing under a tepid shower, he resisted the urge to punch the bathroom tiles. From the next hotel room came the sound of voices, a man and a woman fighting or fucking. Jacob closed his eyes against the shower water but found no guidance in the dark.

Naked and dripping, he flipped on the television. The TV was tuned to a news report, an incident in the city on the plaza of a Catholic church. Mobile phone footage showed a giant man, gun in hand. A crumpled pile of purple on the stone ground might have been a priest, and here came a woman, sprinting at the giant while shouting to her left and right, hands waving as she ran.

Close-up on the woman's face, and Jacob recognized the FBI agent he'd met at New Frontiers. Special Agent Alex Something.

FBI Agent Praised for Avoiding Bloodshed in Ten Worst Killer Takedown.

Good for her. She'd looked exhausted when they met—maybe now she'd be able to get some sleep.

Jacob moved to the window where the New Jersey Turnpike seethed below.

Telling Elizabeth that he was going to make his movie from the outside sounded good when Jacob said it. But now, in this hotel room that smelled of tobacco despite the no-smoking signs, his midday drinking turning rapidly to hangover, it felt laughable.

Stubborn didn't begin to describe his sister. Jacob could lay siege to her life, but she'd never surrender.

As for Floyd . . . inviting Jacob to New York and letting him think a reconciliation with Elizabeth was in the cards, then just when Jacob was making progress with his sister, turning up shitfaced to blow everything up. What was Floyd's deal? Shoveling coke up his nose and hiding away in his bedroom with that spooky van Buren and the wraithlike Chloe Zhang. What was *that* about?

Jacob lay on the bed and closed his eyes, willing sleep.

* * *

He woke to a bronze dawn, five AM, his mind clear. He pulled on his jeans and his cleanest tee, and slung the Lumix around his neck. Floyd had brought Jacob to New York. Floyd had made him sick with worry about Elizabeth, then torpedoed any chance of reconciliation between brother and sister. Floyd had long owed Jacob an explanation—and Jacob was done waiting.

CHAPTER

27

Sean Wannamaker wasn't talking, even to confirm his breakfast preferences. A psychological assessment diagnosed catatonia with reference to an underlying schizoaffective disorder. In the interview room below the Thirteenth Precinct, Alex gazed into Wannamaker's dilated pupils and wondered if his catatonia was nothing more than a double-dose sedative pumped into his ass because he scared his jailors shitless.

"Do you know this man?" The image of Leonard Harris that she slid across the table may as well have been a playing card. No movement in the oversized pupils. "How about this one—Councilor Tyrell Dixon? How about Luca Benedetti? What about the rest of Ricky Talon's list, Sean? Is that why you won't talk? Are you buying time for someone else to act?"

Wannamaker stared straight through her.

* * *

Alex took the longer route to the 23rd Street subway to avoid the media gathered on the precinct steps. Pat Coombs had called three times while Alex was in with Wannamaker. She returned his call a block from the precinct, her knee already giving her shit. Today was going to be a bad knee day.

"Pat, what do you have?"

"Final confirmation—Talon's alibis are rock solid."

Alex hadn't expected anything else, but she nevertheless felt the vibration as yet another door in her investigation closed. "Jeez, Pat. You could at least try to cheer me up."

"That's why I've been calling you. Wannamaker's story checks out. He was a pupil at the Saint Sebastian Academy up in New Rochelle, and there *was* a police investigation around that time. No convictions. I pulled the file."

"And?"

"How far are you from the office? You're going to want to see this."

CHAPTER

28

Floyd had deadbolted the door to the apartment. By the time his puffy face appeared in a crack between the door and the jamb, three neighbors were in the hallway telling Jacob to stop the damn banging or they'd call the damn cops.

"You shouldn't be here." Floyd's red-veined eyes scanned the hallway.

Jacob pushed past his brother-in-law. The apartment made him shiver, the air conditioning set to max. In the kitchen he found Roland van Buren wearing tight black jeans and a black tee with a human skull and two crossed guitars. Chloe Zhang leaned against the balcony door.

"I need time with Floyd," Jacob said.

Van Buren pretended to study one of Floyd's *Time* posters. "Floyd?"

Floyd scratched at his scalp. "Uh, yeah, Roland. Maybe give us a minute."

"You sure, Floyd?" Zhang offered Jacob the same smile she'd given him before—an invitation, but to what? "Roland can make him leave if you want." Said without aggression. A statement of fact.

"Roland can try," Jacob said, already measuring the distance his right hand would have to travel to connect with van Buren's lean gut.

With surprisingly steady hands, Floyd pushed the plunger of a French press. "I'm sure. We can pick up later."

Van Buren turned from the poster to look Jacob up and down with cold eyes. He sniffed—*okay, no biggie*. Then he took Zhang under his arm and headed for the front door, making a detour to whisper something in Floyd's ear. Floyd nodded. The apartment door closed behind them. Jacob and Floyd were alone.

* * *

Floyd lifted his coffee mug, then lowered it without taking a sip, his chin sinking to his chest like a robot powering down.

"Floyd, something happened four years ago that made Elizabeth cut me off. You're going to tell me what it was."

Floyd mumbled into his chest. "She's trying to protect you. If that's worth anything."

"From what?"

But Floyd's eyes had closed. He stood with coffee mug raised, swaying like a tree waiting for the final axe stroke. Jacob spotted Floyd's coke baggie beside the coffee grinder. He used an ATM card to drag out a lumpy line on the kitchen counter, rolled a ten-dollar bill, shook Floyd until his eyes blinked open, and guided him in.

Floyd snorted on autopilot. The snort became a howl. "Ow. Fucking razor blades."

"I need you to wake up and talk to me."

"Butcher." Floyd pinched the bridge of his nose. "Shit, it's cold in here."

Jacob opened the balcony door and warm fuggy air filled the room. "Floyd, you owe me an explanation. No more bullshit. Why did you install extra security on your front door? Where's Elizabeth? And why are you both behaving like the world's about to end?"

"Some days I wish it was." Floyd started to cut himself another line.

"*Floyd!*"

Floyd dropped the ATM card and yelled back, "*She's in danger, Jacob.*"

The words hung in the air.

"What kind of danger?" Jacob said. "Danger from who?"

"I can't tell you."

"I think you can. Who's she afraid of, Floyd? Is it Henry Duval? She's staying at his place. Does Duval have something on her?"

Before Floyd could answer, the sound of Jacob's phone made them both start. Jacob read the screen and mouthed, *Elizabeth*. Floyd stared back at him.

Jacob answered the call.

"You're a gaping arsehole," Elizabeth said.

"Huh?"

"A gaping arsehole, but I get it. Dad gone, Mum checked out, you think it's your job to be the glue in the family. Uncalled for, unrequested, but understandable."

Floyd mouthed at Jacob—*What's she saying?*

"I wasn't expecting you to call," Jacob said into his phone.

"Well . . . ," a heavy sigh. "I've been thinking. Maybe I overreacted. I have a peace offering. Claude Lemieux."

"The climber guy?"

"I know you wanted the celebrities, but Claude will give good footage. He made an illegal urban ascent in Dubai to protest global warming. It would be a world exclusive."

Jacob locked eyes with Floyd as he said, "Elizabeth, the stuff about the movie was just to get your attention. All I want is to talk."

"Can you be at New Frontiers tomorrow at nine?"

"Of course."

"Great. He'll be ready."

"And you and I can talk after?"

She'd already killed the call.

"Talk after what?" Floyd said.

Jacob turned off the Lumix and the lens retracted with a soft *burr*, an animal snout retreating to safety. "You need to stay off the powder, Floyd. It's frying your brain. You're going to stay here, and I'm going to meet Elizabeth. Whatever trouble she's in, I'll help her. You can stay out of it from now on."

"She won't talk to you."

"Of course she will. She loves me."

Floyd wiped at his eye with his thumb. "That's what I used to think."

CHAPTER

29

Pat Coombs met Alex coming out of the elevator, turned her by the elbow, and walked her back inside. "Lunch meeting."

"Pat, it's ten thirty."

"Trust me." He hit the lobby button.

* * *

Alex waited until they were housed in a red leather booth in the Goodyear Diner, and the waitress had Coombs's pancake order. "Well?" she said, shielding her eyes from the sun-drenched window.

"We confirmed Wannamaker was a pupil at Saint Sebastian." Coombs tucked his napkin into his shirt. "And you asked me how the Saint Sebastian investigation compared to that recent case at the Framingham School up in Mass." He paused while their waitress poured coffee. "In the Framingham case, we have children abused not only by priests but by powerful local men. Old-time monks used to sell honey and wine; these priests sold underage sex. When the case broke, half the notable males within ten miles of Framingham were carted off to jail."

"But at Saint Sebastian there were no convictions."

The waitress returned with a plate of pancakes and four ramekins. When Coombs reached for the blueberries, Alex blocked his hand. "You get to decorate your stack when you finish the story."

"Fascist," Coombs said mildly. "The Saint Sebastian case never made it to court. This was before the *Boston Globe* ripped the Catholic church a new asshole, and I thought maybe the world wasn't ready to believe that priests were operating sex factories. But then I found this." He reached into his satchel and passed Alex a thick, black binder. "Page thirteen."

Alex flipped to an FBI progress report typed on an actual typewriter. Halfway down the page she found the heading "Key Suspects," and below the heading a list of nine names. Four began with the prefix *Fr.* for *Father*: Fr. Donald, Fr. Petersen, Fr. Anadoyu, Fr. Gomez. The other five names had been redacted with a black stripe of ink.

A lightness filled Alex's chest. "Why redact names in an internal FBI report?"

"See why we're not sitting at your desk?" Coombs wielded the syrup jug with one hand, chocolate chips falling from the other like tiny bombs. "Someone in *our* outfit redacted those names. Could be the funny handshake crew looking out for one another. Could be that two of the five names on the suspect list are Dixon and Benedetti."

"The dates work," Alex said. "I wonder how many New Frontiers members are the right age to be victims?"

"Plus the other two redacted names might be on Talon's list. Delase Carter's too young to have been abusing children when Wannamaker was school age, but we could be talking Cardinal Clement or Hertzberg. Bigney's just about old enough, if he started early. Leonard Harris fits like a glove. Harris could be a perp, not a victim."

"Can't he be both? Most abusers are abused themselves." Alex closed her eyes, letting the sun from the window massage her eyelids. "We need a full history of Saint Sebastian pupils to crosscheck against New Frontiers membership. Revenge killings by ex-school kids, Pat? The suspect list could be in the hundreds."

"The request's already in. And it's only a request—we may need stronger medicine. It's only a matter of time before the media traces Wannamaker and Clement back to Saint Sebastian."

Alex checked no one was in the adjacent booth before calling Murphy and telling him what they'd found.

Murphy inhaled with a hiss—his trademark sound when weighing political risk. Next would come the inevitable request to back off, slow down, proceed with extreme caution. But Murphy surprised her. "Saint Sebastian will give us what we need. Those bastards will not obfuscate. Get out there, Alex. I'll have an emergency warrant in your inbox before you arrive."

He killed the call and left Alex staring at a bug crossing the window.

"Where did Murphy grow up?" she asked Coombs.

"Huh? I want to say Pittsburgh."

Murphy. Irish Catholic kid in an Irish Catholic town. Altar boy in the dark days?

In the window reflection, Pat Coombs was out of his seat, speaking on his phone, one hand awkwardly fumbling dollars onto the table beside his half-eaten pancakes. He closed the call and said, "Father Cole will meet us at Saint Sebastian two hours from now."

"You head back to the office, Pat. Dig into that New Frontiers membership list. I'll take Father Cole. Divide and conquer. Let's go."

Coombs tossed up his car keys and caught them, a smirk across his broad face.

"What?"

"Good to have you back, Alex."

* * *

Father Cole was three things Alex hadn't expected: black, leanly handsome, and immaculately dressed in a charcoal suit and dark purple tie. The director of education for the Saint Sebastian Academy met her at the door to the austere Victorian administration building and asked in a voice laced with the Caribbean if she wanted tea. When Alex declined, Cole led the way to an office with pile carpet and a view of a dappled quad. He waved her into a leather chair, and when she said she'd rather stand, accepted her choice with a dip of the head.

"You're here about Sean Wannamaker, an alumni of this school."

Alex passed Cole a copy of the page from the FBI report. Nine names, five of them inked out. "Sean Wannamaker planned an attempt on Cardinal Clement's life. I need to know who these redacted names are. Clement may or may not be one of them. Who are the others?"

Cole studied the list, and Alex thought she might need the warrant Murphy had emailed while she was still gunning the Impala on I-95. She was ready to point out the non-exemption for religious institutions when Cole produced a tiny key, walked around the desk to a wooden filing cabinet, and unlocked a drawer.

The page he handed Alex also had nine names but no redactions. She recognized Fr. Donald, Fr. Petersen, Fr. Anadoyu, and Fr. Gomez. The other five names were all male. Three had titles: Assemblymember, First Deputy Superintendent, Inspector General. No one from Talon's list. No Leonard Harris.

Cole came back around the desk. "The unfortunate business was before my time, but I gather that some kind of deal was struck."

"Deal?"

"We provided the FBI with the external names, and we were permitted to discipline the internal wrongdoers in our own fashion. It appears both institutions agreed to a degree of discretion around the whole proceeding."

Water thundered in Alex's ear canals. "A cover-up."

"We gave the FBI the names they asked for. What you did next was your business."

* * *

Sean Wannamaker's cornflower-blue eyes bored through Alex and out the other side. When the tape was rolling, she said, "Sean, your Google history is full of the Ten Worst People in New York. Cardinal Clement is on that list. So are two dead men. I need you to tell me what you know about the deaths of Luca Benedetti and Tyrell Dixon. Last time I mentioned their names, you became very agitated. I need to know why."

A frown darkened the baby features. "How dare they?" he said softly.

"How dare they what?"

He spoke softly, as if breaking bad news to a small child. "How dare the newspapers compare Clement to some lowlife landlord, a petty crook of a politician, all those other nobodies. How dare they put the devil on the same page?"

* * *

Alex stood at the window of Murphy's office watching two pigeons jostling for space on a rain pipe. "Cardinal Clement and Sean Wannamaker have no connection to Benedetti, Dixon, or Leonard Harris. I've been wasting my time on the Saint Sebastian connection when I should have been chasing down the New Frontiers membership roster."

"We'll deal with Clement," Murphy said from behind her. "I've already passed him on to the cold case division."

"I'm saying that I screwed up again, like I did when I dropped that Tyrell Dixon lead. If you need to take me off the case, I understand."

Murphy grunted something she didn't catch. She turned to find him leaning over his desk, arms like pylons, staring at the nine names Father Cole had given her.

"Sir?"

"I'll make sure Internal Affairs chews this to the bone."

"I said—"

"I heard what you said and the answer's no, you're not off the case. When does the joint task force briefing start?"

"In an hour," Alex said, resetting internally. "The Marshals Service sent two guys, and the ATF team is downstairs drinking all our good coffee. Behavioral Analysis will have a set of profiles in the next twenty-four. Other than that, we keep digging, keep searching, and see what the great American public has to offer. Anything else?"

Murphy had gone back to staring at the report page. "Whoever redacted these names is heading to jail. I don't care who he golfs with."

* * *

It was after midnight when Alex slumped on her couch with a bottle of red and a large glass. Two men dead, no clear suspects, a string of connections that made no sense, and she'd wasted twenty-four hours chasing the wrong lead.

The wine turned her stomach. She tried du Pré playing Max Bruch, but Jacqueline's cello sounded like barbed wire on sheet glass. Nothing could clear her mind tonight.

She stopped the music.

She almost called her dad despite the hour.

Maybe Pat was right when he called Benedetti and Dixon a pair of no-mark bottom feeders. Maybe they didn't deserve justice.

She looked up at her husband's photograph on the mantlepiece and heard his soft voice in her head. *You don't believe that.*

"Where the hell were you today when I needed you?" she asked.

CHAPTER 30

Through the Lumix lens, the vaulted main room of New Frontiers might have been a Viking long hall, a modern adventurer's Valhalla. Claude had met Jacob in the pink gallery. The Frenchman's greeting had been, "Cameras hate me. My skin looks like orange peel."

Jacob had reassured him that he could balance out skin tones in edit, then asked—in the most normal voice he could summon—when Elizabeth would be joining them. Claude had ignored the question and now he squirmed on the chair, his orangey arms twisted into some kind of yogic bind. He'd chosen to wear a striped sweatshirt that would create a distracting moiré pattern on screen, but Jacob didn't care. He wasn't here to film Claude.

"I was surprised my sister called," he said, barely able to hear his own voice over the drumming in his head. "Did she say what changed her mind?"

Through the lens, Claude clenched his fists like a child, thumbs on the inside. "Can we get this over with?"

Claude clearly didn't want to be here any more than Jacob did.

What was Elizabeth up to?

"Tell me about Claude Lemieux," Jacob said. "Give me a sense of what you do."

Claude rubbed at his nose as if trying to remove the freckles, then abruptly launched into a monologue that began with his quest to find the best ramen noodles in New York. Next came how he'd totally own a Staffordshire bull terrier—ten out of ten hound score—if it wasn't for his building's fascistic policy on dogs. After dogs came gigs: a list of all the bands Claude had seen in the last six months, all unfamiliar to Jacob, and a critique of the Lower East Side's punk rock scene. All the gear, Claude said, but no idea.

When Claude stopped—as abruptly as he'd started—Jacob said, "Ramen, Staffies, and punk rock. No mention of climbing?"

"You said tell you what I do." Claude scratched at his scalp. "Climbing is who I am."

Despite everything, Jacob almost laughed aloud. A thudding cliché, but the camera liked Claude and he could get away with being a bit . . . Floydy. Jacob focused in on the freckled face. Time to work another angle.

"Claude, I hope I didn't land you in the shit. Telling Elizabeth about Montauk."

Claude's gaze dropped to his lap. "All good."

"Yeah, well, I apologize. I know how it feels to be on the wrong end of her anger."

Claude stared into the vaulted ceiling. Jacob played for time. "Tell me about the Princess Tower in Dubai."

"I took a banner." The green eyes drifted back to the camera. "*Keep the Oil in the Soil.* Should have said sand, not soil, but I couldn't find an oily rhyme for sand. Flew it from the big silver tit on the roof of the tower. You can grab the stills from my Insta."

"Sounds terrifying."

"My shrink told me that I have an atypically high fear threshold."

"Is that why you do it?" Jacob said. "To feel fear?"

"I guess everything makes sense on the wall." Through the Lumix lens, legs kicking out a rhythm, Claude might have been a little boy waiting for the school bus.

"You okay, Claude? Need a break?"

Claude rubbed at his eyes. "This whole thing—being interviewed—reminds me of a story Floyd told me about an advertising shoot for some watch he was endorsing. They put him in a lineup with a musician and a football player, to represent diverse types of masculinity." Claude pressed his mouth to his forearm and made a surprisingly realistic vomiting sound. "Anyway, the musician was so obnoxious that Floyd couldn't get his line right. He only had to say, 'Be Your Own Man,' and he kept flubbing it." Claude frowned. "I guess I can't find my words today either. I'm done, man."

Claude lifted his shirt so Jacob could unclip the mic battery from his belt.

Jacob wound in the wire. "I'm worried about my sister. You know that, right?"

Claude sucked an invisible straw. "What's Floyd told you?"

"He didn't need to tell me anything. I see it with my own eyes. If you're her friend—and I think you are, despite what you told me when we first met—then you'll help me find her, so I can help her."

The sound of thrashing guitars burst from Claude's hip pocket. He pulled out a phone and held it to his ear.

"Is that Elizabeth?" Jacob said.

Claude pressed the phone against his chest. "Personal call. I'll take it in the den—only be two minutes."

The idea came to Jacob fully formed. "Take your call here," he said. "I wanted to grab a mountaineering magazine I saw in the den when I was last here. Is that okay?"

Claude shrugged. "Knock yourself out, man."

Jacob stepped out from behind his setup. In the beat while his body was between Claude and the camera, he hit the record button.

* * *

Five minutes later, Jacob was back in the main room. For a moment he thought Claude had left, until he saw two dangling Vans sneakers at eye level.

"No luck?" Claude said, from his perch astride the Airstream coffee cart.

"Huh?"

"I thought you went back there for a magazine."

Shit. Idiot. "Couldn't find it. So is Elizabeth coming here? Or do you have new instructions for me?"

"Wasn't your sister, bud." Claude slid forward on the chrome roof and dropped soundlessly to the floor. "Honestly, I'd help if I could. She said to come down here and let you film. Did you get what you wanted?"

I'll know that when I watch the footage back.

"It's fine, Claude. You did your best."

"Told you I was a bad subject."

Jacob picked up his tripod and removed the Lumix. He was headed for the gallery when Claude called out. "Not that way, bud. There's another entrance at the rear."

"Why are we sneaking out, Claude? Who do you think's watching, the FBI?"

Claude showed his teeth in a lopsided smile. "Never walk out the front when you can slip out the back, Jack."

Slip out any way you like, Jack. *You're going to lead me to my sister.*

CHAPTER

31

"IF CLEMENT AND WANNAMAKER are both red herrings, where does that leave us?" Murphy perched on his desk like an angry sparrow. "Did the profiles of the killers come back from Behavioral Analysis?"

Alex nodded. "We're looking for attention-seeking misfits with signature staging behaviors that make their victims look like guilt-ridden suicides. And according to the victimology report, the victims are scumbags. If nothing else, it shows they have CNN down at the Behavioral Analysis Unit in Quantico."

"So we're back to square one with Ricky Talon's list."

"Not exactly," Alex said, glancing at Coombs for backup and hoping her irritation didn't show. "We know Leonard Harris connects to Luca Benedetti."

"But we don't know if that's significant," Murphy said.

"How do you normally feel about coincidences?"

"Hence the re-focus on New Frontiers," Coombs said, stepping in. "We're interested in climbers, obviously—Alex's piton—but half the New Frontiers membership appear to be rock monkeys of one sort or another. I'm talking fifty plus members. So we're focused on anyone at the club who might have known Leonard Harris. Harris is the key."

Murphy made a hand gesture—*speed this up, please.*

Alex took a breath to remain calm. "We started with the founders—Elizabeth Felle and Floyd Shaw. They both knew Harris. His picture's in their gallery, and he was honored in their opening ceremony."

"Elizabeth Felle's interesting," Coombs said. "British like her brother. We found some weapons-grade online bitching about Ms. Felle. A year ago, she purged the club of anyone with sponsorship or ad revenues. The forums say she made members burn their commercial contracts in a kind of purity ritual." He read from his notes. "According to one online post, she's 'into some hardcore radicalized bullshit.'"

"I like her already," Murphy said. "Is the husband getting the same reviews?"

"Floyd Shaw was one of the people she marched out. Shaw has his own quirks. A couple of DUIs about three years back. Cocaine and booze. Managed to stay out of jail, but it cost him his license and his celebrity explorer TV career. Six months after that he was arrested for a bar brawl. He smashed all the windows in the restroom, and when the bar staff tried to kick him out he hurled beer glasses until the cops dragged him away."

"A delightful couple. Does Elizabeth Felle have a sheet?"

"Minor. Glued herself to the lobby of an oil industry conference," Alex said. "But she's no Occupy movement snowflake. Sailed single-handed around the globe and that may be relevant. CCTV confirms that Dixon left the marina alone on his *Sunseeker*, and no one saw or heard another boat nearby. Not many people could guide a dinghy alongside a yacht in total darkness with no engine."

"You'd be surprised," Murphy said. "You know how many yacht clubs there are in the greater New York area? What about the brother, Jacob Felle?"

Alex said, "If he's involved it must be as an impact sub."

Murphy raised a hand. "What's an impact sub?"

"A player who comes off the bench late in the game to damage the opposition." A British soccer term she'd heard William use—maybe that's why it popped into her mind when she was thinking about Jacob Felle. How much more obscure William was buried in her brain? "Felle's tourist visa application lists an apartment owned by

Elizabeth and Floyd Shaw. That's where he was staying until four nights ago when he checked into a hotel in Jersey City."

"You want to bring them in?"

"Too early. The New Frontiers membership list is as long as your arm. Pull in the wrong crowd now and the bad guys will know we have the connection. They'll spook and go to ground."

"So we just wait?"

"We're not sitting on our hands. "

"What *are* you doing, then?"

"For one, I'm assuming Harris-Benedetti *isn't* a coincidence. I'm going back to Councilor Tyrell Dixon's confession to the DoJ—see if we can link Dixon to Benedetti, Harris, or anyone else on Talon's list."

"The NYPD turned Dixon inside out," Murphy said. "Good luck with that."

"Thank you," she said, as if he'd meant it.

* * *

Extraordinary was the word—Tyrell Dixon had treated graft like a calling. Famous and powerful New Yorkers spilled from the Dixon confession like confetti, and Dixon had been staggeringly indiscreet, particularly in early emails when the internet was new and few people grasped the everlasting nature of digital information. By lunchtime Alex had reviewed half the attached emails and found exactly nothing to suggest a connection between Tyrell Dixon and Luca Benedetti or Clearwater Holdings, the company Benedetti traded under.

Coombs walked toward her desk holding a file as thick as a church Bible.

"Printout of all the email attachments," he said. "No one could accuse the man of being lazy." He dropped the file on her desk. "Construction permits, zoning applications, and labor disputes. Dixon was pocketing cash left, right, and center, but he was Queens and the Bronx, and most of Benedetti's empire is Brooklyn and Staten Island. No matches so far."

Alex reached for the file but Coombs slapped down a hand to hold it in place.

"You haven't had lunch, Alex."
"I'm good."
"Let me put it another way. *I* haven't had lunch."

* * *

Tucked into a red-leather window booth in the Goodyear Diner behind Federal Plaza, Alex used a hand to shield her eyes from the sun as she watched Pat Coombs decorate his pancake stack with syrup, raspberries, and a layer of caramel cream, each ingredient applied with precision and panache.

"Pancakes for lunch," she said. "What would your doctor say?"

"She'd say I'm an idiot. *I* say it's a cheap way to load up on calories." Chocolate chips tumbled from Coombs's fingers as he leaned back to admire his creation. "Ever see that old footage of Pollock making splatter paintings? The key to art is knowing when to step away from the canvas. So, Alex, what happens if we don't find anything in the Dixon material?"

"Then we're not looking hard enough. Or not thinking about it right. Dixon attached enough dirt to his email to have half the officials and businessmen in the city scrambling to be on the last chopper out of Saigon. You're telling me Benedetti isn't connected to any of them?"

That had been one of William's phrases—overused and misused. *He'd take that overtime shift like it was the last chopper out of Saigon; he'd have that last slice of pizza like it was the last chopper out of Saigon.* William had kept—now she kept—a bookshelf above the television crammed with military history. He used to joke that he'd chosen to fight fire and read about war, and she should be glad it wasn't the other way around.

Coombs tapped the table with the end of his knife. "Alex, you there?"

"Sorry. You were saying?"

"No, you were. We're not thinking about it right. Okay, so what are we missing?"

Alex's knee ached from sitting too long. She stood to flex the joint.

"I don't know, Pat."

* * *

By dusk, Alex was down to the last attachment to Tyrell Dixon's "suicide note" email. She spun in her chair and, as the FBI office slid by, tried to work out where the day's work had left her.

Honest answer: nowhere.

Coombs appeared at her desk, jacket on, bag over his shoulder.

"You checked everything?" she said.

"Twice."

Alex gazed across the office at the FBI worker bees tapping at their keyboards. "So we busted out on the Benedetti-Dixon connection. I guess we go back to Benedetti and Leonard Harris. Did you pull the official report into the nursing home fire that killed Harris?"

"I'll swing by the fire station and grab it in the morning. Not a lot we can do till then." He hefted the bag on his shoulder. "Want to head down together?"

She spun back in her chair. "The CEO of the nursing home was quoted in the papers. I might try and reach her tonight."

"Can't wait till tomorrow?" Coombs said, and she must have given him a look because he held up his hands in mock defeat. "I get it, Alex. What will Murphy say if our killers take number three while we're stretched out on the couch eating Doritos? Speaking of which, Laurie Cullen—the climate-change-denying professor on Talon's list—plans to speak at a conference tonight at the Park Lane Armory."

"I know," Alex said. "We told her not to."

'You don't look too worried."

"It's at the Armory, Pat—if there's one place in this city we can secure, it's there. The place will be flooded with cops."

Coombs shrugged.

"What?" Alex said.

"Just thinking . . . even if they did get to her . . . I mean, honestly, Alex, how much sleep you gonna lose over any of those lowlifes on Talon's list?"

"Lowlifes have rights, Pat. And we're the line between order and vigilante chaos."

"Here we go. You think if it wasn't for the FBI, we'd have a guillotine in Times Square?"

Alex heard William's voice in her head. *Fire doesn't care if you're a drug dealer or a heart surgeon. Fire doesn't discriminate, and neither do we.*

"We're here to protect everybody, Pat."

"Including the ten worst people in the city?"

"There are no bad people, only broken ones."

Coombs turned his face away. For a moment, Alex thought he might say something, but he'd frozen.

"Pat, are you okay?"

Her partner of nine years seemed to snap back into life, but the smile he gave her was far from convincing. "Alex . . . If after twenty years in this job you still believe there are no bad people, then maybe you should consider a different career."

He shifted the satchel on his shoulder and walked away.

"Pat."

"I'll see you tomorrow, Alex." Said without looking back.

She watched him shuffle to the elevator. Problems at home? Was she riding him too hard? Too many missed family meal times because of his work partner?

She reached for her desk phone.

Kelly-Anne Pinstock, nursing home CEO at the time of the fire that killed Leonard Harris—let's hope you're home.

CHAPTER

32

THE REAR ENTRANCE Claude showed Jacob to wasn't even a door. A coal cellar hatch opened into a refuse yard behind the New Frontiers building, and Claude led Jacob between two fetid dumpsters and along a chain-link fence until they reached a gap that let them out onto a broad and almost silent residential street.

Claude said, "Which way are you going?"

Jacob pointed north toward the subway.

"I'm headed south. See you around, Jacob."

Claude set off at a brisk jog. Jacob let him turn the corner, then headed after him.

* * *

He didn't need to worry about getting too close. He could barely keep up as Claude raced past shuttered auto shops and factories. Disused streetcar rails lay half buried in the brick-lined street, and Claude seemed to glide along them. Jacob lumbered behind holding the Lumix tripod. Up ahead, the orange figure disappeared around another corner.

A few years ago, at fighting weight and fit as a greyhound, Jacob could have run all day. Now he realized how far he'd let his fitness slide. His breath rattled as he rounded the corner and came to a parade of white trucks parked below the concrete ribbon of an elevated freeway. A man in a Mets cap leaned out from one of the cabs, using a pizza box lid to scrape pigeon crap from his windshield.

"You see a guy?" Jacob could barely form the words.

A shrug said the man hadn't understood the question and didn't care to try.

Jacob squeezed between two trucks and emerged under the far side of the freeway in time to see a flash of orange hair as Claude vaulted a metal gate leading into a children's playground. Jacob followed, cracking his shin against the bars of the gate. At the entrance to the playground, he stumbled, the rubber matting squashy under his feet. He slumped against a wooden fort, breathing hard as colored sparks lit up the backs of his eyelids.

Overhead, an airplane cruised east toward Europe. He rested his cheek against the wooden wall of the fort, watching through the Lumix lens as Claude Lemieux dissolved into the distance.

He'd lost him.

When Jacob could breathe, he ran his footage back on the Lumix. On the screen, a tiny Claude Lemieux lowered his wiry frame onto a chair. Jacob ran the footage forward until he saw his own belt buckle appear in front of the camera. He hit play in time to see himself walk past the seated Claude, toward the den. Claude had his phone to his ear but didn't speak until Jacob had closed the sliding door behind him. When Claude did speak, his voice was as clear as rain on a tin roof.

"Yeah, just like you told me to."

A pause, presumably while the other person—Elizabeth?—spoke. Claude said, "Do we cancel? Or forget whore salad and wait for sour lime?" Another pause, then, "Nah, you need to stay out of sight until we figure this shit out. It's not safe."

On the Lumix screen, Claude pocketed the phone and walked out of sight of the camera. A noise like rubber on metal as he climbed onto the Airstream. A minute later, Jacob reappeared in shot and Claude's voice said, "No luck?"

Jacob switched off the Lumix. Still breathing hard from chasing Claude, he googled *whore salad* on his phone. Recipes for spaghetti alla puttanesca filled the screen. He narrowed the search to *salata alla puttanesca* and a couple of entries appeared: small-time chefs being cute on their food blogs. He searched *sour lime* and retrieved a list of lime sour cocktail recipes.

He watched the clip again.

The only bit that made sense was Claude saying, "It's not safe."

CHAPTER

33

You're early, but Maureen is waiting to greet you at one of the side entrances to the Park Avenue Armory. She's here to escort you to the nineteenth-century Drill Hall where your audience awaits, and you follow her bouncing brunette pigtails as she marches you through the lobby, past a poster of your own face, your own blue eyes staring back at you.

> Manhattan Research Group, Annual Conference
> Special Guest: Professor Laurie Cullen, Author of *Climate of Fear—How America Fell for the Environmental Emergency Lie*

Is the Armory always this full of cops? Maureen steers you around an earnest huddle of blue shirts and gun belts, and maybe it's just you, but don't they seem a little on edge?

The Ricky Talon effect.

Not that you need Talon to draw a hateful crowd. Out front you saw more cops, facing off against the massed media on one sidewalk and a rabble of protestors on the other. The protestors wore matching yellow tees and sang songs as they waved their homemade banners.

That was you once, Laurie. Back in the eighties when the only thing bigger than your hair was your sense of outrage. Ban the bomb. Free

Tibet. Meat is murder. The young Laurie Cullen could virtue signal with the best of them.

But that was then, and this is . . . who the hell knows what this is?

Down a wood-paneled corridor and through a room hung with tapestries. Your feet drag behind Maureen's clicking heels—your subconscious telling you that you don't want to arrive at your destination.

What are you doing here?

Earning a sum that starts with a two and has six zeros after it, that's what.

An insane fee for a single interview—don't ask who's picking up the check—and here's another thing: before your book published . . . before you were ousted from your professorship and un-personed by your colleagues and students, before your work was struck from the meteorology curriculum in every major university . . . before all *that*, you could have counted on one hand the scientific conferences that booked you a half-decent hotel, never mind a suite at the Mandarin Oriental. Tonight, there'll be French champagne in the ice bucket, truffle chocolates on the pillow. A chain across the door.

Almost enough to make you forget your inbox full of death threats.

Nothing new in that. But since Ricky-the-hack-Talon started peddling his vicious list, it's like the world went nuts. Suddenly, you're one of the ten worst people in New York and the crazies are lining up to tell you how much you deserve to be raped. *Raped.*

"The Left"—your husband Jules says—"at its compassionate best."

So yay for all these cops and their polished gun belts.

"We're behind the Drill Hall stage." Maureen pauses in front of a stone archway obscured by a velvet drape. "Take a peek."

You fold back the drape and find yourself looking down a vast vaulted space, the ceiling at least eighty feet high. Three chairs on a stage, and what must be two thousand attendees arranged in shallow stadium seating.

Well, Laurie, you picked a side, and here they are. A sea of dyspeptic unfuckable men and their dead-eyed women. Your tribe, heaven help you.

Maureen points to a red light glowing above the archway. "When the light turns green, that's your cue." Mission accomplished, she disappears down the hallway without another word. No "Good luck" for climate-change-denying Professor Laurie Cullen. Maybe Maureen should be outside with the yellow-tee protestors.

You watch the light over the archway. Listen closely and you can make out amplified voices from the stage. Rising in you, like laughter in an asylum, is the urge to turn and flee, back down the hallway, past the cops, past the protestors, down the Long Island Expressway, back to your Bay Shore home . . . back in *time*, if you could—to before you picked a side in this godforsaken war.

Two million dollars, Laurie. You've got two children in college, a mother in a hospice. You give to charity—you'll toe-to-toe with any liberal on how much you give—and even if you did bail, it's not like the other side would have you back. There'll be no reinstatement of your professorship. It's this or nothing. And you deserve better than nothing.

The light above the archway flashes green. Here goes. Your hand is on the drape when you hear the scuff of feet on carpet. You turn into a single hissed word.

"Bitch."

Hot liquid hits your eyes. It stings like acid and the world turns black.

From behind you, a sound like the earth cracking open. Burnt air and a scream that shakes the walls.

You're on the floor—*did you dive, did you fall?*—and your eyes are gummed shut. You scrape at the wet sockets with your fingertips, and the world starts to reappear, but streaked, dirty. Black hands form in front of your face—your own hands—and the smell in your nostrils tells you it's paint. Black paint. Not acid.

Oh, thank you, Lord.

You're staring at the ceiling, and when you turn your head, two lifeless hazel eyes stare back. The girl's head is on the floor, inches from your own, and you're pierced with the realization that she's no older than your daughter Poppy—seventeen at most—with clear sandy skin and a silver stud in her nose. Her arms are flung wide, her oversized yellow tee stretched across her adolescent chest. Text on the tee: *Stop SP**OIL**ING Our Planet*. And where her ribs press against the fabric, a dark stain spreads like a rose opening its petals to the sun.

You twist the other way and now you're staring at a cop, frozen in his shooting stance, gun clutched in his still-outstretched fists. You follow his eyes to the can of aerosol spray resting on the ground a few inches from the dead girl's hands.

Running footsteps, a distant shout, then a closer one. A second cop gently prizes the gun from his colleague's stiff fingers—it's like watching someone disarm a statue.

A third cop kneels over you. A hand supports your head.

"You're okay, ma'am. Ma'am. You're okay."

But you're not okay. And somehow you know that after this you never will be.

CHAPTER

34

Kelly-Anne Pinstock's Facebook page described her as *Retired but active*, as if someone had accused her of sloth and she needed to set the record straight. Alex made the call using a number she'd pulled from the phone directory and a woman's voice answered on the third ring with a sunny, "Who is this?" Alex gave her FBI credentials, established she was speaking with the right Mrs. Pinstock, and explained she was calling about the fire at the Clearwater Community Nursing Home.

The voice hardened. "Am I about to be sued?"

"Not to my knowledge, ma'am. Is the name Luca Benedetti familiar to you?"

Alex heard the scrape of a cigarette lighter followed by a deep exhale. "Of course. Number five on the Ten Worst list when he shuffled off. I must have voted a hundred times for our imbecilic mayor, but he's yet to make the cut. Why are you asking me about Luca Benedetti?"

"Benedetti's umbrella company is called Clearwater Holdings. He was the ultimate owner of Elmhurst Realty, the company that owned Clearwater Community Nursing Home."

"Luca Benedetti?" Pinstock made a *huh* in her throat. "Well, that's news to me."

Alex regretted not doorstepping Pinstock—she'd have given a lot to see if the surprise was genuine. "Tell me about Elmhurst Realty."

"As I told the police at the time, Clearwater was an old building, so we insisted on a pretty tight maintenance contract. But we didn't see too many problems."

"Until the fire."

"Read the report. A freak power surge though the electrical ovens. The electrics were covered under the maintenance contract, and the building was safety-checked every year—I saw the certificates." Pinstock cleared her throat with a smoker's cough. "The real fault was with the fire doors. Elmhurst took a hit and one guy from their Delaware office went to jail for swapping out the recommended fire doors for cheaper alternatives." For the second time, the scrape of a cigarette lighter. A chain smoker, or Alex was making her nervous. Or both. "Is there anything else you need, officer? I have three rose beds still to water before it gets dark."

"We're nearly done. Did you relocate the business to another building after the fire?"

Pinstock made a *pfft* sound. "We were barely profitable anyway. Wrong part of New York if you know what I mean."

"Not really."

"Morrisania is pure Medicaid. Hard to deliver growth to shareholders."

Alex clicked her pen. "One more question, Mrs. Pinstock, if I may. Why did you ask me if you were being sued?"

"Because this is New York. I wondered if some nephew crawled out the woodwork."

Crawled out. Like a cockroach. From the wrong part of New York.

Alex released Pinstock to her rose beds.

She put in her earbuds and turned slowly in her office chair as Alexander Kniazev launched into his crisp interpretation of Chopin's Cello Sonata in G Minor. A few agents were still at their desks, trapped in cones of lamp light as they tapped keyboards and frowned at screens. Cello and piano jostled for position in Alex's ears. She closed her eyes, hoping the music hadn't lost its power, and slowly, as the cello overwhelmed the piano, her mind began to clear. She reviewed her phone conversation with Kelly-Anne Pinstock, wishing William was there so that she could tap his knowledge of how a fire might spread in a nursing home.

Wishing he was there, period.

Something Pinstock had said—or the way she'd said it—snagged in Alex's mind, but before she could capture the thought, her phone buzzed.

"They reach you yet?" Pat Coombs said without preamble.

"Who? What about?"

"Laurie Cullen. Attacked at the Armory."

Alex's stomach lurched. "They got her?"

"No, Cullen's fine. She's down a blouse—unless you can get black car paint out of cotton. It wasn't our perps."

Coombs explained what had happened: Professor Laurie Cullen sprayed in the face, a teenage protester killed, a cop led out the back with tears in his eyes.

"Holy shit," Alex said, dizzy with relief that another person on Talon's list hadn't been killed, but sick at the thought of the dead young girl in the yellow tee.

Alex on the cathedral plaza, shouting for her colleagues to hold fire.

"Murphy hasn't yet found a way to make it our fault," Coombs said. "But I get the sense he's working on it."

Nothing more dangerous than a panicking cop.

"Alex, are you there?"

"Pat, about earlier. You seemed upset."

A small sigh. "Sorry about that. Harriet and me are experiencing a little marital turbulence—the seat belt sign's on, if you know what I mean?"

She'd figured as much. "Need your evenings and weekends back for a while?" she said.

"Nah. A little space is no bad thing. Hey, we'll work through it. We always do."

"I know you do. Look, Pat, if it's *really* okay, then I need you to swing by the fire station for the report on the nursing home fire. My apartment's closer to your place than the office. Meet me at mine when you've got the report. I'll order pizza and open a bottle of red."

And if you want to talk, we'll talk.

"Done," Coombs said, without hesitation. "Is this to do with Professor Cullen?"

"I don't think so. Who the hell knows? Just meet me at mine, okay?"

Her tone must have made her partner's nose twitch. "What you got, Alex?"

* * *

Alex and Coombs faced each other across Alex's coffee table, between them a pizza box, the bloated Dixon file, and a printout of the fire service report into the fatal Clearwater Community Nursing Home fire. Coombs seemed to be back to normal—he'd joyfully inhaled two slices of pie before Alex had touched hers. His way of telling her he was fine.

"You going to tell me what we're looking for, Alex?"

"Kelly-Anne Pinstock gave me the same line she gave the press at the time of the fire. A freak accident, the building regularly checked and all the fire safety certificates present and correct. Then she switched gears, a little too smoothly for my ear, and started talking about how Elmhurst took a hit over shitty fire doors."

"Keen to keep you focused on the doors?"

"The bit she couldn't be expected to know about, rather than the fire certs that she signed off on. See where I'm going with this, Pat?"

Coombs stared at her for a beat. "Give that here." He twisted the Dixon file around and flipped pages until he brought his palm down with a whack. "Here you go."

"What's that?"

"That, Alex, is a faked fire inspection certificate for a bowling alley in Longwood."

"So?"

"We know that in his role as councilor, Tyrell Dixon ran a scam selling fire safety certificates to small businesses. Truth is, there's barely a building in the Bronx would meet the fire code. In exchange for cash, corrupt fire safety inspectors signed off on fire certificates. Tyrell Dixon got a kickback from each and every one."

And Luca Benedetti owned a building that burned down due to faulty fire equipment.

Alex pushed the Dixon file aside and reached for the official report into the nursing home fire that took the life of Leonard Harris. A few sheets from the end she found the fire safety certificate. Same format as the bowling alley example, and when she looked closely . . . Alex spun the Clearwater certificate to line up with the Longwood version, jabbing two fingers onto the identical signature box on both documents.

"Same signature, Pat. Fire Marshal Frederick Parsons."

Coombs leaned forward. "There's our link between Leonard Harris, Tyrell Dixon, and Luca Benedetti. This fire marshal, Parsons, faked the safety certificate for the nursing home Benedetti owned, and kicked up cash to Tyrell Dixon."

Alex glanced up at William's photo on the mantle. He smiled down, but the voice in her head vibrated with anger. *Go get 'em, honey. Scumbags like Parsons aren't fit to wear the uniform.*

She snatched up her keys.

"Where are we going?" Coombs said.

Alex was already in the hallway. "If Benedetti and Dixon are connected, then chances are that Ricky Talon's list isn't randomly generated by the public. And that means someone put those names on Talon's list deliberately. Alibi or not, it's time we paid another visit to our buddy Ricky Talon."

CHAPTER

35

Jacob ordered another Jameson whiskey and tried to focus on the Mexican boxers battling on the TV above the liquor shelf. The fight was a rerun of a classic, and Jacob knew how it ended. In the eleventh, Morales would send Zaragoza to the canvas with a shot to the bowl of his stomach. The veteran Zaragoza would smile and raise a glove to congratulate his young rival. He wouldn't bother trying to beat the count.

After Jacob lost Claude, he'd tried Henry's apartment where he'd met Elizabeth. No answer and when he kept banging, a neighbor appeared holding a tiny white dog and told him that Mr. and Mrs. Henry Duval had gone away for a few weeks, but not to worry because she was watering their plants. He'd tramped back to Floyd's place. Same deal. No Floyd.

Now he was slumped at the bar in a hoppy late-night dive off Franklin Avenue, the kind of place where you didn't leave your jacket on the chair when you went for a piss. Hushed conversations, items passed beneath tables, and normally in this kind of environment the Lumix would be surreptitiously recording, but Jacob sat hunched over his glass. Every time he thought about his sister, he wanted to visit the bathroom to break every mirror with his fist.

Floyd: "She's in danger, Jacob. You have to help her."
How could he help her if he couldn't find her?

Claude on the phone, in the clip Jacob had secretly recorded: "You need to stay out of sight until we figure this shit out. It's not safe."

Claude had been talking to Elizabeth—Jacob had sensed it. His sister was in danger. And here he was, sitting in a bar without a clue where to turn next.

The bartender appeared. "Mind if I switch channels?"

Jacob shrugged. "Seen this fight before. The old guy taps in the eleventh."

Should he call the cops, tell them he was worried about her?

Yeah, she'll love you for that.

The TV screen flipped to CNN. A woman with sharp blue eyes filled the TV screen, under the label "Professor Laurie Cullen." Cut to a throng of men and women in yellow tees, standing in a circle outside an imposing building, holding lit candles and weeping.

"Screw those trigger-happy cops," the barman said. "The girl was just a kid."

Trigger-happy cops. Another reason for Jacob to *not* call them about his sister. He had to find her himself. Somehow.

His phone buzzed. A text from a number he didn't know.

Green Wood Cemetery. Meet me there.

Jacob called the number—no answer.

He texted back, *Who is this?* Then, *Elizabeth, is that you?*

Two minutes later he was in the street, heading south toward Brooklyn.

CHAPTER

36

You're alone in your studio, editing a segment for your evening broadcast of *Dallas Johncock's Interview Hour*. You spent the best part of your morning recording some moon-howler who wanted to talk about alien abductions, and you'll be lucky if you can salvage eight coherent minutes from the footage.

Your phone pings with a WhatsApp message.

Sorry we had to abort. Security is paramount. The senator is still game, if you are.

Now your mind jumps like a frog on a hotplate.

All you can think of are secrets, lovely secrets, spilling like Roman coins through your fingers. This could be what you've been waiting for your whole damn life. The senator is offering you insights that only a select few in government are privy to. He's promised you a peek behind the curtain, validation of your worst fears and your greatest hopes. For too long, you've been dismissed as a conspiracy theorist, a crank, a crackpot... But the truth is out there, if only you can find it.

You remember standing on the 9/11 Memorial Plaza like a rejected Tinder date as the black car disappeared out of sight. You remember deleting the video in which you named the senator—your insurance policy in case you never made it home. You remember telling the indifferent sky that you were done with the senator and done with being screwed around.

And you were. Until they made contact again.

For some reason, you think of your father, self-styled king of the psychic sports pick, running his long cons across a football season. "The trick, son, is to keep them believing the big win is just around the corner." Said over eggs in a diner on parental access day. "The more they yearn, the more you earn."

Now it's you who yearns, as you wonder what the senator can tell you about sonic warfare, parapsychology, chem trails . . .

Is it safe? That's the question.

Your name's still on Talon's damn list, two men are dead, and only last night that lady professor took a face full of black ink. Your radio show guest today—the moon-howler—had a theory about the list. "Rigged," he said. "No way the good people of New York would vote to spear such small fry on their pitchforks."

You let the small fry reference go. "Don't be so sure," you said. "I took a cab yesterday, and the driver was adamant that if you bat a .190 average for the Yankees you have to rank as one of the Ten Worst People in New York."

"Vox populi, vox Dei," the moron guest said. "Ricky Talon claims that the list is the voice of the people, and the voice of the people is the voice of God. But if Talon's list represents the worst of New York, then we live under a petty, stupid God. No, if you ask me, there's something very wrong with Ricky Talon's list."

No kidding, asshole. They—we—keep dying.

The senator is still game, if you are.

You'll go. You know you'll go. But the senator must guarantee your safety, and you'll take your own precautions.

This time, you record your security video without a stumble on the words. The video is scheduled to upload to *DallasJohncockTruth.com* at midnight, your insurance policy if Senator Duval turns out be one of the lizard kings.

The truth is out there. And you, Dallas Johncock, have a duty to bring it home.

CHAPTER

37

THIS TIME, RICKY Talon didn't offer Alex a coffee or interviews that would show her in a "super-awesome light." Seated between two lawyers at a boardroom table somewhere in the clouds above Central Park, he picked at his shirt cuffs and stared through the window, watching airplane trails divide a brooding night sky. Alex didn't need coffee; she needed Talon's attention.

"Good of you to see us so late, Ricky," she said. "I'll get straight to the point. We need access to the online voting system." Both lawyers made notes on their yellow pads. "And a list of everyone who touches it."

"I thought you already spoke to my production team." Talon had the downturned mouth of a child waiting outside the principal's office. "I really do need them focused, Detective. We have to come up with a new feature before tomorrow night or the whole *Talon Tonight* train could come off the tracks."

"*Special agent.* And I thought your ratings could be seen from space."

Talon made a dismissive gesture to the lawyers seated either side of him. "Apparently, *Talon Tonight* is a bar with my name above the door and NBC's name on the liquor license, and owing to the threat of impending litigation from a *fourth* Benedetti wife—how many wives does a man need?—and from Tyrell Dixon's estate, and pretty much every other lowlife on the list, we are about to lose that license."

"No more Ten Worst People in New York," one of the lawyers said. "As of today, the list is dead, if you'll pardon the expression."

"Ever heard of New Frontiers?" Alex said.

Talon shook his head.

"How about Floyd Shaw?"

Talon reviewed the backs of his hands. "One of your little helpers asked me that a few days ago. I never met the man."

"Your paths never crossed? You both work in television."

"Doesn't everybody?"

"And you never met Luca Benedetti or Tyrell Dixon?"

"Why would I?"

"How about Leonard Harris?"

"Who's Leonard Harris?" Talon shook his head. "Never heard the name."

The slight furrowing of the brow as Talon tried to surface Harris's name from his memory banks felt real. Alex was annoyed to realize that she believed him.

* * *

Murphy perched on the lip of his desk. Perhaps he worried that standing highlighted his lack of stature. "Trouble getting past the press?" he said. "Do they have your name as lead investigator?"

"I used the underground garage. So far, no names have leaked."

"Then let's make the most of our time before they do. Hit me."

Don't tempt me. "Okay, we have the full picture on the nursing home fire. Benedetti owned the company that owned the nursing home building. He charged the nursing home to refit Grade A fire-retardant doors, then used a cheap alternative in the actual build. The doors should last ninety minutes in a fire; they were ash in fifteen. But those same shitty doors passed multiple fire inspections. How? Because Benedetti paid off the fire marshal, Frederick Parsons, and some of that money made its way into Councilor Tyrell Dixon's pocket."

Murphy frowned. "We have this Frederick Parsons in custody?"

"Died three years ago. Cancer of the liver."

"No sign of foul play?"

Alex gave her boss a beat to realize what he'd just said.

"Of course, you can't give someone cancer." Murphy rolled a heavy glass paperweight across his desk and back again. "Do we think the CEO you talked to is involved?"

"Kelly-Anne Pinstock was keen to focus me on the fire doors, but that could just be cover-your-ass. We don't think she's significant. For a start, she's alive and not on Talon's list. Our perps are going after the whales, not the minnows."

A knock at Murphy's door and Pat Coombs's head appeared. "Dallas Johncock, number five on Talon's list."

Murphy beckoned Coombs into the office. "What about Johncock?"

"Remember that school shooting two years back at Pinnacle Hills? Dallas Johncock claimed the massacre was faked by the anti-gun lobby."

Murphy nodded. "Johncock's bed-wetting acolytes broke up the kids' funerals."

"But guess what?" Coombs said. "It wasn't Johncock's first rodeo. Four years earlier he was a small-time, local radio jock, claiming that the Clearwater Community Nursing Home fire was a leftist conspiracy to gain support for free healthcare. Guess what happened next?"

The hairs on Alex's arms stiffened. "His troll army ruined Leonard Harris's funeral."

"Tore the place apart. Johncock claimed a victory for free speech and truth. Harris was cremated the next day behind closed doors."

"Why didn't that come up when I googled the fire?"

Coombs shrugged. "You didn't have Johncock's name to correlate. Even then, it's one tiny column buried on the *Bronx Gazette* site. Remind me not to die black and poor."

"Call Johncock and get people to his residence." Alex said.

"Already done. He's at home with a patrol unit parked up on his lawn."

Murphy turned to the window. "What next, Alex?"

"Go see Johncock—we need to accelerate the Leonard Harris investigation. And it's time to bring in the two New Frontiers founders. Elizabeth Felle and Floyd Shaw. Like I said before, we can assume they knew Harris—his picture was in their gallery—and if they're not involved they might have a steer on who we should be talking to."

"Do it. Shake the tree and see what falls out." Murphy didn't look happy. "Here's what's bothering me—and should be bothering you too, Alex. How do all three men end up on Talon's list?"

"We're sure the list was manipulated," Alex said. "We just don't know—yet—whether the hack came from the inside or the outside. Meanwhile, Talon's alibis are rock solid, but that doesn't mean he's not the puppet master. Or maybe he's acting under duress."

"Doesn't have to be Talon," Coombs said. "Could be one of his crew."

Murphy rubbed at his chin. "But why publicize the people they're going after? Surely it just makes their job harder?"

Alex Bedford had no answer for that one. All she knew was that the flywheel of this investigation was now in motion. And she couldn't remember the last time she'd felt this alive.

Coombs's phone buzzed. He listened, said, "Ain't that a bitch," and killed the call. "Dallas Johncock," he said. "The patrol unit we sent to his house found him in his robe eating Ben & Jerry's in front of the hockey, and they've been outside ever since. But we just got a call from Johncock's wife. Dallas Johncock is missing."

CHAPTER

38

"I SCHEDULED A VIDEO," you say from the rear seat, as the car rides up onto the Brooklyn Bridge. "If anything happens to me, Senator Duval's name is out there."

"I assure you, Mr. Johncock, that the senator is looking forward to meeting you," says the distorted voice from the front seat. "He found your show on extraterrestrial encounters fascinating. Perhaps you can further enlighten him when you meet."

You enlighten *him*? "I can tell him that the military covers that shit up all the time."

Or they don't. It's the *kind* of thing the government would do—that's what matters, and that's what people don't understand. Not everything you say should be taken literally. You're like the Bible. You're a mood piece. You're a—

The voice cuts into your thoughts. "We're here."

The car rolls through iron gates yellowed by security lights. You stop with a gravelly crunch. The door opens and you're out in the evening. A stone mausoleum rises out of the ground, surrounded by haggard trees. The driver unfolds himself from behind the wheel. He's tall and wears black coveralls and a mask: Bugs Bunny, a cardboard carrot protruding cigar-like from his oversized teeth.

"Behind the ear," Bugs says.

Before you can work out what he means, the cemetery turns black.

* * *

You taste gravel, the world sideways and silvered with moonlight. You try to clutch your head but can't move your hands. Bugs Bunny crouches in front of you, and behind Bugs a black-clad Minnie Mouse sits on the steps of a mausoleum.

Bugs's cardboard mouth seems to move with his voice. "Dallas Johncock, welcome to your reckoning. We're here to tell you that liberal democracy has failed. Courageous morality is the last frontier."

A woman's voice says, "We believe that nature elevates the best and destroys the worst." You turn to the new voice and moving your head drives an icepick into your skull. Bart Simpson stands under a crooked tree.

"Nature's revenge," you say. "Chinese pandemic programs. That's why I'm here?"

Bugs leans in. "You're here because of Talon's list."

"Talon's . . . The CIA kill list?" You want to hug this lanky rabbit. "That's why the senator wants to meet? But why me? Why does the CIA care about me?"

"It doesn't. That's why we're here." Bugs pats a new-looking marble gravestone. "Did you know that Shona Fitzpatrick is buried right under our feet?"

The name turns your insides liquid.

Bart says, "A victim of the Pinnacle Hills school massacre." He pulls a notepad and Sharpie from a cloth bag. "Final apology?"

Now you know you're going to die. "My video," you say. "My insurance policy."

Bugs nods, solemn rabbit. "The video where you name Senator Duval? The senator has never even heard of you. At least, I assume so."

The senator's invitation was a lie to get you here. And you made it easy for them, crawling out of your bathroom window to avoid the cop car in your driveway.

Bugs waves the Sharpie. "Apology time. How about a simple, *I'm sorry?*"

You hear your father's voice. *The more they yearn, the more you earn.*

"I can put your manifesto on two million screens," you whimper.

Bart looks at Bugs, who—*Oh, sweet Lord*—is screwing a silencer onto a rifle. Bart chews on the Sharpie and says, "Isn't the barrel too long for his reach?"

Bugs snaps in the magazine and racks the bolt. "He used his toe. And stop slobbering your DNA over that pen. Now, hold him steady. I need the angle to blow out the bruise."

Bart holds the back of your head as Bugs works the suppressor between your teeth. It feels like sucking on an oil pipe. Bugs pauses.

"Would you like a chance to redeem yourself, Johncock?"

"Yes, yes." Muffled by the silencer, it sounds like *Weff, weff.*

He withdraws the barrel. The scrape of metal on teeth judders your collarbone.

Bart pulls a phone from his pocket. Your phone. "A filmed denunciation of the lies you've told," he says. "Take responsibility for all the fake news and the doxing and the hate."

"This is a trick. You'll kill me like you did the others."

"They panicked and gave us no choice. For the next ten seconds, you have a choice." Bugs holds your phone at the angle you'd hold it if you were filming yourself. "Confession is a powerful rite, Dallas. It can bring about the most remarkable change of heart, make a man do the most unlikely things." Bugs's cardboard mouth smiles in the moonlight. "We just want you to do what's right."

CHAPTER

39

ALEX WASN'T PROUD that her first reaction to a man's death was a shiver of excitement, but she could live with it. Supervisory Special Agent Murphy's beckoning finger summoned her to the mausoleum. She picked her way over tree roots, steering wide of the yellow tape that formed a triangle around the prone figure in the white fleece, arms starfished like a sleeping baby, a shredded pumpkin where his head should have been. Half past midnight, and the CSI techs worked under mobile police spotlights. Alex looked for their truck, hoping they had a box of coffee on the go.

"Gunshot through the roof of the mouth, everything above the jaw is mashed potato." Murphy nodded toward the body. "Security patrol found Johncock's body just after midnight and amazingly they called 911, not the TV stations. The third death from Talon's list, Alex, and we didn't stop it."

We in this context meant *you*.

"Another faked suicide means we must have the gun."

"A box-fresh Sauer hunting rifle. Three-oh-eight caliber." Murphy stood beside Alex so they could appraise the scene together. Men, she'd noticed, preferred to speak side-on like generals surveying a battlefield, while women tended to talk into each other's faces. She found the male way more efficient. Below them, CSI techs scoured the scene in white paper suits, careful ghosts haunting pools of artificial light. Murphy pointed to a brown leather shoe with a white sock stuffed inside. "He used his toe on the trigger. Awkward."

"Especially when a handgun would do the job. The rifle was registered in his name?"

Murphy shrugged. "No, but that doesn't mean shit. He could've bought it at any Louisiana gun fair if he flashed a library card."

Her boss's shoes caught Alex's eye, white tennis sneakers peeking out from under dark suit pants. Murphy must have left the house in a hurry.

"We have the two-word apology note in Sharpie," she said. "Any other mea culpa in line with Benedetti and Dixon?"

"Two videos. One recanting a lifetime of lies, and the other . . ." Murphy looked like he was chewing glass. "Johncock claims to have been on his way to visit—of all people—Senator Patrick Charles Duval."

"Oh, shit."

"The senator's office denies this, of course, and the senator wasn't even in New York State last night—he was at a gala in Chicago with five hundred other blue bloods. But it's a juicy bone for the media to chew on." Murphy turned and pressed his hands against the stone mausoleum. "Did we haul in the New Frontiers founders yet?"

"Elizabeth Felle and Floyd Shaw. Not yet."

"No?"

"No one home."

"They bailed? Gone to ground?"

"Too early to say. We stationed a team to watch their apartment and I need a wiretap warrant to get up on their phones. I'm putting out a BOLO." A "be on the lookout" notice turned every cop, port authority agent, and airport security guard into a pair of eyes. "I'd like to do the same for the brother—Jacob Felle—just in case."

"I don't like it."

"You want us to sit outside their apartment and hope they show up?"

"I mean I don't like *this*." He gestured to the busy floodlit scene below them. "Whoever runs this show will have a camera crew walking backward ahead of them, everywhere they go. I'm talking daily media briefings and pressure from powers higher than you imagined existed. Suicide cult or murder plot, every hour you don't wrap the case you're an hour closer to being led up the scaffold. And over what? Three dead scumbags."

Alex started to say that Benedetti, Dixon, and Johncock weren't men she'd want to have a beer with, but murder was murder . . . Then it hit her what Murphy was saying.

"You want to replace me on the case."

"You're one of the most effective agents in the Bureau, Alex."

"You lost confidence in me. I dropped the ball on Dixon six months ago, and I'm not making fast enough progress on Talon's death list. That's what this is."

"You've had a rough year."

Oh, you patronizing prick.

"This is my case. And if I'd listened to you, we wouldn't have the Leonard Harris connection and we wouldn't have linked Benedetti to Dixon."

Murphy looked her in the eye. "Pat yourself on the back, Alex, then tell me how—and *why*—these men all found their way onto Ricky Talon's very public list."

"We don't know yet. But you're right. It's probably too tricky for the poor distracted widow to figure out. Maybe it's too tricky for the FBI and we should kick it up to the big boys in the NYPD." The edges of Murphy's nostrils flared, and Alex knew she should stop, but the words on her tongue were too hot to swallow. "This is a triple homicide. It's FBI and it's mine. Don't worry. I won't tarnish your personal brand."

Without another word, Murphy stomped away through the artificial light. From the west, figures approached the crime scene, moving zombie-like between the gravestones with heavy objects on their shoulders. The television crews had arrived.

A trio of NYPD officers held the line fifty yards from the scene. A television reporter called out to Alex. "One of your colleagues behind with his student loans?"

She called back. "What are you talking about?"

"Fox News, honey. Those bastards always beat us to it."

Alex pulled out her phone and googled the Fox News site. On the first page she found a photo of a notepad with *I'M SORRY* written in

Sharpie, next to a brown Oxford dress shoe with a sock sticking out the top. She didn't need the captions to tell her that these were images from the crime scene she was looking down on.

How had Fox gotten hold of them so fast?

Alex texted her boss, Murphy: *I need those warrants.*

Then she went looking for Pat Coombs.

CHAPTER

40

Another bar, this one in Park Slope, Brooklyn, and by one in the morning Jacob was the wrong side of drunk.

What the hell was going on?

The anonymous text had sent him hurtling to Green Wood Cemetery in a cab, and the first thing he'd seen, even before he climbed out of his taxi, was a sea of blue flashing lights. His first reaction had been to run forward—*Elizabeth might be hurt*—but a second, more powerful instinct made him duck into shadow. As Jacob watched, the cops were joined by an ambulance, lights on but siren off, apparently in no rush to arrive.

Whoever was hurt wasn't hurt too bad. Or they were beyond help.

Ironic . . . in the cab on the way over, Jacob had even started to doubt himself. Was Elizabeth really in danger? She'd have told him if it was *that* bad—wouldn't she? Floyd with his coke-addled brain was overreacting. And as for Claude Lemieux—"Cancel tonight" could have been a cinema date. "Whore salad" and "sour lime" might be cocktails, or friends' nicknames, or punk bands. "It's not safe" could have referred to any number of harebrained Elizabeth-style protest actions. Hell, Jacob couldn't even be sure Claude had been talking to Elizabeth in that recorded call.

The police presence at Green Wood Cemetery had dispelled that comforting fantasy.

From his shadow across the street, Jacob had once again called the number the anonymous text had come from. Still no answer. When a TV truck arrived on the scene with its bristling roof antenna, he'd decided enough was enough and jogged back the way the taxi had brought him, no destination in mind, just a need to be moving. When that need wore off, he'd dropped into the nearest dive bar and here he was, raising his hand for a fifth glass of whiskey.

TV truck.

Whatever happened at Green Wood Cemetery might have made the news.

Jacob asked the barman for the channel changer for the TV above the bar. He clicked until he found Fox News: Police tape around a patch of grass in a park. Not a park, a cemetery. Cut to a photograph of a long, drawn face, prominent front teeth and a mane of General Custer hair.

> DALLAS JOHNCOCK: TV Host Found Dead in Green-Wood Cemetery.
> Third Death from Ricky Talon's List of the Ten Worst People in New York.

"You're kidding me," Jacob said out loud.

"I'm with you, brother." The bartender had his eyes glued to the screen. "Copycat suicides my ass. This is some crazy trying to do the world a favor."

Fox flipped to the weather. Jacob breathed a long sigh. The news story hadn't mentioned another death. It didn't mean Elizabeth was safe, and it didn't explain why someone had sent Jacob to the cemetery, but considering he'd half expected to see an image of her body among the gravestones, he'd take it.

The date appeared on the TV along with the Fox News ident. September seventh.

Why was that date familiar?

Floyd's apartment: an invitation under a fridge magnet. A version of the same invitation in Henry's apartment where Elizabeth had been staying. A wedding at the New York Public Library.

Jacob dropped some money on the bar. On the street, under cover of a maple tree, he removed the SIM card from his phone. The SIM went in one hip pocket, his powered-off phone in another.

CHAPTER 41

ALEX CAST A long shadow as she ducked inside the flap of the lab tent erected fifty yards from where Dallas Johncock's body still lay. Coombs passed her a coffee cup.

"The media has images of the suicide note and Johncock's shoe," she said.

"Wonderful," Coombs sighed. "Most likely one of the new CSIs. Think they're walking onto a TV set, then they find out their job is picking up cigarette butts for minimum wage. It would have happened sooner or later."

"Later would have been better." Alex cast her eyes over neatly arranged items on a blue tarpaulin, each item with its own number on a cardboard tent. "Okay, Pat. What we got?"

"Aside from the two videos posted on the website, we have a mint three-oh-eight Sauer Pantera with suppressor, plus carry bag. Leather flip wallet with credit cards, coffeeshop loyalty cards—Johncock was diligent about getting his stamps—and ninety dollars in cash. No texts or calls made or received after midnight. Artists' pad, the kind you can buy in any stationery shop, with a minimalist suicide note on the top sheet. Johncock's prints on everything, no one else's so far. The presence of the cash and the gun rules out robbery, and we expect to find gunpowder residue on his toe."

Alex didn't have to bend to read the tall letters on the pad. *I'M SORRY.* "Do we have anything that would convince a jury this isn't suicide?"

"Guess you need that coffee, Alex."

Alex had to run her eyes over the items twice. "Where's the pen?"

"Correct. No Sharpie found within throwing distance."

"Maybe he wrote the note at home or in his car."

"His car's on his driveway in Queens. And the page is still attached to the pad."

"So?"

"So, you don't write the note at home then bring the whole pad. You tear off the page and fold it in your pocket, especially if you got a seven-pound rifle to carry." Coombs waved at the items on the ground. "If Johncock waited until the last moment to craft his final goodbye, we should have the pen."

"The case of the missing pen. That's rolling-paper thin." A familiar hum began at the back of Alex's brain. No migraine this time, this was her synapses firing up for the hunt. "It won't impress a court, but you know what it tells us?"

"They're getting careless."

* * *

Driving toward the cemetery gates and into the blue wash of morning, Alex's phone buzzed. A text from her boss, Murphy.

Phone warrants ready in one hour. Don't say I didn't warn you.

"Whadda you know? He came through," Alex said.

"Who did?"

"Murphy. He was toying with the idea of reassigning this case."

Coombs rolled down his window and stuck an elbow into the cool dawn air. "Don't kill me for saying this, but it's not the worst idea from your point of view. Let someone else screw the pooch."

"Well, this is me letting you know that the option is open."

"You're asking if I want to be reassigned."

"No shame in it."

Coombs had his hand outside the car, his open palm riding the wind. "That wouldn't be the smart move."

"Why not?"

"Because, Alex, after you crack the Ten Worst case and make Supervisory, I don't fancy spending the next two years running inventory of all the FBI paper clips in North America."

"On night shift," Alex said.

"Settled, then. So, aside from cover-your-ass, what's Murphy's beef?"

Alex sucked on her lip. "Murphy can't coordinate his shoes and pants, but he's not stupid. We have almost nothing we can use in court and our suspects are in the wind. So, where do we go from here?"

Up ahead, the iron gates came into view. Coombs said, "In England, one of the nicknames they have for cops is 'the plod.' I guess police work is putting one foot in front of the other, so let's hit the Johncock family home while the scene's fresh, talk to the wife. At least while we wait for the New Frontiers founders to show their faces."

"The BOLO and phone access should help us locate Elizabeth Felle and Floyd Shaw. If that doesn't work, Murphy will have to let us go public with their photos—he won't like it, but he'll do it."

Coombs wound up his window. "Alex, I know how much you love advice, but I recommend you make a note of every conversation with our glorious leader from now on. Time, date, he said, she said."

"Not my style, Pat."

As they pulled off the curb, a WABC-TV truck arrived at the gates. A camera lens thrust through the open window, and a whiny female voice called, "Hey, Feebies. Johncock's 'I'm sorry' ain't fooling no one. When you gonna admit this is a murder hunt?"

CHAPTER

42

A NGRY SUNRAYS BLASTED the New York Public Library steps, and Jacob pulled at the collar of his newly purchased shirt while the long-fingered security guard checked a printed wedding list.

"I'm afraid your name's not here, Mr. Shaw."

"I have an invitation, I just left it at home."

The guard checked the back of his list. "My mistake, but I'm afraid . . ." He squinted at the sheet to make sure. "Special instructions, Mr. Shaw. You don't get in."

* * *

Jacob headed west along Fortieth to Bryant Park, where two hundred Lycra-clad asses saluted the sun in an outdoor yoga session. At the back of the library, he found a service door beside a white marquee. Jacob took a seat on a low wall where he could watch the door.

After a few minutes, two servers in maroon vests emerged blinking into the light and lit up cigarettes. Jacob was wondering where he could get one of those maroon vests when a pair of youths with hipster hair appeared through the same door. One held a sheaf of papers—sheet music.

"Hey," Jacob said as he approached. "The wedding coordinator told me I'd find you here. Have you guys decided where you want the camera?"

* * *

Refectory tables under ivory-colored cloth waited for guests to stream in from the ceremony, each table ornamented with name card tents, champagne flutes, little boxes tied with ribbon. The bookshelves had been left uncovered, the spines a colorful contrast to the slab floor. *We're not only richer than you*, the room said, *we're more cultured too*. The trio of musicians occupied a quarter-circle plinth in a corner of the vast chandeliered library hall, and Jacob set up slightly behind the band.

Elizabeth probably wouldn't even show. But if she did, he'd be ready.

Voices and footsteps announced guests fresh from the ceremony. His lens a sniper scope, Jacob searched the linen summer suits and bright frocks as they entered the room. He'd just about convinced himself there was no way his sister would attend a *wedding* now, when a tall figure caught his eye—Henry Duval, his long V-shaped body encased in a tweed suit. Henry worked the room like a professional, shaking hands and laughing with that fluid privately educated bonhomie that Jacob—with his brief unhappy experience of boarding school—had always both envied and despised.

He panned left and there she was.

Green dress, hands on hips like a foreman surveying a production line. She was engaged in conversation with a young, good-looking woman in a canary-yellow sari and high-top sneakers.

Jacob stood up behind the camera. He let Elizabeth see him coming so she had a moment to brace. Her smile froze, then immediately recovered.

"Jacob, what a nice surprise. I didn't know you knew Samantha and David."

"Elizabeth, can we step outside for a moment?"

Had that sounded normal? Did he look normal?

"This is Srividya," Elizabeth said. "She's a talented television writer, and one of Floyd's old buddies from his glory days."

"Srividya Parthasarathy." The woman in the yellow sari pushed back her hair. "Pleased to meet you. And Elizabeth is too kind."

"We need to talk," Jacob said to his sister.

Srividya raised an eyebrow at Elizabeth. "Think I'll mingle, hon. Catch you later."

A hand tapped Jacob's shoulder.

"I'm the official videographer." A thin man with a thin tie. "I waived my fee for the exclusive media rights." Emphasis on *exclusive*. "And yet here you are with *your* camera."

"I'm with the band," Jacob said. "But if you like, I can pause filming while you wave your contract in the bride's face on her wedding day."

Jacob turned back to Elizabeth, but she'd gone.

* * *

Sweeping stone staircases led up and down. Jacob took the descending steps two at a time, landing in an empty marbled corridor, his shoes slapping against the stone as he flew past reading rooms, a closed gift shop, utility cupboards. He turned a corner to see a flash of green fabric disappear through a doorway at the far end of the hall.

Jacob called her name as he pushed open the door to a woman's bathroom.

"Sorry to disappoint, Jacob."

Henry Duval stood in the center of a white tiled bathroom, behind his sleek head an exit door with panels of crimson stained glass.

"Was it you sent me to Green Wood Cemetery?" Jacob said. "That man who died. He was on the list everyone keeps talking about. What the hell have you got my sister mixed up in, Henry?"

Backlit by the stained glass, the planes of Henry Duval's face might have been cut from blood-red marble. "It's not what you think," he sighed. "Believe me."

"I believe Elizabeth's in danger. I'm going to help her. Now get out of my way."

"The light in this building is amazing, don't you think?" Henry held out his hands, as if he could feel light trickling through them like sand. "We all just want to be in the light. That's why you're here, isn't it? You want to be back in your sister's light."

Jacob stepped forward. "You're not a tough guy, you're a lost rich kid. And this won't go the way you think it will."

Another sigh from Henry. "I expect it will go exactly the way I think it will. But by the time you make it outside she'll be gone."

CHAPTER

43

A LEX PAUSED IN the doorway to the master bedroom of the Johncocks' two-story Howard Beach home, wondering why she felt like a child. It was the bed, the sheets like icing on a square cake. Alex's mother—a ward nurse from a time when nursing was a paramilitary discipline—would have approved of the hospital corners.

Lights from an armada of TV trucks spattered the windows as Alex searched the front bedrooms. Janine Clara Johncock sat on a leather couch downstairs, being comforted—God help her—by a young male NYPD officer. She claimed to have slept alone from nine in the evening until just after midnight when she'd woken to find the police unit still outside, but her husband nowhere to be found. The occasional fractured wail floated up the stairs.

On her way down to the kitchen, Alex examined the photographs that lined the staircase: the Johncocks drinking cocktails by the ocean, his long face split in a toothy grin, the Johncocks huddled under an umbrella in a European city, Janine Johncock receiving some kind of award. No images of children. Dallas Johncock's technicolor imagination was not in evidence in the décor of his home, and if it hadn't been for one photograph depicting him bellowing into a microphone, this might be the house of two middle-ranked corporate strivers.

Alex found Coombs hunched over his laptop at a kitchen island, his bald skull glinting under a canopy of copper pans.

"No sign of a fight?" he said, his eyes never leaving his screen.

"No sign of anything." Alex looked down a beige hallway to a front door with frosted glass panels as a wail drifted through from the lounge. "Do we have the BOLOs out on the New Frontier founders and Jacob Felle?"

"Up and running, and we should have the phones locked in soon."

A familiar cloud appeared over Alex's horizon as another wail drifted through from the lounge. She tapped out two Excedrin from their bottle. "You buy the wife's Sleeping Beauty act, Pat?"

"Why not?"

Good question. Alex had always known when William wasn't in bed beside her, but was it fair to make the comparison? Shallow sleep was the only kind on offer when your firefighter partner was pulling nights. "I'll speak to her," she said as an unwelcome drumbeat started up behind her temples. "Anything unusual on his social?"

"Before the warning about the senator and the please-forgive-me video, his last upload was at six PM. Something about Chinese weather bombs." Coombs closed the laptop. "Here's a man who claimed President Obama funded a pedophile ring. Screaming chaos on his show, but here . . ." He pulled open a drawer in the kitchen island to reveal the most orderly cutlery tray Alex had ever seen.

"Chaos as a hobby?" she said.

"Or to put bread on the table. Who knows? His last video was pretty convincing."

"He was auditioning for his life. Security cameras?"

Coombs brightened. "The Johncocks have the perimeter of the property covered. At around eleven, you can just make out Johncock breaking *out* of his own house and climbing the fence at the end of the garden. We're checking neighbors to see if anyone saw him get into a vehicle, but this is a quiet part of the city—bedtime by nine thirty. Respectable enough for the mobster John Gotti. You know he lived three blocks east?"

Alex did. She also knew that a few years back, three white youths beat two young black men unconscious for the crime of walking through this neighborhood. Her guess was the perpetrators came from houses with hospital-corner beds and neat cutlery drawers.

"I'll rescue Janine Johncock from the sympathies of the NYPD," she said. "You check in with the team looking into Talon's voting system. Also, Senator Duval. I want to formally rule him out as being in any way connected to this case—one less wound for the media to rub salt into." Alex leaned both hands on the table and tried to roll the tension out of her shoulders. "What have we released to the vultures?"

"Ongoing investigation, the usual," Coombs said. "We got a thousand TV trucks outside. Fox and CNN are both going with copycat suicides."

"Isn't there more mileage in a serial killer?"

Coombs shrugged. "When Marilyn Monroe took the long walk, there were two hundred extra suicides that month. It's been a media fave ever since. When they've rinsed that angle, they'll switch to a gang of Ted Bundys on the loose. At that point, the fun really starts."

Alex closed her eyes, willing the Excedrin into her bloodstream.

* * *

Janine Johncock had nothing to say to Alex that she hadn't already told the NYPD. Did anyone hold a grudge against her husband? Only the whole of New York City, as evidenced by his appearance on that disgusting Ten Worst list. Janine Johncock stopped to dry her eyes, and Alex failed to see the tissue come down noticeably damp. Asked who she'd spoken to since she received the news, Janine Johncock said that her second call had been to her mother in Albany. Her first had been to her lawyer. According to Janine Johncock, Ricky Talon might as well have pulled the trigger and Janine would make him pay. Literally.

Twice during the interview, Coombs put his head around the door and asked for a minute. The second time Alex refused, he said, "No, Alex. I need you now."

Janine Johncock took out a makeup compact as TV truck lights hurled themselves against the curtains.

* * *

Alex stepped into the hallway to find Coombs with his laptop in the crook of his arm. "You're gonna want to buy me a beer," he said.

Before she could reply, the front door opened and a woman in a navy suit entered. Mid-thirties, pale cheeks under ice-blue eye shadow, a masculine jaw, and expensive-looking hair.

Alex flashed her ID. The woman responded with a business card.

"Laura Spelling. Attorney to Dallas and Janine Johncock. Is this a crime scene?"

Alex checked the woman's card, a legal firm with a pricey Madison Avenue address. "Not at this time," she said.

"Then I must ask you to leave." Spelling had a smile like a gamekeeper's trap. "I need to confer with my client."

"As do we. Her husband's just been"—Alex almost said murdered—"found."

"You've caused my client enough distress, don't you think?" A smile plucked at the corners of Spelling's mouth as she pulled an iPad from her handbag and showed Alex the Fox News website. Her manicured finger scrolled from Johncock's suicide note to his Oxford dress shoe with a sock sticking out. "You'll understand I need time with my client to formulate our submission to the Civilian Complaint Review Board."

* * *

Alex's anger carried her out onto the Johncocks' nail-scissor-neat back lawn, where she counted seven cameras poking over the six-foot wooden fence. Coombs trailed behind, still cradling his open laptop. She covered her mouth—those assholes used lipreaders. "Now Janine Johncock won't tell us shit in case it jeopardizes her comp payout. Murphy's going to dump a ton of wet cement on my head." She noticed the smirk on Coombs's face. "What are you so happy about?"

"You heard the saying that good news comes in threes?"

"Not to me it doesn't."

"First, Talon's list. You were right. Hacked with code we traced to a hack-for-hire outfit on the dark web. Relatively unsophisticated—as in, anyone could have used it."

"Can we see who made the purchase?"

"Negative. Crypto sale. But I have something you'll like more. We know Johncock had a meeting booked with Senator Charles

Patrick Duval—a fake meeting, according to the senator's office—but Senator Duval also has a son named Henry. And Henry Duval was a member of New Frontiers."

Alex raised her face to the sky and let the sun sink into her skin. "At last. Someone from New Frontiers we can put in the frame."

"It gets better. We're not only talking Henry Duval." Coombs showed her an image on his phone—a close-up of a residential street. "This is CCTV a block from Green Wood Cemetery. Looks like he was watching us clear up his mess. We can do better than a BOLO, here, Alex. We can go public with this one."

The camera captured the wing of an NYPD patrol car, part of the cordon across the cemetery entrance. On the other side of the street, a young man in a baseball cap leaned out from the shadow of a building. The cap covered the eyes, but it was clearly Jacob Felle.

CHAPTER

44

Jacob pushed through the library doors into blinding sun. If Elizabeth had hailed a cab, he was done, but hailing a cab isn't a quick endeavor on a busy New York Saturday. Pedestrians swarmed at Jacob as he ran to the mouth of the Fifth Avenue subway station on 42nd Street. Already, the fingers on his right hand had stiffened from where he'd driven his fist into the gym-hard wall of Henry's stomach.

The station served one subway line, Manhattan to Queens. The entrance to the eastbound line was closer, and Jacob fumbled his bank card against the reader. The first thing he saw when he reached the busy platform was Elizabeth on the opposite side.

"Wait," he called across. A few people turned their heads.

Elizabeth waved a hand for him to move to the end of the platform. She raised her phone to her ear. Jacob fumbled his own SIM card from the ticket pocket in his jeans. The moment he turned his phone on, it rang.

"What's wrong with you?" Elizabeth said into his ear.

Jacob stepped to the lip of the platform so that the other passengers couldn't overhear. Across the tracks, Elizabeth did the same.

"You're in danger," he said. "I can help."

"You don't know what you're talking about," she said.

"What's whore salad? What's sour lime?"

Elizabeth's face darkened. "Where did you hear that?"

"I filmed Claude at New Frontiers without him knowing."

She glared at him across the tracks as the train hum became a rumble and then a roar.

"Elizabeth, Claude said it wasn't safe for you. What did he mean? Why did I end up at Green Wood Cemetery watching an ambulance cart out Dallas Johncock?"

She turned toward the oncoming train. "You know what's going on. You're just too blind to see it. I can look after myself, Jacob. So do us all a favor and go home."

The steel punch of the train obliterated Jacob's view. He sprinted up the steps, across the bridge, down the other side and along the platform, frantically scanning the windows for his sister until the last carriage had disappeared into the dark.

* * *

The public yoga session behind the library had finished, and a crew in yellow tees busily erected a film screen for an outdoor show. Jacob flexed the fingers on his right hand. The knuckle joints hurt like someone had driven nails into them—he must have hit Henry's ribs.

The service door at the back of the library opened, and one of the wedding musicians emerged, resting against the wall with the sun on his face as he lit a joint.

Jacob approached him. "I need to grab my stuff."

The musician squinted up at him. "Your guy beat you to it by about two minutes."

"My guy?"

"About so high, hair to here. Looked familiar but I couldn't place him. Said you guys had double booked and he gave us a tickle as a sorry." The bass player tapped the side of his nose. "I'd appreciate a hookup. I get 80 percent baby formula from *my* guy."

Jacob ran to the sidewalk in time to see a Mercedes G-Class gun into life and push out into the traffic. Jacob caught a glimpse of a pointed chin and wiry hair behind the wheel. Roland van Buren, with Floyd in the passenger seat beside him. The last thing Jacob saw before the jeep disappeared into the heat haze was a shock of Chloe Zhang's pink hair.

His phone buzzed in his pocket.

"Floyd, where have you been? Why did you take my camera?"

"What's a whore salad?" Floyd sounded high as a Himalayan eagle.

"Tell your mate van Buren to turn his car around and bring me my camera."

"Was Elizabeth at the wedding? Did you see her?"

"It's Henry Duval, isn't it? Henry's got my sister mixed up in something terrible—it's Henry she's afraid of. If that preppy bastard hurts her, I'll turn him inside out."

"You shouldn't be worrying about Henry." Floyd sounded suddenly closer, as if he'd pressed his mouth into the phone. "You should be worrying about Leonard Harris."

"Leonard *who*? Leonard the old guy in the photo at New Frontiers?

A car horn blared behind Jacob's ear—he'd stepped out into the road without thinking and had to jump back onto the sidewalk.

"You can't save your sister if she doesn't want to be saved, Jacob."

"I can try."

"Then be careful. Being famous is a bitch."

"I'm not famous, Floyd. And neither are you, anymore."

"You think? Check out CNN. Safe travels, brother-in-law. You won't hear from me for a while."

"Floyd—"

But Floyd had killed the call.

Jacob opened the browser on his phone and navigated to CNN, where the sight of his own face squeezed the air from his lungs. The first image was his passport photo, followed by a publicity shot from his documentary *Hit Like a Girl*, and finally a CCTV image of him from the night before, opposite Green Wood Cemetery.

"Wanted in Relation to the Death of Dallas Johncock."

Standing on the sidewalk with his face open for all to see, Jacob felt suddenly naked. He dropped to tie a shoelace that didn't need tying as he wrestled to still his racing brain.

A suspect in a murder.

His face on every phone in every pocket in a city of nine million souls.

His breathing came hard and fast.
Relax. Think.
You're no good to her and you're no good to yourself if you don't stay calm.

Jacob turned off the phone and removed the SIM.

He checked his wallet—thirty bucks—then crossed the street to an ATM and withdrew his daily limit of five hundred dollars. He'd had an idea. His first film job—many years back—had been a documentary about the drug trade. A London cop had explained that the smart drug couriers used bicycles, and the really smart ones dressed as joggers. Your average cop sees a middle-class-type jogger, white earbuds in, pounding the streets with not a care in the world . . . If he could manage it without being arrested, Jacob would find a cheap sports shop with a dozy shop assistant who wouldn't look up from their phone. There, he'd buy running shoes, tee and shorts, a running backpack, and a colorful peaked running cap. Everything he needed to hide in plain sight.

Then what?

"You should be worrying about Leonard Harris," Floyd had said.

Elizabeth at Montauk Yacht Club: "I can tell you from personal experience that a life you love can end at any time." Jacob had assumed she was talking about their father. Maybe she'd been talking about Leonard.

Maybe, somehow, Leonard could lead Jacob to his sister.

CHAPTER

45

"THEY WERE *WHERE*?" Murphy stood over Alex's desk, hissing in a failed whisper that guaranteed the attention of every agent in earshot.

"The New York Public Library. Shaw, Duval, and the Felles have kept their phones off since we started tracking, but both Elizabeth and Jacob Felle's phones lit up on 42nd Street—we think they were on the subway line. We ran the facial rec software on a two-mile radius and it picked up Jacob Felle at the wedding, along with Elizabeth Felle and Henry Duval."

"Fifty thousand pairs of eyes on the BOLO and no one sees our suspects?"

"It was a society wedding at the New York Public Library. Not exactly swarming with cops brandishing copies of the FBI's Ten Most Wanted."

"You realize how this makes us look?"

Men had no issue running into burning buildings, Alex noted. But they could be terrible cowards when it came to the prospect of losing face.

Sorry, William, but it's true.

"We need to focus on Jacob Felle and Henry Duval," she said. "Felle wasn't here for Benedetti or Dixon, but we have him at the Johncock murder scene—he's involved, one way or another. Henry

Duval is an ex-member of New Frontiers—the Leonard Harris connection—and we know Dallas Johncock thought he was going to meet Henry's father the night he died. Working assumption is that Henry Duval is calling the shots—he's the one with the resources and he was here for the first two murders. Jacob Felle is playing some kind of supporting role."

Murphy shook his head. Alex knew he was weighing the political implications of making a senator's son the subject of a murder enquiry.

"I know it's ugly, but it is what it is." She pointed to her computer monitor. "Meet Henry Duval, the wealthiest barista in New York. Inherited a fortune before he was eighteen years old and chooses to work in a coffeeshop in Fort Greene, Brooklyn. Duval bankrolled a few expeditions when he was at New Frontiers—never participated as far as we're aware. Classic rich-boy behavior—buying his way in to the club, rather than doing the work."

Murphy came around the desk to see the side-by-side images on the screen. Father and son were both almost comically handsome. A Republican firebrand from old plantation money, Senator Charles Duval had carried the burden of his looks throughout a long political career. William—a nice-enough-looking man, bless him—always said that beauty raised hackles on other women, while men dismissed good looks in other men as a sign of weakness. *Trust your wife with the movie star*, William used to say, *but don't leave her with the funny-looking poet*.

"Well?" Murphy said.

"Well what?"

"I just asked you a question. You said Henry Duval inherited his fortune, but Senator Duval's still alive, isn't he?"

"Correct." *No more drifting, Alex.* "Duval Senior gave Henry his full inheritance on his seventeenth birthday, on the understanding that there would be no further contact."

"What did young Henry do to deserve that?"

"No one's quite sure. The super rich keep these things behind closed doors. We know Henry Duval had trouble at his single-sex boarding school—something about experimenting with other boys— and he had an accident when he was young, lost the pinkie finger on his left hand. Again, unclear exactly what happened, and getting the Senator's office to answer a straight question is like trying to pick a lock with a herring."

"So Senator Duval cuts contact with Henry," Murphy said. "And revenge on Daddy is to work in a coffeeshop. How does all this fit our case?"

Alex had known this was coming. "The pieces don't fit yet. Maybe they won't until we have both the Felles, Floyd Shaw, and Henry Duval in custody. Since the wedding, they've all turned off their phones, but Jacob Felle's phone records show him calling his sister multiple times over the last few days and her not picking up. Sometimes minutes apart. He did the same with Floyd Shaw. Felle's been trying to get hold of his sister and brother-in-law and they've been avoiding him."

"So?"

"Maybe they're not the cohesive unit we've been imagining. The fact that they've turned off their phones suggests they're all involved, but are they all in it together?"

"Let's hope they attend another public wedding at a landmark New York building so we can take them and find out." No humor in Murphy's tone as he selected a pencil from the jar on Alex's desk and rolled it along the desktop under his fingers.

"I was thinking we go public with Duval too."

Murphy rolled the pencil off the desk and glared at it lying there on the floor. His way of saying *no chance*.

"Then what do you suggest?"

"I suggest you find your suspects and bring them in." Murphy turned away, so she didn't see his face when he said, "You sure you're up to this, Alex?"

For once, Alex Bedford wasn't certain of the answer.

CHAPTER

46

They weren't called internet cafés anymore. From behind a pair of oversized running sunglasses, the peak of his new cap pulled low, Jacob paid ten dollars cash for an hour in the Rockstar E-sports Lounge on 49th Avenue in Queens. He was shown to a terminal at the back of a long basement room, his guide enthusing about Rockstar's 144 Hz monitors and something called Roccat peripherals. Jacob didn't tell her he just needed Google.

He sent a list of LinkNYC free phone and Wi-Fi stations to the printer at the front desk, then, unable to help himself, he googled his own name.

British Fugitive Wanted in Connection with Ten Worst Deaths.

His face next to an image of Tyrell Dixon's body being loaded onto an ambulance. His face side-by-side with Dallas Johncock bellowing into a microphone.

He clicked on what looked like a video link and realized he was watching a clip from *Talon Tonight*. A minor movie star he recognized leaned forward in her chair to tell Ricky Talon, "I don't want to talk about my new movie, I wanna talk about Jacob Felle."

Talon squirming in his chair. "No can do, Angela. Even for a friend of the show like you."

The woman refusing to let go. "We had the Ten Worst Terminator, now we got the London Liquidator, and I'll tell you, Ricky, I'm rooting for Jacob Felle. I'm not alone, right, ladies? He's cute and he takes out the trash without being asked—that makes him husband material. And here's a question I have to ask as a good feminist. Why is it only the men on your list getting the axe? When's it ladies night?"

Enough.

Jacob googled *Leonard Harris.*

Barely a page of entries, but a name in the header of the third link caught his eye: Dallas Johncock. Jacob opened an article from the *Bronx Gazette.* "Funeral of Fire Victim Disrupted by Radio Jock Audience on Rampage."

Ten minutes and several linked articles later, Jacob knew that a fire in a nursing home had taken the lives of three elderly residents—the CEO of the home called it a freak accident—and Leonard Harris was one of the victims. Dallas Johncock had incited his listeners to break up Leonard's funeral, and, many years later, Johncock had suddenly appeared on Ricky Talon's list of the Ten Worst People in New York.

Also on Talon's list: Luca Benedetti and Tyrell Dixon.

Three men dead, and Jacob in the frame.

Jacob had to move. He found the restrooms, locked a cubicle door and sat clutching his head for what seemed like an age but was probably no more than five minutes. The nursing home fire that killed Leonard was four years ago—the same time Floyd and Elizabeth stopped taking Jacob's calls.

Back at his terminal, he navigated back to the article with a quote from the CEO of the nursing home. Her name was Kelly-Anne Pinstock, and moments later Jacob was scrolling her Facebook feed: images of a family gathering, a pink rose bed, Pinstock receiving a pair of garden shears with a pink bow around the blades, two pug dogs, more garden, some kind of reunion, more dogs. He googled *US version of Directory Enquiries* and found a link to a site called Whitepages.

Two minutes later, he was jogging in his new running gear toward the nearest Link machine to make a call. Then he was in a yellow cab heading toward Hunts Point in the Bronx, changing awkwardly into a cheap pair of jeans and a new tee, and trying to figure out what he was going to say to Kelly-Anne Pinstock.

* * *

Pinstock was waiting for him on the porch of her boxy wooden colonial. She'd dressed for his arrival in a pristine gardening apron with an embroidered sunflower. Her welcome smile faded when Jacob emerged from the cab alone and without a camera in his hand.

"Mr. Robinson?"

Had she seen his face on the news yet? Jacob searched her eyes for recognition and, seeing none, let himself in through a white gate. Pink roses flanked the gravel path to the porch.

"Mrs. Pinstock, I'm not here to photograph your garden, though it does look lovely. I told you I was from the *New York Times* because I needed to speak with you and I didn't want you slamming down the phone before you gave me your address."

Pinstock came to the edge of the porch and removed a white straw hat, leaving a hat-shaped imprint on the crown of her hair. Jacob was glad she wasn't carrying her prize shears.

"I have life insurance and I'm not interested in any crypto bullshit," she said. "You have ten seconds to leave my property or I set my dogs on you."

"I'm here about the fire at Clearwater Community Nursing Home."

As if responding to a bell, Pinstock turned and marched toward her door.

"Seen the news?" Jacob said. "Ricky Talon's list. People are dying."

Pinstock turned back with hooded eyes in a face like a fallen cake. "What's that got to do with me? Who are you? If you were law enforcement, I'd have seen a badge."

"I'm looking for my sister. She's in trouble. She needs my help."

"What's that got to do with *me*?"

"Leonard Harris was one of the victims of the fire."

Her face iced over. "I know the victims' *names*, thank you very much."

A scrabbling at the window made them both turn. Two tiny pugs pawed at the glass.

Jacob said, "I need to know everything you can tell me about Leonard Harris."

"And if I don't want to talk to you?"

"Then I come back tomorrow, and the next day, and the next, until you do."

Could she see he was bluffing? She'd only have to dial 911 and an army of cops would descend in seconds.

Pinstock glared at Jacob as if he was a blight on her roses. Then she jammed the straw hat back on and thumped back into the house. The two pugs scrabble-skated their way out onto the porch and banged their fat bodies against Jacob's ankles. A minute later, Pinstock was back.

"A private investigator looked into the fire." Pinstock handed Jacob a scuffed business card. "I don't know who she was working for, before you ask."

The card said, *Hannah Perlman, Private Investigator.*

"She promised I'd be okay if I helped her," Pinstock said. "But here we are four years later and I have people on my porch scaring my dogs."

Jacob was at the gate when she called after him.

"I've done nothing wrong, and I'm *retired*."

* * *

A block from Kelly-Anne Pinstock's house, Jacob slammed into a wall of fatigue. Forty-eight hours since he slept. At a bodega across the street, he bought an energy shot, two chocolate bars, a copy of the day's *Enquirer* and a ballpoint pen, then found a tree in a nearby dog park that he could change behind. Back in his running gear, his other clothes stuffed into the backpack, he shook out his legs and set off running south.

* * *

Back in the Upper East Side of Manhattan—a safe distance from Kelly-Anne Pinstock's house—Jacob found a quiet alleyway between two apartment blocks, fed his SIM into his phone and waited for signal.

Missed call from Floyd. A voicemail, but when Jacob checked, no voice message, and when he called back, no answer.

Nothing from Elizabeth.

He wrote their numbers on a piece of paper torn from the *Enquirer*, and he was about to eject the SIM card when he remembered another number.

* * *

Ralph Jotta picked up on the fifth ring. "Jacob fucking Felle. Haven't seen you since editing class, back when you could buy a coffee in Hackney without taking out a mortgage."

"Good times, Ralph." Jacob kept the Link machine between him and the prowling traffic on Westchester Avenue. "I'm doing a little location scouting, and I thought of you. Remember that summer you spent shooting commercials in Manhattan?"

"It was the best of times, it was the worst . . . no, just the best of times."

"Hence the call. What was that skeezy motel you took the crew girls to?"

"Are you being a bad boy?"

"I remember it took cash and rented rooms by the hour."

"Man, you're talking about the Four Jacks Inn at Flushing Meadows Park. That place was savage. Sticky carpets, wipe-down walls."

"Did you need to show ID?"

"Why, did you lose your wallet?"

Shit, why hadn't he said that in the first place?

"Yeah, left it in a bar. I need a place to hang while I work it out."

"Jacob," Ralph said, "if it's the Four Jacks Inn I remember, you could flash a Pokémon card and they'd let you in."

Two blocks up the street, a police car nosed onto Westchester. Jacob hung up and broke into a light jog, forcing himself not to look at the blue and white as it cruised by. He made it around the block without meeting the patrol car again, flagged a passing cab, and slid into the back seat. As the taxi pulled away he turned his face from the window and, for the first time in two moon cycles, allowed his eyes to close.

CHAPTER 47

ALEX LEANED BACK on the diner banquette to allow the server to pour her second coffee and Pat Coombs's third. She'd swallowed a double dose of Excedrin, but it had barely touched the migraine that threatened to separate the two halves of her skull.

"Pat, if we don't make a breakthrough soon, we'll *both* be counting FBI paper clips. What haven't we thought of?"

"Maybe we're too focused on the perps." Coombs swirled cream into his coffee. "The sequence of murders doesn't match the list placings, which is interesting. Benedetti was first to die and number five on the list. Dixon was the second murder and ninth place. Johncock was third and seven."

"You mean why aren't they working down from the top?"

"Or up from the bottom. Put another way, if Henry Duval has control of the list, why not put Benedetti at the top and Dixon second, etcetera? Of course, we're not dealing with a normal mind. If our guy receives instructions from alien overlords via a tinfoil hat, the numbers may mean something we're missing."

"We can ask Behavioral Analysis to look into the numerology," Alex said. "And our seven remaining names on the list? Where are they right now?"

"You'd think they'd be barricaded in their panic rooms," Coombs said. "But apparently, it takes more than being targeted by a serial killer to put a dent in a celebrity's schedule. Bekah Baxter is in Europe doing the far-right TV station circuit. Clara Walter is still carrying out her PureLife Pharma engagements. Delase Carter has some concerts coming up next month that he refuses to cancel."

"Any of them seeing sense?"

"After her brush with death, Professor Laurie Cullen canceled speaker slots in Texas and Kentucky, and Cardinal Joseph Clement hasn't been seen since his plaza appearance—he's under investigation for the Saint Sebastian abuse ring, so next time we see him he'll likely be in cuffs." Coombs raised a hand for more coffee. "Carl Bigney has a history of airing racist views in public, which means he's used to death threats and knows how to keep a low profile."

"Johncock, Benedetti, and Dixon are dead," Alex said. "Which leaves Emil Hertzberg."

"Hertzberg divides his time between his Manhattan town house and his mega-yacht, the *Bella Figura*. Both are protected around the clock by ex-special forces bodyguards. He holds this big celebrity yacht party each year around this time—Farewell to Summer, he calls it—where the rich and powerful indulge in a little mutual back-scratching. The media covers it like a Mafia funeral."

"Surely he won't go ahead this year."

"We asked the question," Coombs said. "No response. Farewell to Summer is scheduled to happen five days from now. My guess is he'll cancel—why take the risk?"

Alex looked out the window onto the street where a disheveled woman with hedgerow hair tried to push a shopping cart filled with cans along the sidewalk. "The analysts found no further connections between the names on the list and Leonard Harris, right?"

"Not a damn thing."

"So, in theory it could be over." Alex watched the woman on the sidewalk shake her cart so hard the cans rattled.

"Feel that way to you, Alex?"

* * *

Alex paused at the top of the subway steps and flexed her knee until the joint ceased to click. The ocean spray in the air suited the music in her earbuds as she turned onto 42nd Street, her feet picking up the polished steel of a disused streetcar rail, her thoughts propelled by the rhythm of Jacqueline du Pré's cello.

Henry Duval and Jacob Felle were in this for sure.

Floyd Shaw and Elizabeth Felle? If they weren't involved, then why had they dropped off the map? Unless Duval had *dropped* them off the map against their will.

A sobering thought: the body count could be higher than they knew.

Another unanswered question: where was this violence coming from?

Maybe Henry Duval and Leonard Harris had some kind of special relationship. Father-son vibe? Lovers? Partners in crime?

Henry Duval, the Felle siblings, and Floyd Shaw had something in common. They'd all—in different ways—lost a parent before they were out of their teens. Was that significant?

It meant they knew loss. It meant they knew blind, unquenchable rage.

Alex found herself staring up at the sun-bleached brick fortress of the Jumping Jack Power Plant. Beltway traffic grumbled in the distance, and the New Frontiers building appeared as she'd expected: the door boarded over with three-inch ply, the parking lot empty.

She'd come here to pick up the scent again, but all she smelled was shipping diesel and garbage.

Her phone buzzed. Her boss, Murphy.

"Sighting of Jacob Felle at a motel in Queens."

"How recent?"

"Sixty minutes ago."

"It took them an hour to call it in?"

"It's not the kind of motel you want to admit staying at. A local unit's watching the entrance until we can get a SWAT team on site. Coombs is on his way. I'll text the address. We'll meet you there."

Alex was already halfway to her car.

CHAPTER

48

Jacob woke to see his own naked body falling face-first out of the sky. He rolled to avoid being crushed and the plummeting Jacob rolled with him. Sprawled on carpet, tangled in silk, the falling Jacob was just the mirror over the bed, the room lined with mirrors, a plastic blind over the window, a wall sign offering four pornographic channels and complementary condoms in the bedside drawer.

Five in the afternoon, he'd been asleep at the Four Jacks Inn for less than an hour.

He splashed water on his face and pulled on his running gear, ignoring the sour hum from the fabric. When he raised the window blind, two cop cars blocked the traffic a hundred yards or so up the street, facing different directions so the drivers could talk. Moments later, an ambulance and a black vehicle that appeared to have a lot in common with a tank pulled onto the curb.

Jacob hit the stairs. In the lobby, he asked the stoned desk attendant if they had a back way out.

"We got better than that," the attendant said with a sleepy smile.

* * *

The corridor took Jacob to a door and then another corridor. Pipework snaked along the ceiling, leading to a second door with a horizontal push bar, and suddenly he was blinking in the jangling light and noise of a teeming shopping mall. Thirty seconds later, he was out of the mall and jogging south toward Brooklyn.

* * *

At a Link machine on Queens Boulevard he tried Elizabeth, then Floyd. He knew their voicemail greetings by heart. He'd stopped leaving messages.

The business card Kelly-Anne Pinstock gave him had a name—Hannah Perlman, Licensed Private Investigator—an email address and two phone numbers, landline and cell. Jacob tried the cell and a robot voice told him the service had been discontinued. The landline rang for sixty seconds before a young female voice answered with a tetchy "Naomi Perlman, who's this?"

"Is it possible to speak with Hannah Perlman, Private Investigator?"

"You want my mom? Sure," the young woman said. "Oh wait, shit, no, sorry. My mom fell in front of a subway train three years ago."

Thoughts hurtled at Jacob out of the dark. "I'm so sorry, I didn't know."

"Obviously."

"I was . . . I need to find one of your mother's old case reports. It's important."

"Not to me. And not to her, right?"

Jacob said, "It could be, in a way. It could save a life. Lives."

"Ha! Bullshit, you're looking for dirt to sue some poor schmuck."

"I promise I'm serious. This could be her legacy. Wouldn't you want that?"

"My mom's legacy is two messed-up kids saddled with a mortgage they can't pay. But you really want to know how to get a hold of her old files?"

"Yes. Please."

"Invent a time machine and go back to before the fire in our garage."

Jacob's stomach dropped.

"Two months after the big splat," the young woman said. "Yeah, the good times just kept a-coming. Lost all her shit, plus all my and my brother's shit, plus half the kitchen. I'm not a superstitious gal, but three years later it still feels like the house stinks of burnt toast."

* * *

Under silver fountain spray, coins of different currencies gleamed, spent wishes from around the world. The odor of horse shit and freshly baked pretzels wafted from the entrance to Central Park as Jacob splashed water on his face and removed his shoes, swinging his legs over the concrete lip of the fountain to lower his throbbing feet into the water. Cool fingers closed around his ankles.

Now what?

The private investigator was dead, her papers burned to dust, and Jacob had no way to reach Elizabeth or Floyd. The smart move, the only move, was to walk into the nearest police station and tell them that Elizabeth was in danger.

And if they don't believe you?

Jacob in jail would be no help to Elizabeth.

"You can't put your feet in there."

He turned to face a woman in her seventies with two small dogs on a leash.

"The birds drink from this fountain," she said. "Think of the birds."

Jacob shook his feet dry and forced his toes back into his shoes. If he could only talk to his sister. Just for a moment. Tell her that whatever she'd gotten herself mixed up in, whoever had scared her into hiding, that it was safe to come out. That somehow—for the first time in their lives—he would protect her, and not the other way around.

He turned on his phone and inserted the SIM. The phone pinged with a message. A four-word text from an unknown number: *The girl rushes inside.*

For a moment, it meant nothing, until Jacob's brain lunged back into the past and came back clutching an answer.

SIM out, phone off, back to pounding the sidewalk.

* * *

The e-sports café on Queens Boulevard took Jacob's last twenty-dollar bill.

The girl rushes inside.

Rushes wasn't a verb, it was a noun meaning raw film footage.

Jacob opened a new browser and typed in the URL from memory, holding his breath until the page loaded. He'd created the site four years ago to store footage for *Hit Like a Girl*, then—after Elizabeth cut contact, but before Jacob had given up trying to reach her—he'd sent Floyd and Elizabeth links to view the unedited interviews. No response at the time, but . . . *there*, above the old WMV files, a new clip, uploaded three hours ago.

Jacob clicked the file. Floyd's face filled the screen.

"Jacob, I found her. Or rather, she called me." Floyd's eyes were maroon at the edges. Behind the lank hair and chin dotted with stubble, a red sheet hung over a window, bathing the room in crimson light. "She promised to meet me in Red Hook—there's a patch of wasteland behind Walcott Street. You can't miss it." His head jerked to the side and mouthed at someone off screen, then he turned back to the lens. "It's bad, Jacob. If you get this message in time, maybe you can help her after all."

The clip ended.

Jacob checked every page on the site twice to be certain there was nothing more.

CHAPTER

49

ALEX—LATE, SWEATY, AND furious from battling Manhattan traffic—had to pull up on the street outside the parking lot of the Four Jacks Inn. The lot itself was crammed with law enforcement vehicles and officers, a sea of blue lights and armored plate. And there was Pat Coombs, walking toward her, the slump in his shoulders saying that they'd missed Jacob Felle.

Alex killed the engine and lowered the window. "No?"

"He slipped out the back," Coombs said.

Alex hit the steering wheel with both hands. She pictured the Jacob Felle she'd met at New Frontiers—quiet, watchful eyes and a stillness that should have told her he'd be hard to find and harder to catch. "Felle's either very lucky or very good—better than he should be with no training."

Coombs leaned against the window frame. "We assume he's untrained. Maybe he spent the last year shooting up the woods at some Waco-style militia camp. Anyway, he's on his toes again—we have a sighting in Central Park from twenty minutes back. Felle cooling his feet in a water fountain. A dog walker called it in when she saw his face on TV, and we confirmed it when his phone lit up. Before you ask, we missed him there too."

"Felle's using his phone again?"

"For a minute at a time, max. But he received a text message from what looks like a burner phone. *The girl rushes inside.*"

"Inside where?"

"Your guess is as good as mine—analysts are on it. By the way, you should know. We had another leak."

He showed her his phone, on the screen a *National Enquirer* news feed with a side-by-side of Henry Duval and his father. "Senator's Black Sheep Son Subject of a Murder Hunt."

"*Shit.* Where are they getting this from?"

"I don't know, but they have our husband-and-wife duo too." Coombs scrolled down to a professional headshot of Floyd Shaw, followed by a close-up from one of his TV shows—they'd found an image of him wielding a machete. After Floyd came Elizabeth Felle, a shot taken at the wheel of a boat, Elizabeth staring at the camera as if she'd caught it sniffing her underwear.

Alex rested her head against the wheel. "Murphy's going to implode."

"Uh, yeah. He already did, but he's gearing up for another blast. CNN was on to him, wanting to know why Henry Duval isn't on our Ten Most Wanted list."

"Duval's their poster boy?"

"All-American son of a senator? Of course he is. Shaw comes second. The Felles are both relatively unknown—at least, they were. Since we went public with their names we've had Floyd Shaw in fifty Manhattan locations at once, Elizabeth Felle sailing past every marina. Henry Duval's face spotted in the moon."

"Where the hell are they?" Alex said. "You think they left the city?"

"With Duval's resources they wouldn't have to. And this isn't impulse killing. A cupboard full of tinned food, a few chest freezers, and they could stay off the street for a year. But that assumes they're all together, or that we've even got the right crowd. Just because they've disappeared doesn't mean they're our guys. New Frontiers had over a hundred members. What have we got on our suspects, Alex, really, aside from a load of circumstantial fluff, the fact that we can't find them, and one grainy photo of Jacob Felle near the Johncock crime scene?"

Over Coombs's shoulder, Alex saw her boss, Murphy, talking to a uniform. He sent the uniform away with a flick of his hand and started walking toward her.

Alex said, "Okay, Pat. Arrange another media briefing. Manhunt underway, task force formed, reward program in place, request for public cooperation, please do not approach."

Murphy stopped three feet from the car. He looked like he was chewing glass. "The papers are calling them the Middle-Class Mansons, Alex."

"Of course they are."

"You're the lead investigator. What are you going to do about it?"

Before Alex could answer, Murphy's phone pinged and he raised it to his ear, wincing as the call connected, then glaring at Alex as he walked away, as if the abuse he was getting was her fault.

She started the engine.

"I'm heading back to the office," she said. "The numerology report came back from Quantico. Summary says there are no discernable patterns in the victims' death sequence, but I want to give it a thorough read."

"No, you don't," Coombs said. "You want to go back to your apartment and get two hours sleep. When you wake up, I'll give you the lowdown on the report."

"You said yourself we've got nothing. You heard Murphy. I've been lead on this case since Tyrell Dixon hit the Hudson and we've got a big fat zero."

"Alex, I can hold the fort. You've been doing the work of two people for the last fortnight. If you don't think I'm right, take a look in the mirror."

She did. William wouldn't have recognized the face staring back at her.

"Two hours, Pat."

* * *

The call woke Alex from a dream of orcas bumping noses in a black ocean. Sunlight burned into one eye, her cheek pressed out of shape against the corduroy cushion of her couch.

"Alex, you awake?"

"Pat, hey. What do you need me to fuck up, now?"

"Quit the pity party." Coombs's tone sliced though her brain fog. "Our hipster racist just dropped off the map."

"Huh?"

"Carl Bigney. Four on Talon's list and no one's heard from him in twelve hours."

CHAPTER

50

HERE YOU GO, Carl Bigney on a secret mission, operation bury your brother, poor ol' Marcus, and fucked if you'll let those freaks dictate how you roll.

"Nut jobs don't write my schedule," you said, when your new PA-cum-girlfriend, the totally-too-young-for-you Jasmine, waved that bullshit Ten Worst list in your face. Besides, no one knows you're in White Plains for your brother's funeral. And here's you showing you're not scared by walking three miles from the cemetery back to the railway station. Yes, in this black woolen suit in this crazy heat. You stop outside a church to light a smoke. Yes, you still smoke, and no, you don't want a conversation about it.

"You took the wrong brother," you tell a life-size plastic Jesus guarding the church. You remember holding Mom's hand as the casket went in. It was your job to stop her jumping down after it.

Up ahead, a faded blue Dodge Ram noses onto the main street and rests for a beat. For a moment it feels like the truck watches you, then it eases onto the south lane and disappears into the heat haze. Okay, you admit it, these freaks have you jumpy. You didn't recognize three of the pasty faces in the paper, but the fourth was Floyd Shaw and you've run into him before. If the other three are like Shaw, you could take them all at once—you just need to stay sharp.

Man, you're forty-eight years old and still beating up guys in your head. Lame.

You really need a beer.

*　*　*

The barman's a black dude and not small. Could be a problem if he recognizes you. Carl Bigney, the most racist man in America, if you believe the moron mainstream media.

The easy way he slides over your Blue Moon then goes back to his newspaper suggests he doesn't know you from Adam. Could be your new Jasmine-inspired look: the beard traded for a Doc Holliday mustache, your beloved three-inch quiff clipped to the skull.

You take a seat at the end of the bar, the door in view. Watching for the Ten Worst freaks, or are you half expecting Marcus to walk in with that nervous smile, always entering a room like he'd come to apologize? You were the cool sibling, no doubt. You were the one who had the girls adjusting their hair when you walked into a room, who forced the teachers to hide a smile when they disciplined you for your endless bullshit. You'll catch up to Marcus in age now and that feels wrong.

You wave for another beer, and it slides into view, glistening in the dusty light.

"Funeral?" The barman's eyes clock the black suit.

"My brother," you say, surprised to hear yourself tell the truth.

"Condolences." The barman leans on the bar. His elbows are white at the tips, like the black rubbed off. "Laid my own father down a year ago."

"Sad to hear that."

"He was ready. Sorry, none of my business, I just saw the threads."

"You're good," you say, and you mean it. This barman exudes a quiet charisma. Not like you, crashing through life like it's a knife fight in a plummeting elevator.

"See this shit?" The barman spins his newspaper for you to read. "Henry Duval. Philipps Academy, Princeton with a year in Oxford, more money than God, and he thinks the best way he can serve the world is to take a few shitheads off the street. Imagine if he and his crazy buddies put their resources into something that mattered."

"The Four Whitest People in New York," you say, and earn a smile from the barman.

How dumb people are, saying you hate black people. What you hate is *white* people's reaction to anything you say that might be semi-fucking-adjacent to racist. Take this barman: nice guy in his Levi's tee, probably grew up eating the same breakfast cereal you did, watching the same dumb cartoons. You'd stand shoulder to shoulder if the slants invaded tomorrow. You're about America, man. You divide by culture not color, but people don't want to hear that. It makes you harder to hate.

"I need to bleed the radiator," you say, pushing up off your stool.

"Outside, hang a left, follow it round the back."

"Set me up while I'm gone."

"Sure thing. This one's on me."

"Appreciate it, man."

The sunlight burns like acid in your eyes as you stumble round the side of the building. The faded blue Dodge Ram waits in the parking lot. No surprise. Where else would you go on a day this hot in a town this shit? The bathroom stinks of cleaning fluid. The urinal has one of those little bee stickers to aim at. You drown the bee in piss, then deliberately turn your hip so the stream splashes the floor. What are you, ten years old? Your piss, you notice, runs dark brown. It's not the booze—you've eased up lately, after a few embarrassing misfires with the lovely Jasmine. Kidney trouble? Liver failure? Maybe you'll be snuggling down with Marcus before too long.

A toilet cistern flushes. A door latch clicks.

"Mind the piss, buddy," you say. "I took my eye off the little bee."

"No problem," says a voice behind you. "I'll be burning these boots, anyway."

CHAPTER

51

Jacob sat for a moment with his back to a hot brick wall, examining a fresh graze on his knee after a stumble had sent him sprawling on the sidewalk. Every muscle in his legs pulsed with pain, his joints scraped like they were bone on bone, and his insides had been scooped out with a spoon.

He was only halfway to Red Hook where Elizabeth had offered to meet Floyd—if Floyd could be believed—and he couldn't go on much longer without water and something in his stomach. Across the street, a bodega offered to restore his blood sugar. A risk he had to take.

He was almost at the door when he noticed the stack of *Enquirers*. Alongside Elizabeth, Floyd, and Henry Duval on the front page, Jacob's own face stared out at him.

"Reward One Hundred Thousand Dollars."

"Clueless FBI Baffled as Middle-Class Mansons Elude Statewide Dragnet."

Jacob turned away from the bodega and pulled the peak of his cap down another inch. The stench of stale sweat stung his eyes as he stumbled down the curb and forced his aching legs back into action.

* * *

Red Hook brought the smell of ocean. Spears of sunlight penetrated the gaps between buildings, and the city seemed to lose its grip on the landscape as he turned off Ferris and into the dead zone of Wolcott Street. The tarmac under his throbbing feet needed resurfacing and green wooden construction boards lined both sides of the street. No cars, no pedestrians, and at nine thirty in the muggy overcast evening, no workmen. Behind the boards, great mountains of sand stretched across an industrial wasteland, a hidden Egypt in a forgotten corner of Brooklyn.

It's bad, Jacob.

What was he walking into? Henry Duval he could handle. Or could he? This wasn't England. What if Henry had a gun? What if it wasn't Henry threatening his sister, but someone far worse?

Maybe you can help her after all.

A part-dismantled scaffold tower loomed against the green boards. Jacob found a two-foot length of scaffold and weighed it in his hand. It wouldn't be much use against a gun, but none of the dead men had been shot, had they?

If nothing else, he felt better with something solid in his hand.

A single-story prefab warehouse behind steel gates overshadowed a patch of weedy ground littered with discarded pallets and lumps of rusted iron. On the far side of the waste ground, almost obscured by weeds, the roof of an abandoned car glowed orange in the setting sun. A gull called out, an ugly mocking cry. Jacob heard a scuffing sound behind him. He turned and instinctively tried to roll under the flat object swinging at his head. Too slow. The object caught him above the ear. Jacob slammed face-first into the dirt and into darkness.

* * *

He woke on his knees, nose inches from a patch of vomit. Scrambling to his feet, a sharp pain in his skull sat him back down on the grass. He was still in the empty plot on Wolcott Street. The abandoned car stood in shadow, and beyond the fence a curve of dirty gold was all that remained of the day. Jacob clambered to his feet again, resting with elbows on knees until he could stand upright. He was alone in the lot. Not quite alone.

The dead man in the driver's seat of the car was male with a shaved head and a large, curved mustache above swollen lips. Jacob recognized the face from the newspapers. Carl Bigney was naked from the waist up, and across the gym-lean chest some kind of crusted brown residue formed crude letters. He had to squint to read. *We all bleed the same.* The tail of the *e* in *same* curled up to what looked like the handle of a kitchen knife located directly over Bigney's heart.

Jacob tasted iron. His eyes blurred, but it didn't feel like emotion, more like an allergic reaction. A voice that sounded like his own told him to run. The same voice told him to clean up the vomit, then immediately told him that he'd never clean it all. A sudden sense of being watched had him spinning on the spot, searching shadows. Panic stuffed his throat. Wolcott Street hummed with silence. Pulling down the peak of his cap felt like jamming an iron hoop over his tender skull. He started to run.

CHAPTER

52

ALEX STOOD UNDER a police floodlight on a patch of weeds, staring at the body of Carl Bigney in a Buick. The stench of excrement made her eyes water, and she hoped it carried as far as the news crews gathered on the sidewalk, held back by a single uniformed officer whose jutting chin said it was too early in the morning to be fucked with.

Careful not to touch the body, she leaned into the car. A kitchen knife—the kind you'd find in any homeware store—still protruded from Bigney's torso. The CSIs had confirmed Bigney's prints on the handle, and no doubt they'd find the tip of the blade had been used to carve the words across Bigney's chest. As Alex withdrew her head, she noted that Bigney's skin was pink behind the ear; he'd just had his fade done. She looked into the flat gray eyes and wondered if they'd looked much different in life. The waxed hipster moustache created a permanent second smile.

We all bleed the same.

Do we, Carl?

Coombs appeared from the back of the CSI truck holding two cardboard coffee cups. As he walked toward her, the police floodlights stretched him up and in, elongating him into alien form before releasing him at normal size.

"Well?" She slugged coffee—cheap, bitter, and at three in the morning, delicious.

"Security patrol found the body an hour ago. We have the chopper up and a random swarming canvas, units checking alleys, backyards, vehicle interiors etcetera, but my guess is they'll be back in their hide by now." Coombs circled the Buick, peering through the rear windows. He pointed a toe at a discolored patch of earth where the CSIs had scraped vomit, leaving a circle like burned grass. "Assuming this doesn't belong to Bigney, we'll know in the next sixty minutes if we have a match in our database."

Alex screwed her eyes shut. When she opened them again, the sky seemed to have lightened. "Bigney was last seen in White Plains?"

"His brother's funeral. When he didn't check in with his PA, she called us." Coombs dropped to a crouch to examine Bigney's body. "She's telling anyone who'll listen that *her Carl* is the sweetest, and never burned a goddamn cross on a goddamn lawn his whole goddamn life."

"His family must have known he was coming for the funeral."

"The mother and two cousins are at a Days Inn. We woke them an hour ago. The cousins say they had no idea Bigney was planning to attend. Bigney's PA says he swore her to secrecy, but she's twenty—top secret means you don't put it on your public Instagram."

"Speak to the mother?" Alex said.

"Sedated. Bury one son and they wake you next day to say you gotta bury the other."

Coombs shook his head and Alex knew he'd had a flash of his own boys, the knock in the night to tell you that two was now one, or none. He shone a flashlight into the footwell then glanced up with a tight, angry smile. "This could be the break we need."

"How so?"

"We all bleed the same, Alex. The same *amount*, anyway, and there's not enough blood in this footwell. We know they brought him down from White Plains. Someone, somewhere, is busy scrubbing a carpet or the back of a van."

"And they'll never get it all out. They never do." Alex stretched out her back. A band of rusty light marked out the horizon. "Better than a missing Sharpie, Pat. But why bring him here?"

"Because it's perfect. The whole stretch of waterline shuts down after dusk." Coombs clicked off the flashlight. "This one feels different.

The DNA left for us to find. Feels like they're getting worse at this, not better."

Alex had twice bugged the CODIS DNA Index Unit to accelerate their search for a match on the vomit. They'd be throwing darts at her photograph before long.

"Maybe our crew rushed this one," she said. "They might have had a plan all along for Bigney, but they can't have known his brother would die four days ago. They found out Bigney had business in White Plains and they scrambled."

"Unless?"

"Forget it, Pat. First thing I checked. Marcus Bigney was definitely a heart attack. No, this was opportunistic." She'd circled the Buick and found herself back at the vomit patch. "The barf looks fresher than the blood. I reckon by the time they set up their little suicide tableaux, the adrenaline had worn off and one of our heroes lost their lunch."

"Four murders. You'd think they'd be used to it by now."

"Is that how many it would take for you, Pat?"

"Won't know until I try." Coombs rested his backside against the Buick's hood. "So, what's rocking their boat? Distracted by the media attention? Too busy jerking off to their handiwork on CNN when they should be crossing T's and dotting I's?"

"Divisions in the group?" Alex said. "One of them losing the faith?"

"We have the blood message across Bigney's chest, but where's the grand act of redemption? Where's the check written out to Black Lives Matter?"

"Maybe he told them to go screw. Or we didn't find it yet."

"Maybe," Coombs said with a shrug. "By the way, are you keeping a record of all your convos with our glorious leader?"

"Like I said. Not my style."

"Sure. Luckily I'm independently wealthy and don't need my FBI pension."

"You know I wouldn't let that happen."

Coombs gave Alex a look that reminded her of Jacob Felle the first time they met: curious, wary, darkly amused.

"Everything okay, Pat?"

He looked away. "Just thinking about the connection—or lack of—between Leonard Harris and Carl Bigney."

"We're still looking."

"Fair. But think about it this way. Benedetti and Dixon were directly responsible for Harris's death, and Johncock ruined Harris's funeral. If this is all about Leonard Harris, then you can see why Benedetti, Dixon, and Johncock become targets. But Carl Bigney's just a Family Dollar Hitler with a megaphone. Even if he has some tangential connection to Leonard Harris, the juice hardly seems worth the squeeze."

Alex gazed into the thickening dawn. "Maybe it's like that TV commercial for potato chips. *Once you pop, you can't stop.* Scramble the joint task force, Pat. Briefing in one hour. I want a geospatial analysis of all possible routes from New York to White Plains and back again. We're assuming a panel truck and the driver might show up on camera—get the biometrics team on it, see if the software can pull a face from the data."

"Done. But you know what's still bugging me?"

"Four dead bodies and no one in custody?"

"Why hack Talon's voting system? Publicizing the list gets us onto them faster."

On the way back to the Impala, they passed the knot of TV trucks behind the tape.

A voice called out, "Why withhold the suspects' names for so long? Does the FBI take responsibility for this one?"

Alex turned to the voice and a flashbulb made her blink.

Her phone vibrated. She read the message and suddenly she didn't care about the press and she didn't need to know why Felle or anyone else would want to kill Carl Bigney and the other weirdos, no-marks, and petty crooks on Talon's list. The message was from the CODIS unit. Jacob Felle's DNA had come back as a match for the vomit on the grass.

CHAPTER

53

JACOB JOGGED NORTH along the Brooklyn Bridge Park Greenway, if you could call his stumbling footsore gait jogging. The side of his head burned where he'd been hit, and his skull felt twice its normal size. But bless these crazy New Yorkers. It was barely four thirty in the morning, the sky still a purple bruise with a thin footnote of gold, and already the Greenway was dotted with early-morning runners—Jacob blended right in. From a distance, anyway. The runner disguise wasn't going to hold if people could smell him from a block away. To the south, the faint beam of a helicopter spotlight still scoured Red Hook. The copter was two miles distant, but every time the beam turned Jacob's way he shivered.

Would they believe that he hadn't killed the man in the car?

Would they care? Would they bury him alive?

He pictured Henry Duval or some other shadowy figure watching from behind the warehouse as he approached the Buick. If he'd been prepared to leave Jacob for dead, what had he done to Elizabeth?

Dawn was taking hold, the Manhattan skyline forming across the water, and the area around Brooklyn Bridge would soon be flooded with people. Jacob left the Greenway and turned onto one of the public piers jutting out into the East River. Gripping the rail at the end of the pier he stared over the water at the winking lights of

Battery Park. Fortress Manhattan. Some kind of seabird hooted. Elizabeth had kept a crocheted owl on her bed until she decided, aged nine, that not even inanimate fauna should be held in captivity.

Maybe you can help her after all.
No. You're too slow, too dumb, too much the little brother.
The trusting little brother.

Jacob lowered himself to the ground, facing the Greenway with his back to the rail, and if he hadn't been so tired, so beaten, so utterly done, then what happened next might not have happened.

Until now, Jacob had felt too exhausted to think. But sitting on the concrete pier, a new sensation overtook him. He was too exhausted *not* to think. Too tired to maintain the barricade he'd erected against the nagging doubt that had been pursuing him for days.

Thoughts, bad thoughts, began to filter through.

Elizabeth cuts Jacob off four years ago, at the same time Leonard Harris dies.

Leonard Harris's funeral is ruined by Dallas Johncock's listeners.

Johncock appears on Ricky Talon's Ten Worst list.

Then Johncock dies.

The bad thoughts coming fast now, as if flowing through a crack in a dam.

Johncock isn't the first person on Talon's list to die.

Benedetti, the real estate guy, falls to his death in early August.

The councilor, Dixon, drowns August 31. Floyd calls Jacob September 1, the very next day. Floyd: "She's sick again. It's back. Tell her to stop before it's too late."

Benedetti and Dixon dead because they too are somehow connected to Leonard Harris.

Stop. Not possible.

Jacob's first visit to New Frontiers. Claude and Henry interrupted preparing for something. Elizabeth sneaking into the office at Montauk Yacht Club.

Jacob assuming she was planning some kind of protest.

Elizabeth trying to make Jacob leave. Protecting him from what she knew was coming.

Floyd had sent Jacob to Green Wood Cemetery for two reasons: to stop the Johncock murder and in the hope that Jacob might save Elizabeth from herself.

Because Elizabeth wasn't in danger. She was the danger.

Staring at the dancing lights of lower Manhattan, Jacob knew with the certainty of a shared bloodline that his sister was murdering the Ten Worst People in New York.

He turned on his phone and inserted the SIM. The cops would be monitoring, but he didn't care. He pictured the pulsing red dot that would guide a chain of silently flashing police cruisers to his location.

Let them come.

His thoughts were interrupted by the judder of an arriving text message.

From Elizabeth: *Corner Mr. Willows and the Ansaris, my favorite B.*

It took Jacob a beat to understand and when he did, a buried part of him smiled in the dark. He scrambled to his feet and blood rushed from his head, firing hot needles into his limbs. He opened a map on his phone and confirmed his hypothesis based on his sister's message, then flung his phone up and over the water. By the time he heard the tiny splash, he was already running toward the Greenway and the sun was halfway over the horizon.

Elizabeth didn't get to play God. Not anymore.

CHAPTER

54

"Corner Mr. Willows?" Murphy asked. "As in back the man into a corner?"

They were back in Murphy's Federal Plaza office, Murphy seated on the edge of his desk, Pat Coombs at the pigeon window, and Alex pacing, too wired to be still.

"More likely a place," Alex said. "Corner of X and Y street. *My favorite B* could be Elizabeth Felle's favorite bar, or New York borough or basketball court or brother."

"Another brother we don't know about?"

"Or a joke, like telling your only child they're your favorite."

"The Bigney murder has to be a team effort," Murphy said. "But we only have Jacob Felle at the scene. Why split up, and why wouldn't Felle already know where to meet?"

"Panicked and ran in different directions?" Alex said. "Truth is, we've no clue. We were too late for a full containment, but we flooded the area with uniforms and we had a chopper up with infrared in case they were hiding under a tarp. Closest we came was the K-9 team tracked a scent to the bottom of the Greenway. We're checking CCTV, but there's over a thousand hours to sift."

"So the best efforts of the FBI and the NYPD can't find one man who doesn't know the city, must be out of cash by now, and has already been on the run for nearly a week?"

"Felle's good at this," Alex said. "Surprisingly so."

"Then we need to be better," Murphy said. "What's your gut feel on where they're hiding out?"

"They're still in the city. My guess is we're looking for a house, not an apartment, so they don't have to worry about noise, with an attached garage so they can exit and enter the house without being seen."

"We have airports, bus and train stations covered," Coombs said. "All local departments are on emergency, ready to descend on a sighting."

"We wait for them to show their faces," Murphy said. "That's the grand plan?"

"The nut we need to crack is Henry Duval," Alex said. "We suspect he has property in the city that we don't know about, but it's all hidden behind a wall of rich-guy shit. We could use some leverage."

Murphy nodded, but he didn't look happy. "What else?"

"We've requested access to the email servers at the TV studios where Bigney worked. Other than that, we're background briefing the media and focusing on intelligence. Jacob Felle's a cypher in the US, but colleagues, neighbors, associates, family might know something, even if they don't know they know. Social media analysis may give us a bite."

"Elizabeth Felle gave nine talks at different yacht clubs across the city in the last twelve months," Coombs said. "Seems to be a recent thing for her. Pulling in cash after the New Frontiers subscription money dried up is our best guess."

"We're checking membership of the yacht clubs," Alex said. "But no connections yet to Harris or to anyone on Talon's list."

Murphy frowned. "Emil Hertzberg pretty much lives on a yacht, doesn't he?"

"Hertzberg's name doesn't pop at any of the clubs Elizabeth Felle spoke at," Coombs said. "But that's no surprise. The man wouldn't lower himself to being a *member* of anything. And when you think *yacht* and *Hertzberg* think less rippling sails and more floating fortress."

Murphy pushed off his perch and fell heavily into his chair. He was one of those men who seemed to get smaller when angry. "And you both still think Leonard Harris is the key?"

Alex said, "The Benedetti, Dixon, Johncock connection to Harris can't be coincidence, and the visitor records from Clearwater Community Nursing Home show both Elizabeth Felle and Floyd Shaw visiting Harris regularly. We're elbow deep in the victims' lives—phone records, email, browser history—but no gold in the sieve just yet."

Murphy slammed a hand down on his desk and his globe paperweight wobbled. "Tell me, Alex. After all our running around, aside from Jacob Felle's vomit, what do you have on this crew that isn't circumstantial? And don't give me pitons and unique sailing skills."

Alex took a breath. "That's why you need to call the senator's office."

"Instead of telling me what I need to do, how about you tell me why Henry Duval would draw attention to himself by publicizing his hit list on talk-show TV."

"Working on that."

"And while you're working on it, another man is dead, we still don't have the ball, and our grand strategy is to hope the other team drops it. Back here in an hour with an update, both of you. And Alex, watch out for the press now that they have you."

Alex looked at Coombs, who shook his head. She pulled out her cell and googled her own name. *Shit.* "Special FBI Agent Alex Bedford Declined to Comment at Bigney Murder Scene."

The accompanying picture caught Alex with her eyes squinting against the flashbulb. She looked a thousand years old.

"Do you need alternative accommodation?" Murphy said.

"I won't be hassled out of my own home."

"What's their current line?"

Coombs answered for her. "'Adrenaline Junkies Seek Ultimate Rush.' Henry Duval is Charles Manson with a trust fund and a movie-star smile."

* * *

Murphy had told Alex to report back in an hour, but he summoned her to his office a mere thirty minutes later.

"Address for Duval." He handed her a yellow stickie. "South Brooklyn townhouse."

"You leaned on the senator. Thank you." *Good dog, have a treat.*

"SWAT's grouping up. Where's Pat Coombs?"

As if on command, Coombs's head appeared around the door. "Breakthrough on Bigney," he said. "We just took a call from the SPLC. They had a tip that the Bigney family was gathering in White Plains."

The Southern Poverty Law Center was a nonprofit based out of Alabama that tracked hate groups. Bigney's anti-immigration rhetoric had put him on their watch list.

Murphy beckoned Coombs into the room. "So?" he said.

"During a routine IT audit at the SPLC last month, a name flagged. A woman named Chloe Zhang did some pro bono paralegal work for them six months back, but she'd been using her password to access their network long after the project ended. At the time, they let it slide—all soldiers together, fighting the good fight—until one of the auditors saw Bigney's corpse on NBC. They checked and Zhang had been back in the files three days ago, looking at . . ."

"The Carl Bigney intel," Alex said.

"The SPLC's company lawyer insisted on calling us before some journalist plastered 'Southern Poverty Law Center Aids Vigilante Death Squad' across the *New York Post*."

"Bless that lawyer," Murphy said. "So who is Chloe Zhang?"

"Still getting up on her," Coombs said. "Born in Boston. A qualified lawyer. Acts as an unpaid advocate for illegals fighting deportation. And best of all, we know from the online forums that she's an ex-member of New Frontiers." Coombs turned his laptop. "This is from an old dating profile."

Alex studied Zhang's slender face and read strength and determination in the wide-set eyes staring out from under a shock of pink hair.

"Find her, bring her in," Alex said. "And I want to know all known associates—friends, family, colleagues—and find out who she connected with on that dating app."

Murphy looked pleased for the first time that day. "Go join the SWAT team on the Duval raid, Alex. An hour from now we might have them all warming cells."

* * *

Alex was digging in her purse for her car keys when the scuff of heel on concrete made her turn. One of the night-feeders—young, female, impossibly straight hair—had made her way past security into the underground car park, the square eye of her camera resting on her shoulder.

"Agent Bedford, can you confirm that Jacob Felle is leader of a British organized crime group?"

Alex started toward the security hut. The camera followed.

"Is Henry Duval the ringleader? What are we dealing with, Agent Bedford? Criminal enterprise? Terrorist cell? Death cult? Our viewers deserve to know the threat they face."

Alex beckoned the guard out of his hut. "Bullshit and disinformation," she said to the reporter. "From people like you."

CHAPTER

55

Jacob stood in white sunlight beside a line of rental bicycles, pretending to read the Citi Bike instructions on an information board, waiting for the screaming tires, the blue lights and shouted command, gravel knee and a face full of asphalt. That it hadn't happened on his twenty-five-minute jog from the Greenway to the intersection of Sixth Avenue and Ninth Street in Brooklyn was a miracle.

This had to be the place, but the bagel shop across the street with its thin line of morning customers offered no clues. Neither did the basement bar with its drawn shutters, or the second-floor windows of the yoga studio.

He couldn't stand on the street corner forever.

The door of the basement bar opened, and a thin man in a bucket sunhat stepped into the sunshine and lifted his head as if checking the weather. Jacob recognized the dense orange freckles and wide green eyes. Without looking Jacob's way, Claude Lemieux retreated into the dark. He left the door to the bar open.

* * *

The taproom smelled of disinfectant and hops. Claude stood behind the bar. Jacob wished he could see his hands.

"Phone off?"

"I dumped it," Jacob said. "Where is she?"

Claude slid a whiskey glass across the bar with two inches of gold. "Breakfast?"

"Where is she, Claude?"

"Ten out of ten for all fucked up, man." Claude thumbed toward the rear of the taproom. "Sorry, it had to be this way."

* * *

The whiskey set fires in Jacob's empty belly as he exited through a fire door into a sunless courtyard. Henry Duval leaned against a door in the far wall, hands in the pockets of his beige chinos and one foot up against the woodwork like a cowboy in a catalogue shoot.

"I hope you're going to be a grownup about this, Jacob." His three-fingered hand drifted to the spot on his stomach where Jacob had hit him in the bathroom at the New York Public Library. "Where's your camera?"

"Where's my sister?"

Henry peeled away from the door. "Come inside. Don't worry, it's safe. For now."

"How stupid do you think I am?"

"Jacob, your sister loves you. That's why, against my better judgment, she texted you from her own phone. Want my opinion?"

"Like I want another smack around the head with an iron bar."

Henry screwed up his eyes. "I won't pretend to know what that means. My opinion is that it would be best for everyone if you just vanished."

"Vanished?"

"Don't be so damn dramatic." Angry, Henry was almost ugly. "I mean you should leave the city while you can. Look, I told Elizabeth I'd invite you in. I've done so. Please make up your mind, I have coffee going cold upstairs."

* * *

The lounge felt smaller than any of the rooms in Henry's DUMBO apartment. Elizabeth seemed smaller too, seated in a wicker chair under a window with the curtains closed, her hair tufty and slept in. When Jacob entered, she dropped her knitting to the floor.

"You're here," she said, springing out of the chair.

"If you'd hit me any harder I wouldn't be."

She seemed about to reply, then scooped her knitting off the floor. When the needles had found their rhythm, she said, "You remembered Rhododendron Drive."

"I remember I was too young to spell Rhododendron. *Corner Mr. Willows and the Ansaris, my favorite B.* Old Mr. Willows lived at Number Nine, the Ansaris at Number Six. You always said Brooklyn was your favorite New York borough, and there's a Sixth Avenue and Ninth Street intersection in Brooklyn, but no Ninth Avenue and Sixth Street. Clever Elizabeth wins the clever prize. Now tell me what was so clever about leaving your brother for dead beside a corpse."

Henry eased into view. "Coffee? Milk, sugar?"

"You told me that we all just want to be in the light, Henry. What did you have to do to get back in Elizabeth's light? Is that how you lost your finger? Elizabeth made you cut it off to prove your loyalty? Or did she make you stab that man in the chest?"

Henry blinked at him but didn't respond.

"Are you hurt?" Elizabeth said, staring at the lump on Jacob's forehead.

"What have you done with Floyd?"

Henry said, "We don't know where Floyd is."

"Forget you left him rolled up in a carpet in the back of your car?"

Elizabeth gave him a look: *Sympathy Wearing Thin.* "You've had a rough night. Now you need to be smart. Where's your camera? Jacob, snap out of it. Your camera. Did you upload your footage?"

"It's on the memory card. Floyd has it."

"Awesome," said Henry.

Jacob measured the distance, trying to decide whether to break Henry's nose or target that perfect jawline. Instead, he walked to the fireplace, picked up a large expensive-looking glass vase from the mantel, and hurled it to the wooden floor. The explosion of shattered glass seemed to thicken the silence that followed.

"I always wanted to do that," said Henry's voice from somewhere behind him.

Elizabeth appeared beside Jacob. "You stink. You need a shower and a change of clothes." She reached for his wrists and shifted him around to face her, turning his palms as if reading his fortune. "You got Mum's artist's hands," she said. "I got Dad's blacksmith's anvils."

"You need help," he said, the words hot on his tongue.

"I won't argue with that." She sounded tired.

"Five people are dead."

"I count four, but it doesn't matter right now."

"You're insane."

"I won't argue with that either. Jacob, you have to understand something. The world's a better place without the dead men on Ricky Talon's list. But we didn't kill them."

"Then who did?"

She frowned up at him. "You really have to ask?"

CHAPTER

56

HUNCHED ON BENCHES in the unmarked truck, the SWAT officers looked like eight sweaty turtles in their bucket helmets and breastplates. In her role as lead special agent on the arrest, Alex closed out her briefing with a plea. "Remember, Henry Duval is the son of a senator, and the senator's weapon of choice will be a five-thousand-dollar-an-hour lawyer. He'll discharge that weapon in our faces if we don't do this by the book. Understood?"

Eight nods confirmed understanding. The SWAT team lead balanced a stinger battering ram between her knees. "It's your show, Special Agent Bedford, but are you going to knock and hope he answers with a Nespresso in his hand?"

Nerves behind the officer's bravado. Good, it might make her more careful. Alex scratched her ribs below the eight-pound, soft armor Kevlar vest. The vest made you sweat like a goat and encouraged the bad guys to aim for your head, but regs were regs. She took a deep breath and held it. One thing William the firefighter and Alex the FBI agent had always agreed on was the watery feeling in the legs when you approached a door with no idea what was on the other side. Today, Alex's legs felt fine. With William gone it mattered less.

"Let's try and do this minus the blood and thunder, okay?"

She let the officers squeeze past her to exit the truck. No need to let them see her struggle with her knee as she climbed down. Fifty yards from the target, the SWAT team gathered in an empty lot between brownstones. The team lead with the stinger nodded to Alex with the look of a daughter waiting for an elderly parent to get in the goddamned car.

Alex smiled at the officers to relax them—stray bullets in cramped townhouses were no fun. "Gently does it," she said, contemplating the staircases she would have to climb and wishing Henry Duval owned only buildings with elevators.

CHAPTER

57

"He almost snapped my arm," Elizabeth said. Or was saying. Or had said a few moments ago. Jacob was in the kitchen at the back of Henry's townhouse. That much he knew. Henry was in the lounge, sweeping broken glass. And Jacob was meant to be listening, but he caught only fragments of what his sister was telling him.

It was Floyd. *Floyd* was hunting the ten worst people in New York. Floyd killed the man in the car. Floyd cracked Jacob over the head. Floyd's grief, Floyd's rage, Floyd's plan.

Jacob floated weightless while Elizabeth described the months after Leonard's death. From the shallows of her own grief, she'd seen Floyd swept away by a raging tide. Lost hours, night terrors, paranoia—amplified by alcohol and cocaine abuse. Of course, Floyd had lost his dad before he was twenty, and maybe she'd underestimated the way he saw Leonard as father, mentor, and spiritual guide all in one. Maybe the rage had always been there. Elizabeth was meant to be the one with the faulty wiring, but suddenly it was Floyd driving drunk, punching cupboards shut, and starting fights in bars, until it had wrecked both his career and his marriage.

"You're telling me Floyd made everyone at New Frontiers burn their contracts?" Jacob said.

Elizabeth sat heavily on her stool. "No, that was me, and I don't regret it. I wanted to honor Leonard and I was sick of the commercial bullshit. That's how I dealt with Leonard's death. Floyd dealt with it by creating Talon's list."

"Floyd did *what*?"

"Remember Srividya? My friend in the yellow dress at the wedding."

"No. Uh, maybe."

"Back then Srividya was on the *Talon Tonight* writing team. Six months ago, I invited her to dinner as part of a campaign to jolt Floyd out of his stupor. Floyd just glared at his plate until we'd finished dessert and he said to Srividya, 'I have something for your show.' He pitched Sri the idea of a list voted for by the public. He called it the Worst People in America."

The earth shifted under Jacob's feet. "Floyd invented Talon's list? Bullshit."

"I can call Srividya right now and you can ask her—if she'll take my call after what's been plastered over the news. I'd forgotten about Floyd's pitch until Talon unveiled his Ten Worst People in New York. They'd refined the concept, but it was basically the same idea."

"Are you going to tell me it was Floyd who hired a private investigator to look into Leonard's death?"

She raised an eyebrow at him. "You know about that?"

"Floyd put me onto Leonard Harris and it led me to Kelly-Anne Pinstock. She was CEO of the nursing home."

The corners of Elizabeth's mouth twitched in what might have been a smile. "Smart old Floyd. And you have been busy, Jacob, haven't you? *I* only found the PI's report six months back when I was putting laundry away. I'd read as far as Benedetti, Dixon, and Johncock when Floyd snatched the file out of my hands. I knew about Johncock, of course—I was at the funeral his troll army ruined. I despised the man. But not enough to do what Floyd did."

"Then Benedetti and Dixon are also connected to Leonard?"

"Benedetti owned the nursing home. Dixon was responsible for the fire. It was all in the report. I told Floyd to go to the cops. He said jail was too good for some people. A few weeks later I see Talon's list in a newspaper, and now Benedetti, Dixon, and Dallas Johncock are in it."

Elizabeth had confronted Floyd, who responded by taking Elizabeth's hair in his fist. She fought him off but not before he twisted her wrist so hard the tendons separated.

"Hold on." Jacob shook his aching head. "You're telling me you had a fight with Floyd and *Floyd* won?"

"He's a different man, Jacob. Tell me you haven't seen that yourself. And all said and done, he's thirty pounds heavier than me. What was it you told me once about boxers? The good big guy beats the good little guy every time."

Elizabeth had run to Henry for sanctuary—to Henry's *spare* bed—and Floyd stopped coming to New Frontiers.

A few weeks later, Benedetti fell from a building and Elizabeth thought, *oh*. Then Dixon leaped off his boat and Elizabeth knew.

"Why didn't you go to the cops?" Jacob said.

"A question I asked at the time." Henry appeared in the kitchen and poured glass shards into a pedal bin.

"The idea of Floyd . . ." Elizabeth said. "I don't know. Then something else happened."

"You showed up at New Frontiers," Henry said.

"I lied to you, Jacob," Elizabeth said. "The night you came to New Frontiers, you did interrupt Claude and Henry getting ready. We'd been planning a protest on that old warship moored off the Upper West Side. Did you know, you can fund nine thousand ambulances for the price of one Virginia-class submarine?"

"You just found out your husband's a murderer and you're unfurling banners?"

"I was in shock. Going through the motions. That's why you saw me go into the wrong office in Montauk. I've been living in a fog, trying to understand what my husband turned into." She looked at her fingers as if they were foreign objects. "Suddenly, you're in the picture and I *can't* go to the police in case Floyd's wrapped you up in it. I tell you to go home. You refuse. The FBI shows up. We're thinking, what is Floyd playing at?"

"We know now, of course." Henry spoke over the top of his coffee cup. "Your job was to *discover* what was going on."

"Floyd was scared for you, Elizabeth."

"That's what you were meant to think."

"I don't get it." The pressure in Jacob's head threatened to blow his skull into fragments. "If that's true, why didn't you talk to me?"

"I almost did at Henry's apartment," Elizabeth said. "Then Floyd appears at the door, calls me a nasty little whore and tells me that the next time it will be my neck not my arm, and not just my neck, yours too. After our last fight, I believed him."

"But then you called out of the blue and told me to film Claude."

"I wanted to know you were okay."

"You wanted Claude to sniff out if I was genuinely worried or working with Floyd." Jacob looked at his sister's wrist, the bandage tight as a boxing wrap. "This is bullshit."

"You sound less convinced every time you say that." She gave him a cold smile. "So, we put our plans on hold. Then Dallas Johncock dies and the next day you show up at the wedding and tell me you were *there*."

"We decided to drop out of sight," Henry said. "Until we could figure it all out. Now Carl Bigney's dead and we don't know if that's good for us or bad."

The bruise on Jacob's skull throbbed. "I saw Carl Bigney's body."

Elizabeth pushed gently at Jacob's shoulder. "Listen to me. Carl Bigney was a nasty little proto-fascist in skinny jeans. I couldn't care less that he's dead, and I can't for the life of me see how Bigney connects to Leonard, but Bigney's death confirmed something we suspected when you showed up at the wedding."

"Floyd's fucking us," Henry said. "If he lured you to Red Hook, *us* includes *you*."

From the other end of the house, a thump on the front door seemed to shake the kitchen. Elizabeth looked at Jacob without expression as another fist landed on the woodwork.

CHAPTER

58

Alex counted to five before she knocked again. One of the officers behind her shuffled his feet. She pressed her ear to the door and heard only her own pulse. She nodded to the SWAT team lead with the stinger.

Two hits and the wood around the lock splintered.

Officers streamed through the doorway, weapons high, filling the air with warning shouts. Alex waited for gunshots. Instead, two-word reports began filtering back. *Lounge clear. Kitchen clear.*

"You're at Quantico," Alex called up, "and this is your Tactical Proficiency exam."

Feet thumped on stairs. *Bedroom clear.*

The team lead appeared in the kitchen doorway. "Take a look, ma'am."

A thin layer of dust covered the steel kitchen worktop. Alex opened a freestanding refrigerator. A few jars lurked at the back of the top shelf. No fresh produce, no milk, no alcohol.

"Nothing but dust, ma'am. No one's been in here for months."

CHAPTER

59

T**HE FOURTH THUMP** on the door jolted Henry into life. Jacob heard feet in the hallway, then the click of a deadbolt and the jangle of a chain. Henry's hissed admonishment carried back to the kitchen. "Moron. What happened to three soft, two hard?"

Claude appeared in the kitchen doorway, obscured under his floppy bucket hat. He dumped two loaded grocery bags on the counter. "This is the last load from the van. When it's gone, we're catching mice for dinner." He pointed at Jacob with his eyes. "Does he know yet?"

"We were getting there," Elizabeth said. "Before you scared the shit out of us."

Claude scratched his scalp through the bucket hat. "What's the smell?"

"That's Jacob," Henry said. "He's back from a three-hundred-mile jog."

Claude placed his hands on the counter and pushed up off the ground. He straightened as he inverted, knees tucking into his armpits until his ass almost touched a set of hanging copper pans. The cords in his forearms rippled like harp strings as he chanted, "Not happening, not happening, not happening."

"Floyd's been laying breadcrumb trails for the police to find," Elizabeth said. "It's small stuff, circumstantial, but cops don't believe in coincidences. Put it together and it starts to feel compelling."

The bruise on Jacob's skull pulsed. "What's your connection with Bigney?"

"We don't have one. But who knows what Floyd cooked up?"

A sound like a gong filled the kitchen, and Elizabeth ducked as if avoiding gunfire. Claude's heel had clipped a copper pan and sent it clanging to the floor.

"Henry, do something with Claude." Red spots blossomed on Elizabeth's cheeks. "Before I do."

Henry walked Claude out into the hallway. Jacob stared at the groceries on the kitchen counter: heritage tomatoes, carrots with the plume still on. Elizabeth put a glass of red wine in front of him. The first gulp made him cough. He took another, and this one stayed down. A tiny stream of spilled wine ran between Jacob's knuckles. He saw bloated red lips in a dead face, a naked torso with letters written in blood. He saw his prone self in the scrub by the abandoned Buick. "Floyd tells the FBI that I've been investigating the connection between you, the death of Leonard Harris, and the dead men on Talon's list. Then my body's found at the scene. It looks like you killed me."

"Makes sense through a cop's eyes, doesn't it?" Elizabeth said.

Jacob's words seemed to be moving faster than his thoughts. "We have to stop him. We have to go to the police."

"That's the plan, but first we have a hole in the roof to fix. A hole you made when you fell out of the sky."

Jacob looked at his sister.

"*Whore salad* was our code for the Intrepid warship protest—random words from a dictionary. *Sour lime* I took from a cocktail menu, and that was going to be the big one, a sit-in on the roof of the New York Public Library."

"We weren't at that gruesome wedding for the food," Henry said, coming back into the kitchen. "The point is this. The whole code word thing is lame, but Floyd can weaponize it with your film. I'm no lawyer, but having Claude say to Elizabeth, 'You need to stay out of sight until we figure this shit out. It's not safe,' is not a good look for us."

A crown of pain now encircled Jacob's head. At Elizabeth's feet, sunlight picked out a glass shard that had missed Henry's pedal bin. "You were talking about Floyd."

"That's not what you thought when you heard it," Elizabeth said. "'Figure what out?' the prosecution will ask. And their answer will be that whore salad and sour lime are code words for the dead men. It won't be admissible, but it might lodge with the jury along with all the other small seeds Floyd's been planting—the piton on the roof that they'll try to pin on Claude, the fact that drowning Dixon took serious sailing skills." She pointed a thumb at her own chest.

"Never mind that Floyd could have found any number of decent climbers or sailors among the former New Frontiers members," Henry said. "Most of whom hold a grudge against your sister." He shrugged on a lightweight linen jacket. "Plus, sad friendless bastards that we are, we can only alibi each other for all the deaths—again, not a good look to a bunch of cops who don't do coincidences." He patted his pockets and called out, "Ready, Claude?"

Claude joined them, in his hand the kind of leather roll that chefs use to carry knives.

"Where are you going with that?" Jacob said.

"Floyd's apartment," Henry said. "Claude has an important job to do, which is fine because Claude's feeling calm again, right, Claude?"

Claude gave a flat salute. "Nine out of ten for calm vibes."

"What are you going to do to Floyd?" Jacob said.

Henry pulled on a hat with a floppy brim. "We're counting on him not being home."

Claude waved the leather roll. "Lockpicks."

"Floyd had a hide he thought I didn't know about," Elizabeth said. "A loose tile under the bathroom basin where he kept his coke. If he hid your memory card, it's there."

"Maybe he already sent it to the FBI," Jacob said. "Or he has it with him."

Elizabeth stared through the window at a cloudless sky. "I think he'll have stashed it somewhere safe. The cops will have people in the lobby and the garage, but there's a defunct fire escape and the fire doors overlook the alley where they keep the trash. The external stairs were removed years ago so the cops won't be staking out the alley."

"Nineteen floors of hard climb." Claude didn't sound unhappy at the prospect.

Henry handed Claude a square box with Lumix Camera branding. "Find the card and erase the bad stuff. Leave the card where you found it."

"You won't need the lockpicks," Jacob said, fishing out Floyd's key and spinning it over to Claude, who caught it. "But you will need me if you want to get in."

Elizabeth stared at him.

"Unless Claude can transform his retina to match Floyd's new scanner, I'm coming too," Jacob said.

"You're staying here," Elizabeth said.

"This is what you wanted, isn't it? Your brother stepping out from behind the camera?" Jacob turned to Henry. "I'll take that shower. And a change of clothes."

CHAPTER 60

Alex called Coombs from the street outside Duval's empty apartment, knowing she had about two minutes to reach the Impala before the TV trucks arrived.

"I guess when you own as much property as Duval, you can lose a three-million-dollar brownstone down the back of the sofa," Coombs said, when she told him about the raid.

"Any luck finding Chloe Zhang, our pink-haired Bigney stalker?"

"Apartment empty and no one's seen her at the restaurant she works at for days."

"Why am I not surprised? What do we know about her?"

"Fired from her first law firm job for tampering with evidence in a human rights case. Lost her license to practice law, and now pays her rent waiting tables. Volunteers as an unofficial pro bono advisor to illegals fighting deportation. A few years back, she embedded in an illegal migrant crossing into Arizona to document mistreatment by US border authorities and private militias. That trip was her ticket into New Frontiers membership."

"So far, I'd like to buy her a beer," Alex said.

"Yeah, well, we're still digging—she doesn't do social media, so it's a slog. We'll have to go public with her too, Alex."

Alex fished for her keys, the Impala in sight across the street. "Time for what the FBI manual calls reevaluation and strategy adjustment, Pat. Meet me at the office in twenty?"

"Make it fifty." Coombs spoke over traffic sounds. "We just got a tip that Floyd Shaw keeps methamphetamine in the back of his washing machine. It's likely a crank call—pardon the pun—but Shaw installed retina scan security on his front door, a very drug dealer thing to do, and the washing machine part feels oddly specific. I've got a master access code for the retina lock, and we're heading over now to take a look. Want us to wait for you?"

"You go. I need to update Murphy."

"Then you should know he's breathing fire. Since the media got hold of Henry Duval's name, people in places higher than he knew existed keep dropping by to tear him a new asshole."

"I hope he knows that blaming your subordinates is not a good look." Alex flashed her badge to hold traffic as she crossed the street. "Did he up the reward like we asked?"

"One hundred fifty each for Felle and the others. Press briefing in an hour." Coombs paused and she heard something in his silence . . . they'd worked together long enough.

"Pat?"

"The *Enquirer* ran a profile on you, Alex."

Alex circled the Impala to the driver's side. "Bound to happen. Let me guess, *FBI Baffled*, accompanied by a photograph of me looking fat, dumb, and old."

"They mention William."

Her hand froze on the car door handle, as if contact with the vehicle had breathed ice up through her arm and into her heart.

"What does it say?"

"It's bullshit."

"Tell me."

Coombs sighed down the line. "Decorated agent tipped for senior role until loss of firefighter husband to brain tumor. Childless and lives alone. Workaholic, no social life. Colleagues fear grief may impede her judgment. Questions over why the FBI gave its most high-profile case to the, uh, Woman in Black."

"Do they print his name?"

"The colleague stuff is pure fabrication. Nobody's saying that. And the nickname won't stick. No one's going to give you a label with the word black in it."

"Pat, do they print his name?"

Another sigh. "Yes, Alex. They printed William's name."

From across the street, an older man with a camera over his shoulder and a young woman with a microphone in her hand waved at Alex to wait. Alex dropped into the Impala and fired up the engine. A yellow bus braked with a screech as she cut out into the traffic. The two reporters appeared in her side mirror. Alex accelerated away, trying not to imagine emptying her Glock into their shiny faces.

CHAPTER

61

H ENRY, HIS FACE hidden by a floppy brim, drove them into Manhattan in a battered Toyota Corolla with tinted windows. Claude scrunched down in the passenger seat, and Jacob sprawled in the back, face pressed against warm vinyl, listening to some jock on the radio describe how the Ten Worst Killers had turned New York into a "community of fear."

The Toyota halted, and Henry's head twisted to check the street. "We appear to have ourselves a community of business as usual and not giving a shit," he said. "Good luck."

Henry was right, not one pedestrian looked their way as Claude and Jacob, hoods up, ducked into an alley that reeked of hops and garbage. Two dumpsters stood against bare brick, and a series of glass doors began five meters above street level.

"Each floor's four meters high," Claude said. "With an eight-meter span-breaker every ten floors. We can't pass in front of the fire-door windows, but we can use the edges and corners of the frames." He shifted his feet, assessing the wall from different angles. "I wish we had more time to plan."

"You don't think you can do it?"

Claude pulled coils of red and black striped rope from the backpack between his feet. "I could do it blindfolded. It's you I'm worried about."

* * *

Jacob had climbed before. But never like this.

The plan was for Claude to free solo until he found a place to fix a rope. Jacob would follow, hand-over-hand, feet flat against the brick—*don't look down, don't let go*. Simple, until the first coil of rope came sailing down, and suddenly Jacob was off the ground, shoulders screaming as muscles he'd forgotten existed assumed responsibility for his life.

Street noises from both ends of the alley told him the world was going on as normal, but as Jacob came level with the first set of fire doors, he'd never felt further from normal. Needles dug into his shoulder blades, sweat salted his eyes and slicked the rope. When he reached the eighth-floor belay point, he saw the tiny metal cam device that Claude had wedged between the brickwork. Knowing that two hundred pounds of body weight relied on those miniature metal lobes gave him a headache that started in his neck and traveled into the roof of his skull. With the headache came the certainty that the building was not, in fact, vertical, but pitched outward at an obscene angle, and the wind knifing in from the north had determined to prize him away from the wall.

Two sharp tugs on the rope meant that Claude had fixed the second cam. Time to go.

Jacob pressed his nose against the brickwork and closed his eyes, but found no refuge in the dark. He forced himself to look up, where Claude moved with indecent speed above him, the rope swinging from the Frenchman's belt like entrails.

Hand over hand. Don't look down, don't let go.

By the twelfth floor, Jacob knew that the universe wanted him to die. Why else would the building suddenly lean out with no warning? Why else would the wind slide icy fingers between his body and the wall? Reaching the second belay, he started to think about letting go.

Just letting go.

At least then his shoulder muscles wouldn't feel as if they were being shredded like crispy duck. A new sensation flooded through him, a strange caressing of the mind. Elizabeth and Floyd, Jacob's career, his longings, his failures, his often-felt sense of trying to run up a down escalator . . . he could let go of it all. Something like excitement prickled his skin.

A sharp voice broke into his thoughts. Jacob looked up to see Claude horizontal above him like a sprinter in the starting blocks, one foot pressed against the fire-door frame, the other leg extended to where the toe had some invisible hold.

"Grip with your left, grab with your right," Claude said, reaching down to take Jacob's hand. "You're almost there."

When Jacob reached up, Claude gently tapped his palm aside and closed his grip around Jacob's wrist. "It's not a business meeting, man."

With a strength Jacob didn't think possible in such a slender frame, Claude pulled Jacob up until one ass cheek rested on the lip of an open fire door. A corridor stretched out ahead of him. A carpeted strip of heaven.

"You're a five out of ten, but you could be an eight in no time." A foot landed in the small of Jacob's back as Claude propelled him through the gap and onto the hallway floor. "Proud to climb with you, man."

* * *

His first steps down the corridor felt like boarding a dinghy. He stopped at the door, listening to the drumbeat in his ears. The clean-carpet smell served up a memory: his arrival in New York still gritty from the plane, mentally preparing to reconcile with his sister after four years. He turned the key in the lock, hit the button to wake the retina scanner and held his eye to the red dot, thinking that it would have been a moment's work for Floyd to delete him from the system, holding his breath until the dot flickered red to green and he heard the soft click of the latch.

Leave the door open or closed? Closed, in case someone came by.
Into Floyd's apartment, listening, listening.

Main living space, empty. Kitchen, empty, the air heavy with the scent of rotting fruit. Floyd's fur-lined face stared down from the *National Geographic* poster as Jacob checked the bedrooms. Floyd's room was no different to the last time Jacob had seen it. In Jacob's room, the stack of razor blade boxes had toppled and clean-shaven Floyds littered the floor. A light patch of wall indicated where the photo of Floyd, Elizabeth, and Leonard Harris had once hung.

In the bathroom, he knelt at the basin, running his thumbnail down the grout between the tiles until he found an indent. The tile came away and he carefully placed it on the toilet seat. The basin stem obscured his view, but his fingers probed a space the size of a matchbox until they brushed against something small and flat. Jacob flipped open the plastic shield on the new Lumix camera Henry had given him, and inserted the memory card. He switched to edit mode, reduced the audio, and ran the scrub bar until he saw himself remove the mic from Claude after the interview at New Frontiers. Jacob selected from that point to the end of the clip. *Delete*. Assuming Floyd hadn't cloned the card or uploaded the footage already, Claude's overheard phone call had never happened.

A scrape of shoe on polished wood had Jacob rising to his feet. His eyes came level with a hand pulling a pistol from a belt holster. Faster than fear came instinct as Jacob's upward motion turned into a curving right-hook. His fist slammed into a shaved jaw and the crack of connection was followed by the thud of the pistol hitting the tiled floor. There was a frozen moment when the gun might have gone off but didn't. Bellowing blue shapes filled the doorway.

CHAPTER

62

ALONE IN THE staff kitchen of the Sixth Police Precinct on West 10th Street, Alex Bedford decided that anyone guilty of finishing the coffee and not putting a fresh jug on the hotplate should get life with no parole. She found a jar of instant and mixed a fierce brew before heading back down to the observation annex where Pat Coombs caressed his swollen jaw as he watched Jacob Felle through the mirror. Felle sat in silence beside his Legal Aid lawyer, a puffy gray-blond fifty-year-old with an unforgivable ponytail.

"Ding, ding." Alex said. "Round two."

* * *

Felle, his eyes hooded with fatigue, muttered a thank you as he took the mug of coffee from Alex with his free hand. He tugged at the chain connecting his other wrist to the table. "Do I really need this?"

"No, we do." Alex pulled out a plastic chair as Coombs let the heavy file slap onto the desk. "Where did we get to, Jacob? Your story is that your brother-in-law has committed five murders, and gone to extraordinary lengths to frame you, your sister, and your sister's friends."

"Correct." Felle massaged his arm below the shoulder where it had been twisted by the first cop to follow Pat Coombs into Floyd

Shaw's apartment. He leaned forward, and Alex could see him summon reserves of energy. It mattered to Felle that they believed. "For a moment, I thought it was my sister," he said. "I was wrong."

"Let's talk about Floyd," Alex said. "He's not doing this alone. Who's helping him?"

Felle shook his head. "I met one of his mates at the apartment. Roland van Buren. Tall man with a thin, sunburned face."

"What does this Roland van Buren do?"

"I don't remember—yes, I do. The first time we met, Floyd said he was a mountain climber."

Alex shot a glance at Coombs who fractionally raised an eyebrow. *The piton found on Benedetti's roof.* When she looked back at Felle, she could see in his eyes that he'd just made the same connection.

"Van Buren's girlfriend was there too," Felle said. "Chloe Zhang. About so tall, pink hair. I saw them again outside the library at the wedding. She was in the back of a Mercedes SUV. Van Buren was driving, and Floyd was in the passenger seat."

Chloe Zhang, the lawyer who tracked down Carl Bigney. Alex and Coombs exchanged another micro-glance. This was starting to stack up.

"Green Wood Cemetery, where Dallas Johncock's body was found," Alex said. "An anonymous text told you to go, and you obeyed because you worried your sister was in danger."

"Floyd made me think that. What would you have done?"

"Called the FBI," Alex said. "Floyd Shaw lured you to Red Hook?"

"I showed you the clip he posted on my website."

"And your sister and her friends have nothing to do with the murders."

"Correct."

"So why won't you tell us where they are?"

"Because I don't know." Felle looked down at his right hand, flexing the fingers. A plum-colored welt had risen across the knuckles.

"Did you hurt your hand on my face?" Coombs said. "I do apologize."

"I thought you were Floyd," Felle said without looking up. "Aren't you meant to shout 'Police!' or something?"

Alex shot another look at Coombs who gave a tiny shrug. Felle's lawyer was busy in his briefcase and didn't appear to have noticed. Alex said quickly, "You climbed the side of a building to break into Floyd Shaw's apartment. Why?"

"We needed to know what else Floyd had on us."

"You knew we'd already searched the apartment."

"You wouldn't know what to look for."

"Like a piton?" Coombs said.

"If Floyd had more of the same, we wanted to get ahead of it."

"Because you don't trust the FBI to do its job."

Felle sucked on his swollen knuckles. "We've done nothing wrong and you have our faces plastered all over the city. We're supposed to trust you?"

Alex said, "Back to your footage. When you interview Shaw, he says, quote, 'It's like chemotherapy and cancer. The worse the sickness, the stronger the medicine required.'"

"He was talking about a trip to Greenland, but it fits what I've been telling you."

"Whereas all your sister had planned was a little light trespassing on a decommissioned warship." Coombs leaned back in his chair. "Do they expect that to bring the government to its knees?"

Felle shrugged. "Perhaps they should start killing people."

"You were helped on the wall by this French climber," Alex said. "Claude Lemieux. Ex-New Frontiers and a friend of your sister. What can you tell us about him?"

"Everything I know about Claude is on the video interview you've seen. Like I said, I last saw him in the hallway outside the apartment. He must have scrambled back down the wall when he heard you coming out of the elevator."

"Where's your sister, Jacob?"

Felle gazed into the ceiling. "I told you. We met in Prospect Park by the old house on the lake. Claude came with me to Floyd's building. I don't know where they went after that."

"I'll rephrase my question. If they're innocent, why go into hiding?"

"Because four men and one woman are dead, and they think Floyd is playing you for fools." Felle scrabbled at his scalp with his free hand. "Why don't you ask that writer woman I met at the wedding? Srividya something, begins with a P. She used to work on *Talon Tonight*. Elizabeth says she can confirm it was Floyd gave her the idea for Talon's list."

Alex had Srividya Parthasarathy waiting in an interview room down the hall, but she wasn't about to tell Felle that. "Let's go back to this female private investigator that you say Floyd commissioned to look into the nursing home fire. Did you see her report?"

"Floyd took the only copy from Elizabeth. I don't know what he did with it."

"But he pushed the private investigator in front of a train."

Felle rubbed at his face. "I suppose he must have."

"Why is Floyd doing all this?"

Felle looked at his hands. "This isn't the Floyd I knew. Revenge, I guess. Anger for what happened to Leonard Harris. Tired of being the good guy. Tired of hiding his bruises."

"Hiding what bruises?"

Felle stared at the steel cuff around his wrist. "Will Floyd get help when you catch him? He used to be a good person."

Alex gave Coombs the nod, and they both stood. "Let's take another break."

* * *

Alex paced the observation room. "He's telling the truth. At least, he thinks so."

"Except for the Prospect Park bullshit. He knows where they are." Coombs rested his forehead on the two-way mirror. "Something's not right. Why's he so calm?"

"Twenty-four hours ago, he thought his sister was a killer. It's relief we're seeing."

"If you say so, Alex." Coombs shook his head as he reviewed his notes. "Okay, so we add Roland van Buren to the BOLO along with Chloe Zhang. Claude Lemieux too?"

"Lemieux's not with Floyd's crew, but he's a climber and he's tight with Duval and Elizabeth Felle, so let's bring him in. They're all still suspects at this stage."

"But you don't believe that, do you? Tell me this. Do you buy Elizabeth's crew breaking into Shaw's place just to see what else he had on them?"

Alex lowered herself into a chair as a wave of exhaustion soaked through her clothes and into her skin. "Sure. Why trust your future to some FBI grunt? Normal rules don't apply to senator's sons, cinematic auteurs, and globe-trotting adventurers. And speaking of normal rules . . ."

Coombs dragged his hands down his cheeks. "I should've announced myself. Thirty years doing this job you get a feeling, and the place felt empty. Felle has an ability to disappear in plain sight."

Alex let it drop. "Where are we with the PI?"

"Hannah Perlman died almost exactly three years ago at Briarwood subway station in Queens. No cameras on that section of platform—convenient—and no witnesses except the driver who said she just sailed out in front of him. Perlman worked out of her garage, and the local cops went through her papers at the time. No death threats, no imminent exposé that might have put her at risk. No mention of a report on Clearwater Community Nursing Home."

"The fire in Perlman's garage?"

"A month or so after her funeral. Looks fishy from where we stand now, but at the time it was just more shitty luck for the Perlmans." Coombs turned a page to find his notes. "Fire department thought it was paint vapor meeting sunlight amplified through the window."

"But how hard were they looking?" Alex spun around on the observation chair. The interview room beyond the glass was empty, Felle back in his cell. "Okay," she said. "Get a homicide enquiry opened on Perlman. They can start with a deep dive on CCTV around the subway station and revisit Kelly-Anne Pinstock, the Clearwater Community CEO. Perlman got her info from somewhere."

"Done. What else?"

"Take another look at the video clip Shaw uploaded to Jacob Felle's private website. Shaw blocked the window, but maybe there's construction noise in the background, airport sounds, something to place his hideout. If we make the clip public, maybe a landlord will recognize the room. Also, in Claude Lemieux's interview with Jacob Felle, he mentions something about a TV advertising shoot Floyd Shaw did with a musician and a football player."

"A wristwatch commercial."

"Check it out, and let's see if there's anyone else Shaw fell out with around that time. Talk to his sponsors, if he still has any."

"Close Shave released a statement. Apparently mass homicide is incompatible with their brand values. You going to update Murphy that we have yet more suspects?"

"First I'll speak with the writer who claims Floyd Shaw gave her the idea for Talon's Ten Worst list. Before we put Floyd Shaw, van Buren, and Zhang in the frame, I need more than Jacob Felle's word."

* * *

Srividya Parthasarathy sipped from a flask of water. "A list of the worst people in America, voted by the public? Ricky almost pissed his spray-on jeans with joy. Some ideas feel manufactured, others are more like found objects. The moment you have them in your hands you're like, yeah, this is killer content."

"It was definitely Floyd who made the suggestion?"

"Pretty much the only thing he said during a thoroughly painful evening."

"Would you describe his mood as dark, angry?"

Srividya sucked on her cheeks. "My word would be numb."

"Did he suggest how the public would vote for the name?"

"As in the mechanism? Nope, and if you're wondering, he didn't ask me to add names to the list. I haven't spoken to him since that dinner. He wasn't at the wedding, of course."

"Of course?"

"Samantha disinvited him after what happened with Elizabeth."

"Which was?"

Srividya glanced up and left, as if asking for permission to speak. "Floyd and Elizabeth had a fight," she said. "Floyd almost broke Elizabeth's wrist. Samantha was all march-him-to-the-cops, but Elizabeth nixed that. Samantha settled for rescinding his invite. Not the Floyd I knew, but I guess you can't be sure with the male of the species."

You never met William.

"Have you seen Elizabeth since the wedding?" Alex said.

"No, and before you ask, if she's not at her apartment or at New Frontiers, I'm tapped. Can't help with Floyd, either. We moved in different worlds after I left *Talon Tonight* and I've been freelancing ever since. On which topic, Agent Bedford, would it be possible to get a quote?"

* * *

As Alex stepped out into the hallway to call Murphy, a woman in a navy suit appeared around the corner. The ice-blue eye shadow and expensive-looking hair belonged to Laura Spelling, the lawyer she'd met at Dallas Johncock's house.

"Miss Spelling."

"Agent Bedford." Everything from Spelling's hair to her velvet heels said that an hour of her advice cost more than an FBI agent earned in a week. "Is he in there?"

"Is who in where?"

"My client, Jacob Felle."

"Felle already has legal representation."

Spelling gave her a dimpled smile. "He's been upgraded."

A wave of fatigue washed Alex further up the beach. "Henry Duval saw your name connected to the Johncock case. I assume you know Henry Duval is still a suspect in this investigation and the subject of a manhunt. Do you know where he is?"

"I do not. But I read the transcript of Jacob Felle's first interview, so I know that the focus of the investigation is about to change. Will you be releasing Mr. Felle today?"

Alex almost laughed out loud. "Jacob Felle climbed twenty stories to break into Floyd Shaw's apartment."

"When the time comes, I will happily no-contest a prosecution for ignoring the building's fire code. As for breaking and entering, I believe he used a key he'd been freely given and his own unique retina scan."

"Felle stays in custody."

"He wasn't in the US when Benedetti and Tyrell Dixon died."

"He was here for Johncock, and he almost puked on Carl Bigney's corpse. Yesterday morning, he assaulted a police officer."

Spelling arched a shaped eyebrow. "Or he was forced to defend himself against an armed intruder in civilian clothes who failed to identify himself as a police officer."

"Felle was on the run for three days before we found him."

"Or he was hiding from his murderous brother-in-law."

An ominous beat began to sound in Alex's temples. Incoming migraine. "Felle stays in custody, Miss Spelling."

"For as long as you can hold him without arraignment."

"Five murders. We'll charge him with something and good luck getting bail."

"Thank you," Spelling said with warmth. "I assume you'll be briefing the press that the focus of your manhunt is now Floyd Shaw and not my clients? I think it's best for law enforcement to be first to the punch, and as we both know, word has a habit of leaking out."

Alex watched the kitten heels until the lawyer turned a corner. Spelling, she realized, was one of *those*. Increasingly rare, but you could still meet a white man or woman who had—or *might have*—their own reasons for giving a black woman shit. In the modern world, they rarely said it outright so you never knew for sure, and that was the problem. That was the weight.

Pat Coombs stuck his head out of the observation room and from the look on his face, she knew what he was about to say.

"Roland van Buren's apartment is empty. Ditto Chloe Zhang. No one's seen either of them for days."

"Okay," Alex said, feeling the tectonic plates of the investigation shift beneath her feet, once again. "Flip the script. Go public with Floyd Shaw and his buddies. Duval, Elizabeth Felle, and Lemieux are still persons of interest. But Shaw, Van Buren, and Zhang are our number one targets as of right now."

CHAPTER

63

Ricky Talon christened the tall lawyer Bert and his shorter colleague Ernie. Five people sat at a board table made for fifteen: Talon, the two lawyers, Talon's assistant Emelda Parsons, bless her badly dyed hair, and Special Agent Alex Bedford from the FBI, who Talon had met twice before and who reminded him of a stern aunt on his mother's side. Bert and Ernie had chosen to sit beside one another, and Talon pictured them in bed together, Sesame Street style, tucked under a double duvet in their five-thousand-dollar suits. That might make a good segment for the show. He needed one.

The FBI agent was writing in her notebook. "And you had no knowledge that the idea for a Ten Worst list came from Shaw?"

"Srividya told me she *dreamed* the idea. She's not missed on the writing team."

Bert said something in his creaky voice about Talon having no prior knowledge of something or other. Talon tried to listen, but *wow*, this view from the Rockefeller Center was ridiculous—Central Park was one big cabbage patch. When he tried to bring his attention back into the room, the air conditioning had a hum that reminded him of a two-stroke moped he'd rented once in Rome.

The idea hit him like a baseball fired into a crowd of forty thousand, only to land squarely in his lap. "A counter profile."

The agent looked up from her pad.

"Ricky Talon meets Special Agent Alex Bedford—exclusive interview with the woman leading the manhunt for the Ten Worst killers. Your chance to set the record straight. I saw that hatchet job the *Enquirer* did on you."

The agent didn't blink. "Goes with the territory."

"Forget the woman in black. We'll make you look like a character from the Marvel Universe. What do you think?"

The agent smiled and closed her notebook. "Appreciate your time, Mr. Talon."

"Why not?"

She slung her bag over her shoulder. "I'll let your lawyers answer that."

* * *

There would be not one more word about the list by Talon or any of his guests, no excuses, no exceptions, until Floyd Shaw was dead or behind bars.

"We're not doing the list," Talon said. "We're just doing list-adjacent."

Ernie said, "The phrase *list-adjacent* literally doesn't mean anything."

"See that rally in Times Square last night?" Talon was on his feet. "Three thousand people singing, 'Floyd Shaw for President.' This is the only story anyone's talking about and we're the *only* show that can't talk about it. We made this story."

"Which is why you'll never mention it again, or you will be fired from NBC, contract terminated. Do you understand, Mr. Talon?"

Talon's phone vibrated. A text from the writers' room. *Celebrities and their animal lookalikes?* He closed his eyes and glared at the dark until sparks flew.

CHAPTER

64

Two heavyset officers walked Jacob past the bars of the general holding area—a soup of inmate chatter, body odor, and flatulence. He estimated twenty male bodies crammed into a space large enough for ten.

As he passed by, voices called out.

"Keep up the good work, man."

"How do I get my ex-wife on your list?"

Laughter followed him down a set of white concrete steps to a windowless coffin-sized cell with a concrete toilet. The yelling and clanging of doors was constant, as was the overhead light. No shoes, belt, watch, or phone. No way to count the passing hours. Jacob closed his eyes and saw Floyd in a room with a red sheet over the window. The FBI had the camera. They knew about Floyd. So why didn't Elizabeth hand herself in? Maybe she already had. Maybe right now she was with Agent Bedford—that was a battle of wills he'd pay to see.

A hatch opened in his cell door. A tray appeared: a single-serve box of corn flakes, an individual carton of milk, and a plastic spoon. The hatch clanged shut.

"Hey," he called out. "You forgot the bowl."

More laughter, this time close by. A voice said, "Hey, *feesh*, pour it straight in."

Jacob opened the top of the plastic bag in the corn flakes box and poured in the milk. When he took his first spoonful, the taste was of childhood and somehow comforting. He thought about Agent Bedford, who radiated a gentle competence. He thought about his new lawyer with the big hair, who'd arrived in a waft of Chanel and told Jacob he was about to be moved to central booking in Brooklyn, a place she cheerily called "the Tombs." Big Hair said she'd have him out in forty-eight hours, so hang tough and say nothing without her in the room. Her last piece of advice was to empty his bowels before they moved him from the precinct.

Jacob had failed to heed her warning, and now he had no option but to use the pan in one corner of his cell. A smear of excrement lined the concrete bowl and the thin roll of toilet paper bulged on one side where it had made contact with piss or toilet water. Jacob did his best and retook his seat on the bench.

He sat in silence, trying to identify the feeling in his chest, a lightness he hadn't expected. It took a minute to figure it out.

He'd done it.

He'd convinced the FBI that Elizabeth was innocent. Elizabeth had told him to tell his own story, and he had. Not from behind a camera, but in Kelly Pinstock's garden, running the streets of New York City, in Red Hook staring at a body in a car, hanging from his fingertips fifty feet up a wall, chained to a police desk facing the FBI. He'd told his story perfectly. And the best thing? It was true.

CHAPTER

65

Murphy and Alex watched on Murphy's laptop as a young Delase Carter walked toward the camera flanked by a six-foot-nine football player and a teenager holding a surfboard. The three men presented their wristwatches and said with one voice, "Be your own man."

Fox News cut from the decade-old commercial to the modern Delase Carter wearing crimson sweats, sitting across from a man in a suit, in what looked like a warehouse. The words *Secret Location* flashed on the screen.

The interviewer leaned forward on his chair. "Mr. Carter, the interesting thing about that ad is who *isn't* in it, correct?"

"Was meant to be me and the shitkicker, plus you know who."

"Floyd Shaw."

"Mr. Ten Worst himself. Only he weren't no killer back then. Man could barely get a word out his mouth, except to bitch at me. Wasted half a goddamn day, if I recall."

"And it wasn't until you saw Shaw's photograph on our award-winning *Fox Morning News Show* that you remembered the shoot."

"We had words. Shaw couldn't get his line right, so they canned him and drafted the surfer."

"Did Floyd Shaw threaten you?"

Carter sniffed. "Wouldn't be no Ten Worst killer if he had. I just know the man took an instant dislike." He drew a finger down the side of his face. "Why would a man like him take a dislike to a man like me?"

Murphy closed the laptop.

"How long's Delase Carter been sitting on this?" Alex said. "He must have recognized Shaw the moment we went public with his picture."

"Long enough to negotiate the right deal with Fox." Murphy's chair squeaked as he spun it away from the desk. "The real question is why didn't we find this first? Claude Lemieux mentions it in his video interview with Jacob Felle, an interview Fox News doesn't have. Not cool, Alex."

A rap on the door stopped her replying, which was probably for the best. Pat Coombs's head poked into the room. His face said he had something. Murphy beckoned him in.

Coombs cradled his laptop in the crook of his arm. "In Jacob Felle's video interview with Floyd Shaw, Shaw mentions an expedition on K2, something about how the trip went bad. Turns out there were three of them on that expedition. Shaw, a young novice called Gregor Messick, and one more experienced climber." Coombs turned his laptop for Murphy and Alex to see a photograph of a thin, heavily sunburned male face.

"Roland van Buren," Alex said. "Went bad how?"

"Gregor Messick didn't make it down," Coombs said. "He and van Buren became separated from Floyd Shaw in a snowstorm. Later, van Buren told the enquiry that Messick slipped and their connecting rope frayed on a jagged spur. An alternative view is that van Buren didn't want to risk freezing to death waiting for a rescue so he cut the cord."

"Maybe Floyd Shaw wasn't as lost in the snow as he later claimed," Alex said. "Maybe he saw van Buren cut the cord and that's his leverage. He's forcing van Buren and Zhang to help with the Ten Worst murders."

"Or it was Shaw cut the cord and van Buren has the whip hand."

Coombs shut the laptop. "We can debate it later. In more good news, van Buren has an aunt with an apartment over in Sunnyside, Queens. Pays her rent on the nose every third of the month by direct debit."

"Good for her," Murphy said. "So?"

"So she died two years ago."

Alex started for the door. "Pat, you go with the arrest team to Sunnyside."

"Where are you going, Alex?" Murphy said.

"Central booking," Alex said. "If anyone can help us find Floyd Shaw, it's his wife. Jacob Felle did a fine job convincing us to turn our attention to Floyd. Maybe he can use his powers of persuasion on his sister."

CHAPTER

66

Jacob remembered Agent Bedford's simple hoop earrings from their previous meeting, the gold against the gray of her lobes a useful anchor as his mind turned somersaults in the aftermath of his arrest. Now he was sitting across from her again—his new lawyer Laura Spelling by his side—while Agent Bedford explained that for as long as his sister and her friends refused to hand themselves in, the FBI would have to consider the possibility that they were working with Floyd, Roland van Buren, and Chloe Zhang.

"I told you they're not," Jacob said.

"And if you're right then she has nothing to fear," Agent Bedford said. "Trust me."

Spelling made a noise in her throat.

"Jacob," Agent Bedford said. "Your sister can help us find Floyd Shaw and the others. She knows her husband better than anyone else alive." The agent turned her attention to Jacob's lawyer. "Fugitive from justice with extenuating circumstances. No opposition to bail. In court, we'll recommend no jail time."

Spelling laughed. "Hiding from a serial killer makes you a fugitive?"

Agent Bedford turned back to Jacob. "Your sister knew Floyd was behind these killings *before* Bigney died, and she kept it to herself. That's bad, but if she can help us find Floyd Shaw, we can work it out.

Henry Duval can match whatever bail the judge sets for all four of you. Terms will include no contact with the media, and you'll have to stay where we can find you, but you'll be free. And if you're worried about Floyd Shaw, we can provide protection."

"What about your partner's failure to announce in Shaw's apartment?" Spelling tapped the tip of a gold pen against her front teeth.

"Factored into my offer, Miss Spelling. I assume you can contact Henry Duval?"

"I'm not cognizant of his whereabouts."

"Not what I asked." Agent Bedford turned back to Jacob. "This is the win-win. Your lawyer knows it. I think you know it too."

* * *

"Did you get hurt when they arrested you?" Elizabeth sounded light, free.

Alone in a side room with Spelling's phone to his ear, Jacob turned his back on Agent Bedford, who watched him through the glass door. "Where are you?"

"We're safe," Elizabeth said. "Spelling filled me in on Roland van Buren and Chloe Zhang. Makes sense. Van Buren loathes me and he's a towering cunt of a man. Zhang I barely remember—which says a lot. I didn't know they were together, but I'm not surprised. Mediocrity attracts mediocrity. Look, I don't want to be on this line for long, so skip to the part Spelling thought would be better coming from you."

Jacob outlined Agent Bedford's offer. In the micro-pauses between sentences, he probed the aural landscape for telltale sounds. Was that the creak of a rope?

"This FBI agent guaranteed no jail time?" Elizabeth said when he'd finished.

"She didn't guarantee anything."

"I'd have called bullshit if she had. You trust her?"

"Does it matter?"

"Do you, Jacob?"

"Yeah. Actually, I do."

"Thank you."

"For what?"

Her answer was a sigh. "When this is over there are things we can do together. I know a messed-up rich kid who could bankroll a movie." A beat, then, "It's funny. Or tragic."

"What is?"

"Floyd almost broke my arm and tried to pin five murders on me. In Red Hook, he came close to killing the person I love most in the world, and there's still part of me that wants to see him walk away from this." She exhaled with force. "Tell your agent squeeze I'll think it over."

Agent Bedford came through the door. "Well?" she said.

Floyd almost killed the person Elizabeth loved most in the world.

"It's all going to be okay," he said.

CHAPTER 67

Alex called Coombs from the basement canteen in central booking. Through a street-level window she watched the neat ankles of the TV crews milling in front of the building.

"We missed van Buren, Alex."

Alex refrained from kicking the pastry counter.

"Minutes before our guys arrived, a neighbor saw him get in the elevator with some kind of gym bag in his hand. She thinks he's been home all week."

"How would she know that?"

"Jazz coming through the walls. She almost called the cops, but felt dumb telling them her neighbor was playing Charlie Parker too loud. We tossed the apartment. Cupboards full of clothes and we found his passport in a drawer. Only bit of good news—it's the apartment where Floyd recorded his clip for Jacob Felle. Checking for prints and DNA. Oh, and we pulled van Buren's bank records. No major withdrawals in the last twenty-four."

Alex reached the front of the line and pointed at the largest coffee cup size. "Floyd Shaw and van Buren grooving to Parker like they don't have a care in the world. Then, twenty minutes after Jacob Felle calls his sister, van Buren vanishes. Pat, did I just screw up again? I gave Elizabeth Felle van Buren's name."

"I don't think so, Alex. Jacob Felle gave us van Buren in the first place. And us chasing van Buren is a good news story for Elizabeth Felle."

She carried her coffee down to the subterranean parking lot. "What about van Buren's Mercedes, the one Jacob Felle saw outside the library?"

"We have it leaving the garage below his building around the time the neighbor says she saw him with the gym bag. Camera doesn't capture the driver or other occupants."

"Any news from the Hannah Perlman homicide investigation?"

"Zero. And no trace of that report on Clearwater. Looks like Shaw has the only copy and it's probably ash by now."

Alex stared into the dark corners of the underground lot. "What should we be doing that we're not doing, Pat?"

"Praying. You a lapsed Catholic by any chance? Lapsed Muslim? Mormon?"

"Optimist," Alex said. "Keep me updated. I'll give Murphy the good news."

* * *

Alex had Murphy on speaker in the Impala as she waited to merge onto the Brooklyn Bridge.

"Press briefing in sixty minutes." His voice dripped ice. "I told the communications team that you personally would make the next public statement. As the face of this investigation you can inform the press that our suspect list is still growing, and that we missed our man. Again. My office in thirty to prep."

Murphy hung up. Alex slammed the wheel and accidentally hit the horn.

A fat male head emerged from the window of the car in front. "You think I'm sitting here for my fucking health?"

Alex pressed both hands down on the horn.

CHAPTER

68

Ricky Talon let his writers present for three minutes before he silenced the room with a howl. Six faces drained of color. Talon's assistant, Emelda, didn't look up from her iPad.

"Hands in the air," he said. Six pairs of hands rose slowly. "Now, put them down if you were unaware that we face a ratings slide that could make a Himalayan avalanche blush."

Two of the writers' lips began to quiver.

"The biggest story this city has seen in a decade and we're the *only* show that can't talk about it. But instead of bringing me the next Ten Worst feature, you come with bruised fruit you picked up off the floor. Game-show hacks? Fucking musical comedy? If I want bad ideas, I have my own. We could do prank calls to politicians, dogs that look a bit like Hitler . . . None of that is going to keep us on air."

The writers' arms started to sag. Talon saw the truth in their startled eyes: the Ten Worst list was a once-in-a-lifetime ratings phenomenon and they knew it, they just didn't know if he did. A girl whose name Talon could never remember stumbled from the room.

Emelda was on her feet. "Ten-minute break, people."

As the writers sloped away toward the canteen, Talon readied himself for a broadside. The hands-up thing hadn't been cool, but hell . . . filmed hobo fights?

Emelda passed him her iPad. "Look. They offered her up as a blood sacrifice."

A live news stream was playing on the iPad screen. The FBI agent who'd interviewed him—Agent *Bedford*?—stood behind a lectern on a set of stone steps. Talon increased the volume and heard her say something about a partnership with Crimestoppers... increased rewards... how advanced technology, forensic analysis, and behavioral profiling were providing insights into the fugitives' behavior and movements.

"Is the FBI soft pedaling while the Ten Worst killers clean up the city for you?"

"Special Agent Bedford, are you concerned that the lack of progress might see you replaced as lead investigator?"

A gloss of sweat glinted on the woman's forehead and collarbone. She looked tired and out of ideas.

"I'd have made you look like Eliot Ness," Talon said out loud.

On the screen, a balding man in a brown suit appeared and spoke into the FBI agent's ear. She retreated into the building, bringing the conference to an abrupt close. Talon looked up to see Emelda holding out her phone. The last time he'd seen that look on his assistant's broad useful face, she'd pulled him out of a meeting to tell him that his father had died.

"He says he's Floyd Shaw," she said, handing Talon the phone. "Calling to offer us the biggest eyeball share since the moon landing."

CHAPTER

69

"Seriously?" Alex said, the moment they were back inside the Federal Plaza.

Coombs couldn't keep the smirk off his face. "Elizabeth Felle, Henry Duval, and Claude Lemieux are warming cells in Precinct Fifteen. Walk-ins. Almost gave the desk sergeant a coronary."

"Jacob Felle came through." Alex peeled off her damp jacket. *Urgh.* "Let's go."

Coombs shook his head. "Let them stew. Alex, I say this in love, but you look like microwaved shit. Next time the press snaps a shot of you, it's in a clean shirt with a freshly scrubbed face looking like the killer agent you are, okay?"

"Was I that bad out there?"

Coombs gave her a thumbs-up and a Hollywood smile. "You were marvelous!"

* * *

She emerged from the shower to five missed calls from Pat Coombs. Phone wedged between shoulder and cheek, she poured freshly brewed coffee into a travel cup.

"Pat?"

"Today's your day, Alex. First Elizabeth Felle strolls in, now this."

When he told her why he was calling, she made him repeat it. Twice.

"A live confession on *Talon Tonight*?" She could barely process the idea.

"It may not be Shaw," Coombs said. "But whoever called Talon knew the brand of kitchen knife used on Bigney, and that's a detail we never released. You obviously impressed Talon, he asked for you by name. He's waiting for us at the NBC offices at Rockefeller."

"Shaw must know there's no way we'd allow a live confession."

"Don't second-guess crazy. The media started calling Shaw the Trashman because he takes out the New York City trash. Maybe it went to his head and he wants his big moment."

"Platform for the great manifesto. What does Murphy say?"

"Murphy's a mouse slavering over cheese that's sitting on the jaws of a trap. Grab Shaw with no bloodshed and he's an FBI Hall of Famer. Screw it up, he's the story you tell freshman agents around the campfire with a flashlight under your chin. Worry about Murphy later. Meet at Talon's Rockefeller Plaza office in thirty?"

Alex rummaged in her other jacket for her keys. She should eat, but her stomach refused to open for business. "Tell Talon ninety minutes."

"Something more pressing than a televised confession from our murder suspect?"

Alex dropped a packet of Excedrin caps into her bag, though she likely wouldn't need them. If the pharma companies could bottle the effect of a homicide case hitting escape velocity, they could retire all other products. She clipped her firearm to her hip and paused for a moment in the doorway to the lounge, electrified by what the next few hours might bring, and unable to meet William's eye.

"I'm going to stop by Precinct Fifteen," she told Coombs. "I don't want Shaw calling the tune. And if anyone can tell us where he is right now it's Elizabeth Felle."

* * *

Alex pulled up a chair opposite Spelling and Elizabeth Felle, the lawyer as immaculate as Elizabeth was scruffy in her jail sweats and messy scrabble of gray-black hair. Alex wished she'd brought Pat Coombs to even up the contest. This was going to the mat.

No, for heaven's sake, Elizabeth had no idea where Floyd could be, but had the FBI tried his mother in Oakland? Did they speak to Srividya, the writer on *Talon Tonight* who could prove Floyd Shaw invented the Ten Worst list? Speaking of *prove*, could they prove that Elizabeth had been framed by her husband, and if not, why not? How long would she be caged without charge and when could she speak to her friends? Most importantly, when would they reopen the case on the Clearwater Community Nursing Home fire? Would Benedetti and Dixon be prosecuted posthumously for Leonard Harris's death? Would justice finally be served?

Alex ran through her assurances. The FBI was doing everything it could to find Floyd. They were actively reexamining all the evidence that appeared to point to Elizabeth and her friends. And yes, there would be a time to look back at the Clearwater fire. She would personally see to that, but only when Floyd Shaw was in custody.

"Or dead," Elizabeth said. "You can say it."

"We're very much hoping it doesn't come to that. Did Floyd ever talk about Carl Bigney before Bigney appeared on Talon's list?"

Elizabeth gave a tiny lift of the shoulders. "Anti-fascism was our love language for a while. Bigney's name might have come up. Nothing specific that I remember."

"What about Delase Carter?"

"His interview on Fox was the first I'd heard of them falling out."

"Floyd had a fight with a famous rapper and he didn't mention it?"

"We didn't discuss his sponsor engagements, even back then. I was never a fan."

"But it wasn't until later that you made him and other members of New Frontiers torch their commercial contracts."

Alex had hoped the comment would knock Felle off guard, but she didn't flinch. "Exactly right, Agent Bedford. When you need people to step forward, rituals matter. Whether you burn contracts, crosses, or books, rituals signify boundaries an individual must pass to attain growth. Some of our members had become overly concerned by the financial opportunities. I wonder, how important is money to you?"

"Not at all, when I have it."

Elizabeth drummed her fingers on the table. "You're rather good at this, aren't you?"

"At what?"

"Agent Bedford will personally ensure the case into Leonard's death is reopened. She's *very much hoping* Floyd doesn't die in a hail of FBI bullets, but she doesn't disrespect my intelligence by sugar-coating coating the truth. And she just let me know there were times when she didn't have money, which builds empathy or sympathy depending on my perspective."

Spelling's lips pinched into petal shapes. She didn't like the way this was going.

Alex said. "Bekah Baxter, Laurie Cullen, Clara Wilter. Did Floyd ever talk about the women on Talon's list?"

Elizabeth tilted her head. "I never caught him smeared in pig's blood, dancing naked around their photographs, if that's what you mean?"

"Is this amusing to you?"

"No, but neither is it shocking. And if you expect me to feign horror to prove I wasn't involved, I'm afraid I won't make it that easy for you. My husband has tried to frame me for murder and it's your job to prove it, not mine."

"You seem unconcerned that five people are dead."

"Not relevant," Spelling said, shifting in her seat.

"It's okay, Laura." Elizabeth placed a hand on the lawyer's arm. "Agent Bedford, if the private investigator is dead because of Floyd, that's obscene. But the others? Tell me, how much sleep have *you* personally lost over those men?"

Alex took a breath to recalibrate. How interesting to sit across from these two women. Spelling, sharp as a sushi knife, but predictable. Elizabeth Felle emitting a more challenging intelligence. Happy to own her cultish behavior. Happy to use language that made her sound pompous and strange. Happy to express her lack of concern over five homicides. Happy to make Alex do the work.

Time to switch gears. "Tell me about Roland van Buren."

Elizabeth's eyes rolled up to meet Alex's gaze. "What about him?"

"Is he close to Floyd?"

"Is he close to anyone?" Elizabeth's tongue traveled along her lower lip. "You might as well know that he hates me for booting him out of New Frontiers. And before you ask, I know Chloe Zhang, but we were never close. She's a little creepy, and she can't keep her knickers on. How well Floyd knew Chloe, I couldn't say. Are you married, Agent Bedford?"

The punch you don't see coming is the one that knocks you out—William used to say that. Alex's cheeks tightened as she smiled into Elizabeth Felle's hard gray eyes.

Try to use William against me and I'll shatter your nose bone on the table and hand my badge to Spelling on my way out.

"Not anymore," Alex said.

"Children?"

"No."

"Choice or you weren't able?"

Even Spelling flinched at that, glancing at her client with something like horror.

Alex drew her resources in tight and said, "Choice. The wrong choice, as it transpires. What's this got to do with finding Floyd?"

Felle studied her for a moment. "You *are* good at this. The point, Agent Bedford, is that I've been married fifteen years, but I only recently met my husband, if you follow? And thankfully we never bred. But even with Floyd's newfound rage, his sense of injustice over Leonard's death, his willingness to do things like this," she held up her bandaged wrist, "my husband is too much of a pussy to be killing people on his own, and he doesn't have the brains to frame me and my friends."

"But van Buren does. Okay, so where should we look for van Buren?"

"Under rocks, in sewage pipes, coiled around a tree branch over a bird's nest?"

"You've no idea where Shaw and van Buren might be?"

"Would they have told me?"

"Floyd might. Or you might guess—you were together a long time."

Pinkish stains blossomed on Felle's cheeks. "You think I know where they are, don't you?"

A reaction at last. Alex pushed. "I think you're in no hurry for the killing to stop and I *know* you like to control the pieces on the board. I read your friends' statements before I came here. Henry and Claude appear to have memorized the same script."

"The truth isn't a script."

"Your power over them is palpable. And over your brother."

"Floyd pulled my brother into this, not me."

Spelling coughed. "Elizabeth."

"Does that make you angry, Elizabeth?" Alex said. "Our counterparts in London tell us that you're no stranger to rage. You almost took a teacher's eye out with a colored pencil."

"Enough," Spelling said. "Irrelevant. Not useful."

Felle glared at Alex. "Floyd might have killed my brother and you want to know if that makes me angry?"

"*You* might have killed your brother when you made him climb a twenty-floor building."

The pale lips curled into a sneer. "His choice. We're not like you, Agent Bedford. Pushing ourselves to the mental and physical limit goes with the territory. Don't pretend you understand us. You don't and you never will."

Alex felt her own breath quicken.

Ever been shot at, Elizabeth? You want to push yourself to the limit, try facing off against a home-grown terrorist, or a drug dealer who knows his next arrest buries him for life.

Spelling whispered something in her client's ear, then snapped her folder shut. "I'm terminating this interview. Please confirm the charges, Agent Bedford, if you have any. And let's see what the judge has to say about bail."

"Do your job," Elizabeth Felle said in a flat voice, "so I can go home."

CHAPTER

70

JACOB HAD BEEN determined not to sleep, but the soft leather, sunlight diffusing through smoked glass and the gentle undulations of the suspension conspired against him as the vintage chauffeur-driven Jaguar wove through Manhattan. Memories of his recent bail hearing invaded the shallow slumber: escorted in handcuffs from his cell to a subterranean parking garage and the back of an unmarked car, a glimpse of television crews gathered on the station house steps, reunited with his lawyer, Spelling, in a drab windowless office, given a script and twenty minutes to learn it. More corridors and polished floors until he was ushered into a wooden box facing a judge with a face like a deflated beach ball.

Spelling had done most of the talking.

Jacob Felle was an innocent man, a victim of Floyd Shaw, Roland van Buren, and Chloe Zhang who had conspired to frame him for the murder of Carl Bigney and left him with head injuries, the severity of which were still unknown. Jacob Felle strongly rejected the charge of fugitive from justice and if the FBI persisted down that path then a court of law would ultimately see him proved innocent. Before his arrest, Felle had been evading his brother-in-law, not the police, and contrary to being a flight risk, he was now actively assisting the FBI with their investigation. He would remain in New York until the investigation was concluded. The court would withhold his passport. Where could he go?

With a sour expression, the judge granted bail at nine hundred and fifty thousand dollars, and Jacob was removed to another tiny cell. With bail set at nearly a million dollars, Jacob settled in for a long wait, but less than two hours later Spelling reappeared with his wallet, belt, and his Lumix camera, hurried him down more corridors and out a back entrance where he slammed into a wall of sunshine, then into the caress of one of the most beautiful cars he'd ever seen.

"Who paid my bail?" he asked. When Spelling declined to answer, he said, "Henry Duval. It must have been. Where's my sister?"

Spelling had banged on the roof to tell the driver to haul ass.

Now he jolted awake as the Jag pulled up beside what appeared to be abandoned factory buildings. A harsh white sun ricocheted off canal water and burned Jacob's eyes.

"This is you," said the chauffeur.

In the rearview, Jacob saw aviators, a Bluetooth earpiece and clippered light-brown hair. He tried to speak, but it must have been ninety degrees in the car and his throat was parched. He managed to croak out, "Where are we?"

"Take that path to the right. And sorry about the heat, AC's a joke in these old Jags but I had to close the windows a mile back. You'll see why when you open the door."

Jacob was halfway out of the car when the stench of sewage struck him. He bent at the waist to control a heave in his gut, and when it was safe to stand, he started down the canal path. He expected to hear the Jag reverse away, but it hadn't moved by the time the path bent around the corner and brought him to a cobbled dock. The tall athletic figure of Henry Duval stood by the water, a canvas bag at his feet.

"You made it." Henry came forward with his arms wide. When he saw that Jacob had no intention of stepping into a hug, he turned the motion into an awkward handshake.

"When did you get out?" Jacob said, still trying to override the urge to vomit.

"This morning. We've all been charged with some kind of withholding information bullshit. It's just to keep us local so they can screw with us when they want to. Bail was a stretch, but what's money for, if not to get out of jail? And sorry for the tour of Manhattan. We have the dubious honor of being pursued by both the media and your brother-in-law." He waved to indicate their surroundings. "This toxic wasteland is Newton Creek. The locals call it Shit Creek. I figured no one would bother us here."

"Where's Elizabeth?"

"She wanted me to give you this." Henry slung the canvas bag to land at Jacob's feet. "The clothes are mine. You'll also find a new phone and some cash."

"You didn't answer my question."

Henry looked across the water toward Manhattan. "Your sister wants us to sit this one out in separate locations. Harder for Floyd and van Buren that way, and if they do find one of us, better that poor bastard can't give away the others."

"Didn't the FBI offer police protection?"

"You're a trusting soul."

"Don't patronize me, Henry."

Henry held up his palms. "Elizabeth's royal decree, okay? You of all people know how that goes. If you want to argue, she put her new number in the phone. The good news is that under your bail conditions you can leave the city provided you stay in New York State. My driver, Jeff, is taking you to a house in Beacon, fifty miles north of here. Jeff's ex-something-or-other, you'll be safe, and he'll drive you to your check-in at the local police station each day."

"I don't need a babysitter. I'm not scared of Floyd."

"That's exactly what Elizabeth said. So, I'll tell you what I told her. First, the media will swarm you if they get even a whiff of your whereabouts. Second—and I can't stress this enough—if you're not afraid of Floyd Shaw by now, then you haven't been paying attention."

"Is Elizabeth in the city?"

Henry's answer was an expansive hand gesture that took in the canal. "You know what's ironic? Tyrell Dixon funded his early campaigns with donations from factory bosses. In exchange, he looked the other way when they pumped chemicals into the creek." Henry held up his three-fingered left hand. "My friends and I skipped our insanely expensive school and swum off this dock as a dare. I caught a splinter and the wound got infected with toxic waste. They had to amputate. I don't want to sound callous, but I'm not sad to see Dixon gone."

"Henry, you helped my sister, and I'm grateful. But if you're not going to tell me where she is then I don't know why we're still talking."

Henry managed to arrest his smile before it slipped completely. He smoothed at his hair. "Travel safe, Jacob. And don't miss a bail check-in. A million bucks is money, even to me."

* * *

Jacob's new phone only had two numbers, Elizabeth and Spelling. He tried Elizabeth. No pick-up, no voicemail option. The Jag was halfway across the George Washington Bridge, air thundering through the open windows, when the phone rang in his lap.

"Some messages for you, Jacob," Spelling said. "Now a good time?"

"Go on." The Hudson below shimmered with sunlight.

"Your mother saw the news, is worried, call her. Elizabeth will call tonight, so keep this cell on. Aside from that, you've had three marriage proposals and a few vague threats, nothing to be concerned about. A guy in Staten Island offered to pay your mortgage. Some girl in Queens says she's ready to talk about her dead mother's legacy, and one unnamed correspondent wants you to know that she—or he—can suck a golf ball through a garden hose. Pretty standard nutjob stuff now that you're a TV star. Anything else you need from me?"

"I just sit on my arse in Beacon until the FBI finds Floyd and van Buren?"

"Think of it as a chaperoned vacation. Don't be glum, Jacob. You did good. You're out, your sister's out, and the FBI are focused on the right man."

And Elizabeth would call him later that night. He should be elated. So why did he have that butterfly-in-the-chest-cavity feeling like he'd left the oven on?

Spelling said, "Okay, gotta go. This cell's always on and I sleep light."

Two minutes later, they came off the bridge and a jolt in the Jag's suspension triggered Jacob's memory. A phone call with an angry girl who'd lost her mother and who thought Jacob had telephoned to rake up dirt on some poor adulterer.

He called Spelling back. "The girl who wants to talk about her dead mother's legacy. Did she leave a number?"

CHAPTER

71

Alex had asked for a quiet office to focus on logistics, but quiet focus wasn't Ricky Talon's style. While Pat Coombs met with the NBC security team, Talon insisted on giving Alex a tour of the TV studio. His assistant Emelda walked behind her boss like an Upper East Side nanny trailing after a high-value infant.

"This is where the producers drip bullshit into my earpiece." Talon had led them to a booth with a bank of TV monitors and audio-visual mixing boards. "You'd think this room would be bigger, right? Everyone says that."

The booth had a strip of window overlooking the auditorium, and reminded Alex of the bloodless observation annex attached to a police interview room. "Let's run it one more time," she said. "When Floyd Shaw calls, what do you tell him?"

"That I want to lick his face for saving my ratings."

"Ricky," Alex said. "We've been through this. There'll be no live broadcast. Shaw won't even make it into the building."

"Come on. Dramatic on-air takedown? You'll be famous."

"Another reason why it isn't going to happen. Ricky, you get to be the man who helped catch Floyd Shaw, or the man who refused to. Your call."

Talon slumped into a producer's chair and mimed a phone at his ear. "Mr. Shaw, your request to broadcast from the New Frontiers building in Brooklyn has been accepted. The FBI guarantees that provided you arrive unarmed, and behave in a calm and nonviolent manner, you will not be arrested until after we conduct your live television interview. When you arrive, park in the parking lot and enter the building alone. Armed FBI agents will make themselves known once you are inside."

Talon flicked his eyes at Alex, hungry for praise.

"Perfect, Ricky. Thank you. Now, we have to assume Shaw might be watching the Jumping Jack building. He'll see agents getting into position—which he'd expect—then an hour before the supposed broadcast, you arrive with one camera operator and one sound guy—in reality, two more FBI agents."

Talon was out of his chair, nervous fingers pushing filters up and down on the mixing desk. The audio-visual guys must hate his guts. "Appreciate this isn't a writers' room collab," he said, "but do we want to say *armed* agents? Shaw was adamant he didn't want to see any guns."

"He's going to see guns," Alex said.

* * *

She met Coombs at the lip of the *Talon Tonight* TV set. Her partner perched on Talon's desk wearing the same grin as when he'd told her Elizabeth Felle had walked into a police precinct.

"Pizza Suprema offering two-for-one on slices?" Alex said.

"Better even than that." Coombs presented her with his laptop. "We trawled the email servers at the TV studios where Bigney works. Guess who shows up?"

"Floyd Shaw?"

"The man himself. The first email is a response to a joke Bigney made on his TV show about the destruction of the Amazon rainforest. Something about how we should cut down all the trees so the pygmies—Bigney's word—will have nowhere to shelter and it'll force them to wear clothes like normal people do."

Alex remembered the Buick, the blue lips, the neat fade behind the ear.

"Shaw mails Bigney," Coombs said. "Says he has an eco-awareness trip planned down the Amazon and challenges Bigney to a debate on his TV show. Bigney replies, thanks but no thanks. Shaw pushes for a meeting to talk it over. Bigney doesn't take the bait. End of correspondence."

Alex took the laptop and scanned the exchange. Bigney's last email was two sentences long: *Screw you, Heartbleed. Let's see how the bunnies do without their jungle.*

"Why didn't we find this sooner, Pat?"

"Shaw didn't use his primary email. The mailbox was set up just before he initiated the conversation with Bigney, and not used since."

"Created specially. Bad plans for Bigney from the start." Alex approached the *Talon Tonight* backdrop, a panorama of the New York skyline—touching her finger against the canvas made the Freedom Tower ripple. "What are we saying? Bigney makes a bad taste joke about indigenous Amazon peoples and Shaw adds him to the kill list? As motives go . . ."

"Think Delase Carter. Piss off Floyd Shaw and you make the list. Since Benedetti and Dixon the bar keeps getting lower, but maybe that's what happens when you're mad as a frog in a jar. The others might be on the list because Shaw didn't like their hair."

"So what's Shaw's play with the emails? Get Bigney to agree to a meet in some out-of-the-way bar, then snatch him when he turns up?"

"And when Bigney refuses to meet, he switches to Plan B."

"Tracking Bigney via the SPL with the help of his buddy's girlfriend, Chloe Zhang." Alex rejoined Coombs at the lip of the stage. "But we're still assuming Floyd Shaw's pulling the strings here. Elizabeth Felle was adamant that van Buren's the driving force."

Coombs stared up into the lighting rig. Watching him scratch his hairless scalp, Alex experienced a rush of affection for her partner. When they worked well, it was two people thinking with one mind.

From behind Alex came a woodpecker noise. She turned to see Ricky Talon tapping at the glass window of the mixing studio, waving his phone in the other hand and making *Oh-my-God* faces. Floyd Shaw had called ahead of schedule.

CHAPTER

72

JACOB FLIPPED NEWS channels, trying to get comfortable on Henry's chocolate corduroy couch, a monster bag of salt-and-vinegar chips in the vee of his crotch. The occasional clunk of a barbell said that Jeff—the chaperone Henry had appointed to protect him from Floyd—was still pumping iron in Henry's garage with a view of the driveway. They'd arrived at dusk to what Jeff called Henry's winter palace, a tall Dutch-style residence on the edge of Beacon, with too many rooms and poor natural light. Jacob had made his private arrangements for later that evening while Jeff was upstairs changing for his workout.

Meanwhile, both CNN and Fox News agreed that Floyd Shaw and Roland van Buren were the most exciting fugitives since Osama Bin Laden. The NYPD was incompetent and the FBI baffled, just look at that disheveled Special Agent Bedford they had leading the case. Ricky Talon was a fool and the occupants of Talon's Ten Worst list were reaping what they, in their own unique ways, had sown. Experts were wheeled on to speculate about Floyd Shaw's state of mind, and Jacob noted a change in tone. Murder was murder, and that was *bad*, but if you could go back in time and take out Adolf Hitler in 1936 . . . ?

The back door creaked. Jeff was done working out.

Jacob fed himself a fistful of potato chips—they might have been cardboard in his mouth. CNN pivoted to Emil Hertzberg, number one on Talon's list. Hertzberg was thought to be inside his Upper East Side townhouse, surrounded by a hundred armed Jeffs. The coverage lingered on an unflattering photograph taken at a Republican donor's garden party in Savannah. Hertzberg held a glistening champagne flute and smiled at the camera. Small round eyes, long lashes, pink cheeks and plump lips . . . No wonder they called him Miss Piggy. Would Hertzberg's annual celebrity-studded Farewell to Summer yacht party go ahead? CNN said watch this space.

Overhead, the sound Jacob had been listening for: water pipes groaning as Jeff started the shower. Jacob rolled off the couch and into the kitchen where Jeff had left his jacket alongside a bag of groceries. He lifted the car keys from the jacket and scribbled a note on a scrap of takeout menu. *Business in town, back later.*

Jacob closed the garage door gently behind him.

Henry's Jaguar crouched in the dark.

CHAPTER

73

Assuming Floyd Shaw didn't earn himself a bullet in the thorax, he'd be cuffed and in the back of an FBI truck within thirty seconds of entering the Jumping Jack parking lot. In the back room of New Frontiers, Alex Bedford stared at an expensive coffee machine as she pictured Shaw pulling up in the lot—her imagination had him driving a battered Hyundai—and walking through an invisible honor guard of sniper rifles. When he was ten yards from the door, an unmarked van would seal off the parking lot exit. Two roof-mounted spotlights would flood the lot with light, and armed agents would make themselves known from all angles. Then it would be up to Shaw: cuffs or coffin.

A voice jolted Alex out of her reverie.

"Murphy wants a word."

She turned to find Coombs in the doorway. "Tell him I'll call him back in five."

"Tell him yourself. He's here."

She followed her partner into the long room. Murphy stood by the Airstream.

"Sir," Alex said. "Everything okay?"

Murphy wore a bright pink button-down shirt. The shoulders of his suit sloped at the edges and the pants broke clumsily over the tassels of black leather loafers. "All teams in place, Alex? No sign the media has wind of what we're up to?"

"So far so good. Talon's on his way in an unmarked. All he has to do is walk into the building flanked by agents carrying film equipment."

"You think Shaw's watching us?"

"I think we'd have found him. But if I'm wrong, he'll see some secretive FBI shuffling and he'll see Talon enter the Jumping Jack—exactly what he should be expecting."

Murphy nodded. "Kid gloves with Talon, okay? Creatives can be difficult to manage."

Creatives? That's why Murphy was dressed like a child auditioning for Bugsy Malone. He wanted to look his best for Ricky Talon.

Murphy lowered his voice. "Did I tell you I'm off to training academy?"

"You did not. Sorry to hear that."

"It means a supervisory post will open up." He gestured to the empty room. "Get this right, and we'll both be forgiven for chasing shadows."

And if I get it wrong?

Alex found Coombs in the corridor staring at a photograph in the gallery, a grizzled man in a woolen rollneck sweater. Stephen Allen Reynolds, sailor, whaler, soldier.

"I just googled this guy," Coombs said. "The Reynolds family owned half of Louisiana and Junior here was a playboy compared to his old man. Reynolds Senior built the family fortune *and* found time to hunt Moby Dick and lead a battalion in the Mexican-American War."

"Sailor, whaler, soldier, slaver," Alex said. She moved down the line to where Leonard Harris bared his teeth for the camera. "Interesting company you keep, Mr. Harris."

Noises filtered up from the ground floor. Alex reached the stairs in time to see Ricky Talon come through the door flanked by two FBI agents in plain clothes, one carrying a camera and the other with mic stands over his meaty shoulder.

"Where do we set up?" Talon said. "I know, I know, we're not doing the interview. But I can record a piece to camera, right? From inside the villain's lair."

"Alex." Coombs's voice from halfway up the staircase made her turn. "Hear that?"

She listened. A faint *whump, whump* came from directly overhead.

"Morons." Alex backheeled the wall. "They sent the Black Hawk up too early."

Coombs shook his head. "That's not a Hawk. Too light."

She listened to the rhythm of the blades. "If it's not us, then who the hell is it?"

CHAPTER 74

JACOB RECOGNIZED THE young woman from the description she'd given him over the phone: "Look for the shapeless goth with milk bottle glasses and skin to give a dermatologist nightmares." He joined her at the foot of the steps to the Metropolitan Museum of Art.

"Thanks for meeting," he said from inside a gray marl hood. "Do you have it?"

Naomi Perlman, daughter of the late private investigator Hannah Perlman, had one earbud in, the other dangling from its cord, hissing music. She reached into a tatty backpack and produced an envelope with an old-fashioned string and washer fastener. "After Mom died, I found this behind the water tank. Looks like she hid it along with some personal papers."

"Did you read it?"

"At the time, no. Looked like boring Mom work stuff." She arched a thick black eyebrow. "Then you called asking after one of her old case reports and said it was her chance at a legacy. I dug it out and—*whoa*—you weren't kidding when you said it could save a life."

"But you've been sitting on it since I called?"

"Not a life I particularly wanted to save—you'll see when you read it." She handed Jacob the file. "You think Floyd Shaw and this van Buren guy murdered my mom over the file?"

"It looks that way," Jacob said, resisting the urge to open it there and then on the steps of the museum.

Naomi Perlman called over her shoulder as she walked away. "If this helps find your brother-in-law, make sure it has Mom's name on it, okay?"

Jacob checked his phone as he jogged back to where he'd left Henry's Jag parked under an ash tree. Four missed calls from Elizabeth—she must have heard he'd absconded from Beacon. Resting Hannah Perlman's report against the steering wheel, he began to read about the Clearwater Community Nursing Home fire.

Five pages in, he'd learned nothing new. His phone vibrated again. Elizabeth again. He let it ring and flipped to the back of the report. The last sheaf of stapled pages provided a summary of Perlman's investigation timeline.

> Feb. 1—Interview Kelly-Anne Pinstock; Pinstock claims no prior knowledge of faulty fire doors and no responsibility for fire/deaths.
>
> Feb. 9—Interview Elmhurst employee from Delaware office—Stevie Williams—at Rikers Island prison. Williams jailed for installing low standard fire doors. Bitter at being made "fall guy." Won't say more.
>
> Feb. 10—Obtain copy of official report on nursing home fire. Fire service contact suggests (off record) that I look into fire safety certs.
>
> Feb. 13—Connect with my contact at city hall. Off-record confirmation that fire cert fraud is "worst kept secret in local government"; obtain copy of fire certificate for Clearwater Comm Nurse Home.
>
> Feb. 14—Back to Rikers Island. Second interview with Stevie Williams. Williams confirms cert fraud is commonplace and offers to trade name of city hall official involved, in return for keeping his name out of it. I agree (verbal, non-binding). Williams names Tyrell Dixon.
>
> Asked why he didn't share this with the police, Williams says bad enough being in jail without a contract on his head.

> Feb. 15—Obtain company information and annual reports for Elmhurst Realty. Luca Benedetti is beneficial owner.
> Note that company records show drop in employee numbers around time of fire.
> Feb. 16—Interview former nurse at nursing home. Orderly confirms low staffing, and remembers overworked staff forgetting to check fire-resistant bedroom doors were closed. Also suggests low staff-to-resident ratio inhibited evacuation on night of fire.
> Feb. 18—Confront Kelly-Anne Pinstock with low staffing numbers as contributing factor to deaths. Pinstock claims her hand was forced by parent company, Apex Equity Partners, who demanded 45% staffing reduction three/four months before fire.

Jacob turned the page to find a handwritten flowchart. Clearwater Community Nursing Home P.C. connected to Apex Equity Partners L.P., which connected to Vision Inc. Hannah Perlman had added a handwritten footnote: *Companies owned by Apex Equity were subject to 45% staff cuts, mandated by parent company, Vision Inc. Beneficial owner of Vision Inc.: Emil Hertzberg.*

Jacob exhaled—*whoosh*. Emil Hertzberg, number one on Talon's list, had ordered the staffing cuts that contributed to Leonard Harris's death.

It took another ten minutes to be sure there were no other names in the report. On the inside cover he found a handwritten note from Perlman.

> This note to serve as a written record that while this report was compiled for a private client, the nature of the findings mean that I am compelled under license as a Private Investigator to share this information with the NYPD. This goes against our initial agreement, but findings are too big to ignore. Ramifications enormous. Best, Hannah Perlman

Jacob closed the file. Perlman had written her own suicide note, she just hadn't known it at the time. His phone buzzed again. This time he answered.

"You stole Henry's car?" Tornado warning in Elizabeth's tone. "You're lucky he didn't report you to the police."

"Borrowed it. Elizabeth, I have Hannah Perlman's report."

A beat, then, "You're kidding me. How—? Never mind. What does it say?"

"Emil Herzberg is named alongside Benedetti and Dixon. His staffing cuts meant they couldn't get the residents out of the burning nursing home fast enough."

"Herzberg." Another beat. "Did you tell that FBI agent you've got the hots for?"

"Not yet."

"Call her now. Floyd might be using Ricky Talon as a distraction."

"Ricky Talon?"

"You haven't heard? It's all over the news. Floyd offered Talon a secret televised confession at New Frontiers and somehow the press got hold of it. New Frontiers is swarming with FBI and TV crews."

"The FBI would never let an interview go ahead with a murder suspect."

"I guess they figure Floyd's dumb enough to think they might. A month ago, I'd have agreed with them. Where are you now?"

"Sitting in the Jag on Madison Avenue, near the Met."

"Okay—change of plan. Meet me on the slipway at the Boat Basin marina on 79th Street. Your FBI agent buddy will be at New Frontiers, and the best thing we can do right now is get this report into her hands."

"Shouldn't I call it in first?"

"The FBI are tied up with Floyd and every New York television network. Meanwhile, I want to read this report before the FBI weaponizes it against us. Oh, and bring your camera."

"You hate when I film."

"I know you trust this Bedford woman, but I want a record of the conversation. Besides, you found the report. This is your story, now. You can't miss the final scene."

CHAPTER

75

THE ROTOR BLADES cutting air above the Jumping Jack Power Plant belonged not to an FBI Black Hawk, but to a long-range Bell 206 helicopter operated by ABC Television. Within minutes of the chopper appearing, TV trucks from all the major networks converged on the Jumping Jack. Alex and Coombs watched from an upstairs window as reporters jostled FBI agents who struggled to hold a perimeter at the edge of the parking lot.

"Why would Shaw set this up and then leak it to the press?" Alex said.

"So he can go out in a blaze of very public glory?" Coombs didn't sound convinced.

Alex slapped a palm against the glass window. "Get the Black Hawk up, clear the sky. All agents to withdraw."

"Want me to have Ricky Talon escorted back to 30 Rock?"

Alex's stomach tightened. "Not just yet."

She found Talon in the long room, doing a piece to camera.

"Was it you?" She was in his face, close enough to make him step back.

"Hey, we're filming here," Talon started to say, before he clocked the look on Alex's face. "I didn't tell anyone, I promise. I don't know who leaked." A flush rose from his neck to his hairline. "This will *destroy* me. It looks like I threw a party and nobody showed."

"Alex," someone called out.

Alex turned to see Murphy walking toward her, an expression on his face that she couldn't read. Behind Murphy, Pat Coombs stood between two agents. She couldn't read her partner's face either.

"It's Pat," Murphy said.

She looked at him, uncomprehending. Over Murphy's shoulder, she saw Pat shuffle out of the room, flanked by the two agents.

"Pat Coombs has been leaking our investigation to the media."

Alex felt the walls of New Frontiers bend. "Bullshit. Not Pat."

"Internal Affairs have been on to him for a while. He remortgaged twice in the last two years and it flagged. I only just found out. It's why I came down in person."

"Not Pat," she said again.

Alex's phone buzzed. The perimeter team lead.

"Agent Bedford, marine service just picked up a two-seater powerboat leaving Gowanus Bay, heading our way like a bullet. Hard to see out there, but we have what looks like two men in the cockpit. Could be Shaw and van Buren. Please advise."

CHAPTER

76

THE CHAMPAGNE RESTS on ice, the canapés are arranged in the galley, your staff are waiting on deck, and you, Emil Hertzberg—cocooned within the polished walnut, sparkling chrome and soft leather of the *Bella Figura*—need to make a decision. Farewell to Summer is more than a yacht party you throw each year, it's a statement, a gilt-edged reminder of why you are not to be messed with.

From your cabin window, you see the winking lights of the cruiser with its cargo of politicians, CEOs, media moguls, one justice of the Supreme Court, movie stars, a royal or three—your *friends* gathered at the Manhattan Yacht Club waiting for the green light to come aboard. They have no more love for you than you for them, but like protects like. You should give up your annual show of power because some crazy assholes put you at the top of a kill list?

Your security team—of course—told you to cancel. The police told you to cancel. Your lawyer told you to cancel. Maybe they're right. After all, you didn't get this far by taking unnecessary risks. And there's political capital in calling it off at the last minute—*Can't our idiot governor safeguard the city's most prominent citizens at a cocktail party?* Also . . . *wicked Emil* . . . wouldn't it be fun to send a cruiser-full of distinguished guests home with no supper?

"I assume we're going ahead with the party, sir?" says a male voice behind you.

You didn't hear the door, with these ex-special forces ghouls you rarely do. The hallway light silhouettes the short, powerful figure of your security coordinator, Tommy, ex-Green Beret from Utah, fists like engine blocks.

"Tommy, come in. How's Maria?" Maria is Tommy's fat wife with a thyroid problem. You've found it pays to remember details about your more valuable employees.

"Uh, good, they've balanced up her meds a little better. We're ready for the cruiser, sir. We can bring the guests on two at a time so we can scan for weapons and verify ID. My guys are in position. Just say the word."

As Tommy steps into the light, you can't help but imagine those enormous hands at your neck. This man kicked down doors in Afghanistan and now he babysits soft-bellied city rats in three-thousand-dollar suits. You look at Tommy and you think about his ferocious security team, and you think about the minimum-wage waiters and cooks and cleaners all lined up on deck awaiting your approval like a Victorian house staff, and you know the media morons are wrong when they call you a poster boy for the widening equality gap. It's not a gap, it's a piece of elastic, stretched beyond breaking and still stretching. One day the elastic will snap with a sound like a rifle shot, followed by a deathly silence, then carnage. And the fact that you remembered your employee's wife's thyroid problem will count for nothing.

"Why assume?" you ask Tommy.

"Sir?"

"You said you *assume* we're green-lighting the party?"

Tommy wears an expression like a cow staring into a bush. "You've seen the news? Floyd Shaw's busy on the far side of Brooklyn. According to the TV coverage, he's due to make a live confession, and right now he's driving a speedboat straight at the FBI."

CHAPTER

77

Jacob lowered the window of Henry's Jag and warm air buffeted his cheek. Even now, as he headed for the marina to meet his sister, Floyd might be approaching the Jumping Jack building, preparing for his live broadcast, a final moment in the spotlight that the FBI would never allow to happen. Jacob's chest tightened.

The Floyd Shaw he knew just wasn't that naïve.

Jacob tasted salt and shipping diesel in the wind outside the car. He had a sense of a memory—vivid, filled with flavor—that threatened to materialize, but remained just out of reach. He turned on the radio and flipped channels until he found a news station.

Maybe Floyd *was* that naïve, because the news announcer had just learned of a possible sighting, two men in a fast boat off the west Brooklyn coast. Jacob pictured Floyd behind the wheel, the hard sunburned face of van Buren beside him, the bounce of the boat, spray smashing against Plexiglass. What could they hope to achieve except a bloody wet death in front of the cameras?

In related news, the radio announcer confirmed that Emil Hertzberg's annual Farewell to Summer party on the *Bella Figura* would go ahead as planned. Hertzberg was determined to show the world he wasn't afraid of Shaw, and why not, when the *Bella Figura* was a fortress with a private security army and an ocean for a moat? No one boarded that yacht without Miss Piggy's say-so, and if they somehow did, there was little chance they'd get off alive.

Miss Piggy, Jacob thought. *Emil Hertzberg.*

Claude's voice in his head: "Do we forget whore salad and wait for sour lime?"

Dallas Johncock with his long toothy face and mane of hair.

Jacob aged seven standing in the doorway to his sister's bedroom. Elizabeth and her friends curled on Elizabeth's bed in their pajamas. Elizabeth letting Jacob know in their special way which one of her friends she was angry with that day. The other girls laughing. Someone saying, "Was that meant to be Italian?"

Jacob on the subway platform, Elizabeth turning toward the oncoming train. "You know what's going on. You're just too blind to see it."

A truck horn blared and the memory that had been out of reach arrived in his mind fully formed, and with the force of knowledge you realize you've had all along. Jacob almost swerved the car into the concrete barrier. Up ahead, taillights glowed—red wounds bleeding into the dark. Jacob regained control of the car, and after a mile he could breathe again. Steering with one hand, he found the number he needed in his phone. His finger hovered over the call button, then he threw the phone down on the seat. Once he made the call, it was all over.

* * *

He didn't see the sailboat until a hulking outline separated itself from the darkness twenty feet from the jetty, forming slowly into triangle sails and a deep hull. Now he heard the lap of displaced water against wooden pilings, the creak of a rope pulled taught. The boat pushed a breeze of rust and salt ahead of its prow, approaching at an angle until it came to rest with a fender squeak no louder than a seagull cry, the name *Ocean Spray* level with Jacob's eyes.

Whump. Something landed at Jacob's feet. Another *whump*, further up the jetty.

"Figure-eight around the cleats," Elizabeth said from the dark bow.

Jacob wrapped the first rope over the horns of the nearest cleat and walked ten paces to secure the second. He straightened to find Elizabeth at the rail, feet planted wide on deck, red tracksuit and a red scarf covering her cropped hair.

"Are you sailing this solo?" Jacob said. "With your wrist like that?"

"I've managed bigger." She reached down with her unbandaged hand to pull Jacob on deck. "I just need to pack the sails and we can head. Any news on Floyd and that speedboat?"

"Last I heard the boat was heading for New Frontiers. The radio jock said the FBI have a blackout in place. The TV crews can't get close enough to see what's going on."

In the yellow wash of a bulkhead lamp, Elizabeth looked younger than her thirty-seven years. "We'll head out that way—see if we can find your Agent Bedford. I'll read the Clearwater report in the car."

She turned her back on Jacob and started to tug at sail covers. "Do me a favor and grab my bag from the galley," she said. "I only need a minute here."

Jacob paused at the entrance hatch to the lower deck. He checked his sister still had her back turned before he pulled out his phone and hit send on the text he'd composed in the car. Setting the phone to silent, he tucked it under a pile of canvas seat covers, then hit record on the Lumix around his neck.

Light broke from the hatch as Jacob slid back the cover. The steps were so sheer he had to back his way down. *Don't you usually climb up a ladder to reach the noose?* His skin shivered as he reached the final step, knowing what he'd see when he turned around.

Floyd sat cross-legged on the floor like a child ready for a story, his hands bound in front of him with plastic ties. At the back of the galley, Claude Lemieux stood with his shoulders against a wooden door. Behind Floyd, Henry Duval rested on his haunches at one end of a bench and at the other end sat Chloe Zhang. She pushed her pink bangs from her eyes and gave Jacob a smile that chilled his bones.

Floyd mouthed a single word at Jacob. "Run."

CHAPTER

78

ALEX PEERED INTO the darkness from dockside, trying not to think about Pat Coombs—*I knew something was wrong. Why didn't you tell me you needed money? Why didn't I make you tell me?*—trying instead to figure out which of the tiny bobbing red, white, and green lights represented the speedboat that the marine service had confirmed was heading their way with two men behind the wheel.

Beside Alex, an FBI agent relayed the information coming into her earpiece. "Target is a two-seater Bayliner. *There.*" Pointing to a tiny green spark. "We have a police launch standing by, but a Bayliner can leave our launches for dead. Unless we blow them out of the water, they're getting through."

Alex watched the green spark grow brighter and larger. "They'll use the pier to come ashore. Stay out of sight. We'll take them when they hit dry land."

She watched from behind a concrete stanchion as the sleek powerboat approached. Two men in the cockpit, both wearing sailing caps, their faces obscured. As the boat came alongside the pier, she saw the man behind the wheel retrieve something from a bag at his feet.

"Firearm," Alex shouted.

Dazzling spotlights flooded the speedboat. Screaming FBI voices told the man behind the wheel to *drop his fucking weapon now.* The man fell back into his seat and the object in his hand bounced off the powerboat's curved hood, lighting up in a perfect iPad-sized rectangle before it slid down into the water. The other man threw up his hands. Alex could see their faces now. No Floyd Shaw, no Roland van Buren.

"What's that on their shirts?" Alex barked at the agent closest to the boat.

"Some kind of logo," the agent called back. "Luxe Marine Boat Delivery."

Her phone buzzed with an incoming call. "This is Agent Bedford."

"Agent Bedford? Raul DeToro, FBI political liaison."

Jesus, that was fast.

"Is this about Pat Coombs?" Alex said. "Why don't you save us all time and trouble and just run with 'Corrupt clueless FBI screws up again?'"

"Huh? No, ma'am. We just got a call from Senator Duval's office. He's reporting a break-in at his property in Bonneauville, just outside Gettysburg. I thought you'd want to know."

Alex watched as FBI agents hauled the two Luxe Marine Boat Delivery employees onto the pier, their hands already cuffed. "The senator's silverware isn't my number one concern right now," she said.

"Not silverware, ma'am. Believe me, you need to know what was stolen."

Alex's phone buzzed again. A text that chilled the breath in her lungs.

She turned to the agent with the earpiece. "How far away is that police launch?"

CHAPTER

79

B ELOW DECK ON the *Ocean Spray*, Henry Duval stooped to accommodate his long frame under the wooden ceiling as he held out his three-fingered hand. His other hand dangled a chrome pistol, its snub barrel pointed at the floor.

"Phone, please, Jacob."

Jacob faced a narrow galley kitchen, a cooking hob on the starboard side and a bench seat to port. Floyd, docile as a Labrador, sat pretzel-legged on the floor with his bound hands in his lap, gazing at Jacob with moist brown eyes. Claude blocked a door that led into the bow, and Chloe watched him steadily from her seat on the bench.

"You switch sides?" Jacob said to Chloe. "Or you were Elizabeth's all along?"

Chloe smiled back as if it was a great question. "Do you have *any* idea how disgusting it was sharing a bed with Roland van Buren? The things we do for love, even unrequited love."

"You're in love with my sister?"

"It's no secret—I'm not ashamed. I met Elizabeth at a Pride march. I told her she looked hot. She told me I looked lost. She was at Pride in solidarity, she said, because people who want to make a difference should stick together. She was right." Chloe dabbed her eyes with a sleeve. "Thanks to Elizabeth, I *am* making a difference. She rescued me. Claude and Henry too. We were all just lost, angry kids looking for something to damage. Elizabeth gave us purpose. Your sister rescued us all from ourselves."

Jacob turned to Floyd. "Did they take you at Red Hook after they killed Bigney?"

Floyd blinked back at him.

Jacob said to Henry, "Looks like you're the man in the light. At least, you're the one she lets play with the gun."

"Phone, please," Henry repeated.

"I left it in the car." The boat leaned gently to the seaward side. Elizabeth was casting off from the jetty. "How long to the *Bella Figura*?"

Henry smiled without warmth. "Chloe, check that Jacob's telling the truth."

Chloe rose from her bench to pat Jacob down with firm hands, helping herself to his wallet and the keys to Henry's Jag. "No cell."

A waft of diesel rose from the bow as the engine coughed into life. With his gun hand, Henry waved Jacob toward the ladder. "Upstairs."

* * *

The deck gleamed under a wash of moonlight. Elizabeth had the wheel in a glass-sided wheelhouse and Henry herded everyone inside, keeping Jacob and Floyd together ahead of him. Stars glittered in the clear night, and both banks of the Hudson sparkled as the boat carved through the water. Elizabeth's pale hands gripped the wheel, the bandage missing from her wrist.

"You healed up fast," Jacob said.

"And *you* cracked the code." She sounded happy as a child. "I told Henry you would."

"Whore salad and sour lime," Jacob said. "It took me a minute."

"What's that?" Claude shifted from sneaker to sneaker.

"They don't know?" Jacob said to Elizabeth.

She shrugged. "Henry and Chloe know. I didn't get around to telling Claude."

"Didn't get *around*?" Claude kicked with his heel and the window behind him rattled. "What do they know that I don't?"

"They know that you misheard whore salad and sour lime," Jacob said. "Just like I did. You thought they were random code words for Elizabeth's targets, but it's a secret language from when she and I were children."

"You're kidding me," Claude said under his breath.

"Take a person's first name and run it backward," Jacob said. "Add the animal they most resemble to the front. Dallas Johncock, long face, big teeth. *Horse*. Dallas backward. *Sallad*. Horse Salad. Emil Hertzberg, Miss Piggy, a female pig, then Emil backward. Sow Lime."

Claude hissed at Elizabeth. "Ten out of ten for messed up. Why didn't you tell me?"

"She doesn't trust you," Jacob said. "She thinks you're a useful idiot. Do you know this is all about personal revenge, not some grand statement to the world?"

Elizabeth answered first. "It's one in service of the other. So many bad people in this stinking city, and Leonard's death helped me select a few to make an example of. If only all evil men could make amends as they shut the door behind them."

Jacob's gut lurched with the tilt of the boat. "What's tonight's plan, Claude? Or did they keep that from you too?"

"Leave him alone." Chloe lifted her head, her skin translucent in the moonlight. "We're not you, Jacob. We don't need to know everything all the time."

"Here's something I know, Claude," Jacob said. "I know why Herzberg has to be last."

"This won't do you any good," Elizabeth said.

"She left him for last, Claude, because Hertzberg is a suicide mission. How will you do it, Elizabeth? Storm the boat and try to get to Hertzberg before his security detail blows you back into the water? Ram his yacht and hope he drowns before you do?"

"You'll never make a mission planner, Jacob." Elizabeth sounded almost amused.

"Ask her, Claude," Jacob said. "Ask how she plans to get you out of this one alive."

Claude's head began to nod in rapid jerky beats. "What's in the crates, Henry?"

Henry dismissed the question with a wave of his pistol. "I told you. Provisions for when we head up the coast."

"I loaded five wooden crates onto the deck, all with the lids nailed down." Claude's green eyes were shot through with yellow moonlight. "What's in the fucking crates, Henry?"

"We're nearly there," Elizabeth said. "Won't do any harm to tell them how you really lost your finger, Henry."

Henry shifted his feet so the pistol at his thigh could now cover Claude as well as Jacob and Floyd. "When I was twelve years old, a Civil War reenactment musket fired while my beloved father was showing me how to prime the pan. He made me tell the doctors that it was my own fault. The whole thing was hushed up, of course."

"What's that got to do with anything?" Claude's voice was high and thin.

"Black powder," Henry said with a smile. "Raw gunpowder used in reenactments to fire cannon and muskets. My father keeps more than enough to blow up a house, a bridge, even a yacht if you know where the fuel tanks are located."

"We're going to die," Claude said to no one in particular.

"You could have died climbing the Burj Khalifa," Chloe said. "Elizabeth could have drowned alone in the middle of the Pacific. And for what? We've all risked our lives to satisfy a selfish urge—it's what we do. But this is different. This *matters*."

The *Ocean Spray* leaned into the turn and again Jacob's stomach lurched. A bank of glittering lights came into view. He turned to Claude. "You don't have to do what she says."

"Two minutes to go." Elizabeth pulled the wheel to the port side. Claude licked dry lips.

"She lied to you," Jacob said. "You have a choice."

"They don't want choice," Elizabeth said. "They want clarity."

Claude seemed frozen in time.

"Henry can't shoot us all," Jacob pleaded. "We decide how this ends."

"Claude won't help you," Henry said. "He knows we have to pay for what we've done—we all know that. Confession is a powerful rite, Jacob. It can bring about the most remarkable change of heart, make a man do the most unlikely things. What we do tonight is our confession—the world will know what we've done—and when we sail into the hull of the *Bella Figura* and ignite the powder, it will be our redemption."

"And yours, Jacob." Elizabeth spoke without turning from the wheel. "We couldn't have done this without you."

"This is *nothing* to do with me."

She gave him a flash of smile over her shoulder. "Montauk Yacht Club is also a boatyard. The *Bella Figura* had a refit the year before Hertzberg bought her. While you were distracting the receptionist by asking for dinner recommendations, I was back in their office filing cabinet learning where the *Bella*'s primary fuel tanks are located. Then there's the fine job you did convincing the FBI that this was all Floyd's doing."

A weight settled in Jacob's stomach. "You're insane."

"Define insane."

"There are innocent people on Hertzberg's boat."

"Define innocent." Elizabeth stared out into the night. "Crooked politicians and judges? Heartless bankers? Hypocrite movie stars? Leonard was the best of us, and if a man like Leonard can die the way he did, then nothing's right in this world. One minute to go."

"The wait staff," Jacob said. "The security guards. Ordinary people."

Elizabeth said, "Henry, I'm going to hand you the wheel. Anyone moves, shoot them. I'll be on deck." She gave Henry a sweet smile. "And thank you, Henry, for everything."

Jacob grabbed his brother-in-law by the shoulders. He might have been handling wet clay. "Floyd, I know you can hear me. You can't let this happen."

Floyd's eyes flickered into life and the muscles bunched along his jaw. Then the puffy features sagged again.

Elizabeth gave Jacob a look he hadn't seen since they were children. *I'm your sister, trust me.* "You took control of the narrative, I'm proud of you," she said. "Today is our statement to the world, and I'm glad you're part of it. I'd ask you to film, but I doubt your camera will make it out the other side."

"You hear that, Claude?" Jacob said. "Nothing makes it out the other side."

Claude covered his face, muttering into his palms.

"You tried, Jacob," Elizabeth said. "But now it's time."

Henry squeezed past Elizabeth to take the wheel. To pass he had to raise his gun above his head, and two things happened. Without warning, Floyd launched himself at Henry, his bound hands clubbing down on Henry's head. In the same moment, Jacob dived for the doorway, shoving Elizabeth aside as he stumbled out on deck. A cracking sound chased him through the door, too loud to not be a gunshot, followed by a scream that could only be Floyd.

Two hundred yards ahead of the *Ocean Spray*, a yacht hull rose out of the black water, deck lights sparkling like champagne bubbles, the faint trace of music in the wind.

Jacob hurled himself across the deck, slipped and landed on his knees, clambered forward as the *Ocean Spray* cut a relentless passage through the water. Wooden crates, each the size of a case of wine, rested against the stern rail. Jacob got his fingers under the nearest box to lever it off the ground. It took all his strength to heave it onto the rail and over the side. The splash was lost in the bellowing from Jacob's own lungs. He had his fingers under the second box when footsteps echoed on the deck behind him.

Claude landed with a gymnast's grace in front of Jacob. His silver tears glinted in the moonlight.

"Take the box at the far end," Jacob yelled. "The powder won't survive seawater."

Jacob didn't see the wooden baton in Claude's hand until it arced down toward his temple. He dropped his shoulder, trying to slip the blow, but Claude was faster. As Jacob's world went dark, Elizabeth appeared in the wheelhouse doorway, a bright orange flare gun in her hand.

CHAPTER

80

YOU STAND IN the prow, Manhattan across the water, preferring to gaze at the city lights than watch those fat lumps guzzle your champagne and swallow your canapés. And they call *you* the pig? Miss Piggy. Ridiculous. You're an ugly man—who cares? Your women aren't paid to look at your face. They're too busy zooming in and out of your belly button.

Speaking of which, a waitress caught your eye. She must be eighteen if she's serving alcohol, but she looks younger and you didn't arrange any alternative entertainment . . . You'll ask Paula, your chief of staff, to whisper in her ear, see if the girl's amenable to a little extra cash.

Here comes Paula now, with her earnest waddle and her pinched efficient face.

"Paula, darling, I have a little ask—"

She cuts you off. "Coast Guard just called. We have to evacuate."

"What are you talking about?"

"The RIB's standing by. We need to go. The police may not get here in time."

"In time for what?"

Your answer is a sound like snapping timber from the water off the *Bella Figura*'s stern. You peer over the rail as a shape forms in the darkness, a sailboat less than a hundred yards away and running on its engine with no lights. Twin masts, sails furled, the prow pointed at the exact center of your hull. It's coming straight at you.

It's them. Somehow you know it's them.

The sailboat swells in size as it approaches. Paula tugs your sleeve, but you're frozen at the rail.

Blue light on water as a police launch appears from the north, bisecting the water between the sailboat and your beloved *Bella Figura*. The *badda-badda* of a helicopter swoops overhead, and you duck instinctively. The police launch glides into place to block the approaching sailboat. The sailboat yaws east. More launches appear. The sailboat pulls around—churning circles in the water. The helicopter drops low. The sailboat is surrounded. In the lit interior of the helicopter, a police marksman leans out in a harness. The launches forge a ring around the sailboat, but they don't approach.

"What are you waiting for?" you scream into the wind.

A spotlight from the chopper picks out four figures on the sailboat. Two disappear inside the wheelhouse, leaving a tall man and a woman on deck. The tall man aims a pistol into the beam from the helicopter. A flash of gold from the helicopter is followed by another sound like timber snapping. The tall man falls back onto the deck.

The woman also holds a gun of some kind. She aims into the sky, but away from the helicopter. The night explodes in a cascade of red fire. A flare gun. She reloads and points the muzzle at something at her feet.

Still the police launches won't approach the sailboat.

Why didn't they shoot her when she was reloading the flare?

Megaphones scream. The woman with the flare screams back, but her words are lost in the wind. One of the police launches breaks from the cordon. A single figure stands on the deck of the police launch, another woman, this one wearing a bulky life jacket, her empty hands high in the air.

The police launch comes alongside the sailboat. The women talk. The woman with the flare gun keeps it pointed at something between her feet. The chopper circles overhead. The marksman's rifle never wavers.

Still they talk. Eventually, the woman in the life jacket makes a signal to the helicopter—urgent, demanding. The helicopter peels away. The woman in the life jacket reaches up to grab the rail of the sailboat. The other woman draws back her arm and flings the flare gun into the sea, then reaches down to help the woman in the life jacket climb aboard.

A strong hand grips your arm. Tommy, your security manager. "Let's get you inside."

CHAPTER

81

Morning on the Williamsburg Bridge into Brooklyn, supposedly post–rush hour but no one told the traffic. Alex drove the FBI-issue Corolla despite her knee, her leg rigid as a walking stick over the gas. She got in lane for the Brooklyn-Queens Expressway, heading north toward Rikers Island as Jacqueline du Pré's carefree cello softened the atmosphere in the car. Beside her, Jacob Felle brought his cuffed hands to the window button to let in warm gritty air.

She turned the volume low enough to talk. "Okay there?"

"Very civilized," he said. "I expected a cage in the back of a patrol car."

"I can arrange a cage for the return trip." Alex slid into the overtaking lane to pass a truck grimed in dirt. "How's your head?"

Felle touched the pulpy bruise over his right eye. "No lasting damage."

"For what it's worth," she said, "I'm sorry about your brother-in-law."

Jacob Felle had woken in an ambulance to learn that Floyd Shaw lay in the mortuary with Henry's bullet lodged in his heart. Henry had suffered a similar fate moments later on the deck of the *Ocean Spray*, when a sharpshooter's .308 bullet tore through his throat. Jacob's first question had been, *What about Elizabeth?*

"Well?" He sank down into the car seat. "What do you want to know that you couldn't ask in there? I assume FBI special agents don't typically pull escort duty."

Smart. But she knew that already.

"I thought you might have questions," she said. "Then I have one for you."

"Questions." Felle kept his face to the window. "Here's one I know the answer to. Elizabeth won't come out, will she?"

"Six bodies, Jacob. Could have been a hundred more. Be glad New York State doesn't have the death penalty."

"Benedetti, Dixon, Johncock, Bigney, and Hannah Perlman. That's five bodies."

"We found Roland van Buren in the trunk of his Mercedes in a garage in Gowanus."

"Van Buren. How does he fit?"

"He was your brother-in-law's coke supply. Van Buren started dealing when his media career collapsed, and he used Floyd's bedroom to bag up his deals. He was part of Elizabeth's plan from the start, that's why she had Chloe Zhang pick him up. She needed Floyd to have a credible accomplice. After Floyd leaves to meet your sister in Red Hook, van Buren gets an anonymous call telling him the cops are on their way. He takes his stash to the garage and they grab him there. While we're filling in warrant forms and polishing our nightsticks, Duval's vacuum-wrapping van Buren's body for the trunk."

The traffic was moving now, Brooklyn unfolding below the expressway.

"Why didn't Floyd just tell me what was going on?" Felle said to the window.

"We can't ask him, so we'll never know for sure, but I suspect he was trying to protect your sister, just like you were. He knew Elizabeth had commissioned the report, he knew she was behind the murders, but he didn't dare tell you the truth in case you came to us, or dismissed him as a coke-addled lunatic." Alex paused. "Or maybe . . ."

"Or maybe he was scared of what Elizabeth would do to me if she knew I knew."

"It's possible. So he prodded you and gave you little clues. Perhaps he thought that just seeing her brother in person would be enough to jar her out of her madness."

"Some hope." Felle's cuffed hands lifted to the bruise over his eye. "Why share all this with me?"

Alex decided not to answer that one yet. "If it helps, Elizabeth never wanted you involved. I think that's why she cut ties four years ago. She knew what was coming."

"Except I did get involved," he said. "I insisted."

"And Elizabeth's smart and adaptable enough to take advantage. She gets you to film Claude so she can drop the Delase Carter nugget for us to find. Her genius move was using you to convince us that Floyd was framing her, not the other way round. Henry called in the anonymous tip that sent us to Floyd's apartment while you were there—and you set us onto Floyd."

Another long silence as they passed the off-ramp for the 25A road to Citi Field. William had taken Alex to a Mets game years ago, one of the most tedious experiences of her life, bless his heart. William occupied her head even more than usual this morning.

"I still don't get it," Felle said. "It was Floyd who pitched the list, not Elizabeth."

"Floyd's biggest crime was having thirty IQ points less than his wife. Elizabeth convinced Floyd the concept would sound better coming from someone with his television background. Floyd agreed, to keep her happy. A month later, he sees Benedetti and the other names on *Talon Tonight* and knows he's been duped."

"Why publicize the list at all?" Felle said. "Why draw attention?"

"I thought you'd have worked that out already," Alex said.

Felle stared at his hands. Half a mile later, he said, "Distraction. She knew you'd connect the victims to Leonard Harris. Talon's list gave you a different connection to chase."

"Suicide pact, crazy guy targets random list, with a handful of female red herrings to keep us all guessing . . . she didn't need to fool us forever, just until her big finale, Hertzberg's Farewell to Summer yacht party."

"So framing Floyd was always the plan?"

"Of course." Alex took the off-ramp onto 81st Street, square brick houses and tidy lawns—suburbia with all its gentle menace. "We were meant to find Bigney murdered and Floyd dead by his own hand, leaving a suicide note saying his work was done. The FBI has everything it needs to close the case, the rest of the list breathes a sigh of relief and Emil Hertzberg thinks it's safe to go ahead with Farewell to Summer."

Bitterness in Felle's voice. "Except I spoil the plan."

"Claude told me he pulled the blow when he hit you in Red Hook. He likes you. Before he could check if you were breathing, headlights appeared at the end of the street. Just a random car passing, but they panicked. Ten seconds later they're driving Floyd to a boat Henry had stashed in some two-bit marina, and you're waking in your own vomit. They even forgot to leave Bigney's redemption letter at the scene—a list of high-profile secret donors to his racist TV channel."

"And now they need another way to make Hertzberg think he's safe," Felle said. "So Floyd Shaw offers a live televised confession on the night of the yacht party."

"A voice analysis of the call made to Ricky Talon matched Henry Duval's voice from his police interview. Like I said, Elizabeth's smart and she thinks fast. The speedboat delivery kept us guessing right up to the last second."

"Why tell me all this?" Felle asked again as they hit the Rikers Island Bridge.

Alex still chose not to answer that one.

"The thing is, Jacob, Elizabeth was a great planner, but she and her friends were amateurs when it comes to killing. On their first outing, Claude left one of his pitons on the roof by mistake. After your visit, then mine . . . it shook them into making more errors. Claude says they had to dump the Sharpie used for Johncock's suicide note because Chloe chewed on it."

The security gates for the Rose M. Singer Center women's facility came into view. A cluster of TV trucks huddled by the entrance. Alex pulled in fifty yards from the gate so the news crews couldn't identify her or her passenger. She killed the engine.

Felle gave her a long, cool look that seemed to last minutes. "What did you say to Elizabeth that made her drop the flare gun?" he said.

"You can ask her yourself in a moment."

"I'm asking you."

Alex weighed her answer and opted for honesty. "I told her she'd have plenty of opportunity to take her own life in jail. But she didn't need to take yours too."

Felle winced, then his features set hard. "No. She wanted me to die with her."

"Not without purpose." Alex reached into the glove compartment and pulled out the camera she'd retrieved from the evidence bay. "The media will say she's crazy, but your sister believed she was doing the right thing. And for what it's worth, I think she really wanted to keep you out of it. Problem is, you're as stubborn as her." Alex handed Felle the camera. "A lot of what we know comes from your footage. You knew you'd most likely die if you got on that boat, but you went anyway. You saved lives."

Felle cradled the camera in his cuffed hands. "I can't do anything with this now."

Not true, and they both knew it. Felle had the whole story captured in that small box in his lap. Within a year, he might be sitting in a soft chair on a show like *Talon Tonight*.

"You said you had a question for me," he said.

Alex stared through the windshield. The boxy facade of the women's prison could have been a bowling alley if not for glimpses of barbed wire behind white fence slats. "Why text me?" she said. "And why hide your phone so we could track it?"

"Does it matter? You got what you wanted."

"It matters if I want to sleep again. Your sister could have blown up Hertzberg's boat while I was in the wrong place, waiting to arrest the wrong person. I'm getting slapped on the back so hard I can taste my collarbone, but without your text message a hundred people would be dead and I'd be hanging in an FBI gibbet in the Federal Plaza lobby."

Felle stared at the camera in his hands—good hands, she noticed. "I wanted it to be you."

"I don't understand."

"If I couldn't stop her, the police would have to. I saw the footage of you at the plaza with the cardinal. You could have shot the giant with the gun. You chose not to and he's still alive. So is my sister. For now, at least."

Alex on the deck of the police launch, blasted by salt spray and knifing wind, screaming into her radio to hold fire, ignoring the frantic warnings in her earpiece as she stared up into the burning eyes of Elizabeth Felle.

She settled back in the car seat as a familiar throb started in her temples. She had no Excedrin in her bag, but never mind. Her migraines had arrived on the same train that carried William away and she'd live with them a while longer. She checked her phone. One missed call from Pat Coombs, two from Murphy, one from her dad.

So Pat had reached out. She'd call him back eventually. You can be perp and victim at the same time—*she'd* told *him* that. And those poor boys of his. Pat had stood by her and she owed him the same. She'd wait until the Pat Coombs mix in her bloodstream was more pity than anger, then she'd make the call.

Murphy on the other hand. Murphy had been scheduled to meet Senator Duval that morning, and now he wanted either to bawl her out or promise her a promotion. If the former, she had some choice words ready for her boss. If the latter, she'd already decided to accept. There was, she knew, a tiny chance that Murphy had had her best interests at heart all along. She wasn't quite ready to accept that possibility.

She'd return Dad's call later, arrange a visit, be their little girl for a few days.

"Do you know what you'll say to Elizabeth?" she said.

Felle peered out through the windshield. "I'll tell her she still has a brother. I'll tell her that it *is* a fight over who gets to sit in the front seat of the car, and I should never have let her win."

Alex followed Felle's eyes up into the empty sky. She remembered standing below Clearwater House thinking about the call of the void—a call she'd never been tempted to answer—trying to convince herself that continued existence wasn't a betrayal. She needed to stay alive to do her job—a job worth doing.

William would understand.

Wouldn't he?

Alex started the engine. "I'm ready if you are," she said.

ACKNOWLEDGMENTS

A *THANK YOU* FROM the author.
To Elana, for your endless support, ruthless honesty, and careful editing. You get it, you know how much it matters, and you make the space I need.

To my agent, Dan Conaway at Writers House, New York, for your persistence, resilience, and skill. And for knowing when to produce the whiskey bottle from the bottom drawer.

To my editor on this book, Sara J. Henry, for your uncanny ability to identify the fixes that make the difference. You understood what I was trying to do and you helped me do it better.

To Matt Martz, and the Crooked Lane team, for the opportunity and for the induction into the world of publishing.

Thank you, also, to my first readers.

David Murphy, poet, playwright, and friend over at jdmurphy-writing.com, your expert opinion and honest feedback on those *many* drafts helped me more than you know.

Ness Carter, you are an excellent first reader. Taking on a friend's unpublished manuscript is no small thing, and you've done it more than once. I'm afraid the next one will also be coming your way.

Linda Marshall, thank you for your eagle-eyed input in the final stages.

Paris and Nick, your enthusiasm, suggestions, and your help in finding the fifth knuckle added some much-needed polish.

I also want to thank four mentors and champions who helped shape my writing.

Jonathan Santlofer, your tuition—like your writing—is inspirational. A mix of craft, creativity, and compassion that is rare and valuable.

Rob Redman at The Fiction Desk, you were the first editor to publish my stories in a real book. The pathway you offer to new and emerging writers is enduring and special.

Allison Williams, your coaching left a lasting impression on how I write.

Alex Keegan at Bootcamp Keegan, you taught me that the only feedback worth having is the unqualified, diamond-hard truth.

Finally, thank you to my parents, Adrian and Bridget, and to Joe, David, Kate, Ben, and Rafa. Your support and joy in everything I do ensures that you are always in the room with me.